THE
SUPERNATURAL
Diet Club

THE GOLDEN BOWL BOOK TWO

MAEVE
CHRISTOPHER

The Supernatural Diet Club

The Golden Bowl Book Two

Maeve Christopher

Published by HNI Books
Copyright © 2017 Paula M. Scully

Editor: Janet Hitchcock
Cover: Dar Albert of Wicked Smart Designs
Formatting: Nina Pierce of Seaside Publications

ISBN 978-0-9993905-1-1

Acknowledgments

My thanks to Janet Hitchcock, Chris Senechal, and
Tracey Quintin for helping me make this book
the best it can be.

ONE

~ Buck ~

Annie didn't know I'd returned to Marberry, Maine, the place I almost lost her—and may still. Waves slammed the rocks where I sat, some freak storm out at sea churning everything up. It might have been better if they swept me away. *Less painful.* I remained on the rocky cliff, defiantly waiting, sweating in the cool of the night, mashing a tangle of prayers in my hand.

Prayers from The Golden Bowl. The trademark of Annie's restaurant. It probably would have been better for Annie if I never took on the job of transforming her business into a profitable enterprise. The nausea, the sweat, the sea lashing at me—it might have been better for me, too. So said the vicious voice in my head.

The wind whipping me carried another voice—the first prayer I'd taken out of that gold bowl almost a year ago, as a joke, really. *God is doing a new thing.* That proved true. I'd fallen hopelessly in love with Annie. I've never loved another person in my life, not truly. How could I go fifty years without loving someone?

I can't not be with her. She was an irresistible beacon to my dark soul. I tried tearing the papers in my hand, but they remained indestructible. Mocking my malevolence with truth, the wind said.

The last of the moonlight disappeared in the crash of a wave. Silence and stillness shocked me.

"The truth will set you free."

I turned to see Cat. I'd never known what to make of her. Annie called her a modern-day prophet. "I suppose it's no surprise you're here."

She took a seat beside me. Her smile lit up in the inkling of sunrise. "Good morning, Buck. I'm so glad you could join us on holiday."

"I suppose my client's cancellation was your doing. Not that I mind. I can use the break."

"Indeed." Cat's smile told me she knew the word should have been "breakdown," not "break."

Cat often spoke in riddles and double meanings. Annie called it "speaking prophetically," which sent a shiver up my spine. Whatever it was, Cat was a force to be reckoned with, despite her diminutive stature. I noticed how the raging sea had now calmed, and the first rays of sun lit up her smile, her golden hair.

I handed her the ball of prayer slips I'd frantically plucked from the bowl hours ago. Words that convicted me, frankly scared me, now mashed into a sweaty mass. It seemed I was compelled to take one after another, as though hoping to get a fortune cookie with a better fortune. "Perhaps you can give me some advice on these."

She smiled. "Almighty Buck, the truth will set you free." She took the paper ball and turned back to the spectacular colors of a July sunrise.

A bolt of heat spiked up from my gut and watered my eyes. I thought they might boil. I pushed my thumb and forefinger across them to stop this madness. But now the heat was threatening to choke me.

I noticed Cat's head was bowed, her eyes closed, the mass of paper cupped in her hands, as though she was offering them—to whom?

It was fear choking me. Red-hot fear. Fire spun through me, vertigo overtook me. I saw the blood on my hands. I saw my college friends, now my business partners. I heard the words of our blood pact.

I felt Cat grip my hand, the crumpled papers slicing at my skin. "You cannot worship God and money, Buck. You chose money. You have everything in this world. Every material possession you've ever dreamed of, and more. You've done business with the wealthiest, most prominent clients, enjoyed the pleasures of this world. You've done it your way, tasted the lust of the flesh, the lust of the eyes, the pride of life. You've sold your soul. You're like Satan himself—masquerading as an angel of light and righteousness. You have everything but love."

Remorse choked out one of the prayers I'd pulled from the gold bowl. "Love does not delight in evil but rejoices with the truth." In truth, I didn't know what that meant. What possessed me to even remember that line?

"Yes."

Cat obviously knew what it meant.

Nausea began to diminish. I tried to focus on the gold light outlining pink and purple clouds. My hand shook around the unruly paper ball. "I've never felt such a mess in my life."

Cat's hand was still on mine, a gentle touch now. "The Precious Blood protects Annie. God won't let you take her. Holy Spirit is convicting you."

Despair gripped me. "What am I supposed to do?" *Think.* I was the expert everyone consulted to solve problems. I should be able to solve this. "Our firm is having its best year ever. What if I donate all my salary to The Golden Bowl's charities? Wouldn't that please Annie *and* God?"

The morning light shone in the deep blue of Cat's eyes riveted on mine. "Your money cannot save your soul, Buck."

"So I'm damned, is that it? There's nothing I can do?" Indignation flared on another wave of nausea. "You've got a bloody fortune, Cat. Why does God like you so much? You make at least ten times what I make in a year."

Her eyes sparkled up at me.

Guilt took over. "Sorry to be so nasty."

"Buck, God loves you as much as he does me. Nothing can separate us from God's love. Nothing. He knows how you've lived your life. He sees you've chosen money over him. He saw the blood pact you and your partners made—a deal with the devil, whether or not you knew that at the time. That grieves God, but it doesn't mean he doesn't love you. He brought Annie into your life so you could see a better way. So you could turn your life around before it's too late."

My head was splitting by the time the sun had risen. I had renounced my deal with the devil and made a new one with God. Despite the headache, my gut told me I was on a better path. Perhaps Cat would allow me to see Annie now. And how did such a tiny thing as Cat have the ability to stop anyone from doing anything? It was beyond me.

While Cat sat in silence, praying I suppose, I took it upon myself to flatten out each paper I'd pulled from the prayer bowl. Then I stashed them in my suit jacket pocket. No doubt I'd need them. I used the handkerchief I found there to wipe salty sweat, sand, and sea from my face and hands. Having been doused with the spray of a rogue wave, despite my efforts, I'm sure I looked a sight.

My legs had long since fallen asleep, so I took some time getting up. Cat bounced up, agile and strong. I decided her energy was due to youth—I had twenty years on her.

She took my hand. "Buck, I hope you plan to join us at Annie's. Everyone's on holiday in July, it seems. There's not a hotel room available, I'm sure."

"You've got such a crowd of family, I can't imagine there's a spare room."

She giggled. "It's a massive old farmhouse. We're still discovering new rooms. Cisco's office on the third floor was just as he left it last October. At the least, you can sleep there."

I looked down at her, and those eyes mesmerized me again. "Thank you, Cat. For everything. I feel I have hope."

She squeezed my hand. "You most certainly do, Buck. Let's go get some breakfast. Annie will be thrilled to see you."

I don't know who was helping whom off that ledge, but as we reached the packed dirt pathway known as Miller's Way, I caught sight of Nathan Rhodes. "What's he doing here?" I couldn't keep the disgust out of my voice.

Cat glanced up at me. "Cisco's rules. I have bodyguards at all times." She pointed. "There's Billy, too."

Billy waved. Rhodes scowled. After a nod I tried to ignore them both as we walked up through the parking lot of The Golden Bowl. Cat kept me distracted from thoughts of what they might say about me to the wrong people. By the time we reached my car, I had the news on most everyone in the extended family.

Cat let go of my hand. "Annie told me she might go for a drive with you in your Lamborghini. But Doc said he'd be afraid Nathan would never be able to catch you in that car." She smiled up at me.

It was a smile that kept me dutifully in line behind their SUV on the drive to Annie's.

~ *Annie* ~

My day began at 3:00 a.m. when Joe Harris, agent to the mega-stars, pounded on my bedroom door. "Annie!"

Half asleep, I threw my robe around my shoulders and opened the door. "Is something wrong?"

He thrust a cup of coffee at me. "Paulo's decided he's doing your show. Let's not give him a minute to change his mind. I think he's on a sugar high from all that blueberry ice cream. Get dressed, and let's go."

I was suddenly wide-awake, the cup trembling in my hand. "Joe! I thought we're doing the first show with my sister. I memorized everything. I'm thinking I can do this—she's my sister. I'm not prepared to interview Paulo. *Paulo Clemente*! What are we going to talk about?"

"Ice cream. What else? He loves your ice cream. You'll show him how you make it at The Golden Bowl. No problem, doll, you can do that in your sleep. Get dressed. The stylist'll be at the studio, ready to do your hair and makeup." Joe stalked off.

I chased him down the hall, clutching my robe, splashing coffee. "The script!"

He turned around, and I almost crashed into him. "You can use your script with Debbie. No one has to know you filmed the first show second. It'll be our little secret. Go get dressed."

There was no use arguing. I ran to my room, showered in a flash, and dressed in the outfit I'd carefully laid out. Forty minutes later I was in the foyer with Paulo Clemente, the world's hottest young rock star. His wife, Ellen, stood in front of him, his arms wrapped around her, his straight black hair falling into his bright blue eyes.

Ellen smiled at me. "We're sorry, Annie. Paulo still gets nervous doing television interviews. He's decided he can do it now, if that's okay with you."

Joe threw a bag full of Golden Bowl aprons at me and turned to Ellen. "That's perfectly great. No time like the present. Let's go."

We piled into a black SUV and pulled out of the driveway in a motorcade with a contingent of bodyguards and assistants. It was a six-mile drive to my studio, located in a converted fish-processing plant that now housed my new prepared foods facility.

Things had changed enormously since my sister, Debbie, and I met for the first time a year ago. Through her, I met billionaire businessman and philanthropist, Cisco Clemente, and his amazing wife and rock star, Cat. She had convinced Cisco that The Golden Bowl was a worthy cause to invest in.

Now Cisco's youngest brother, Paulo, and Cat and the rest of their world-renowned band were touring to raise money for our charities. They called it The Golden Bowl Tour, bringing money and publicity to my mission of feeding people: body, soul and spirit—and spreading the word of the power of prayer.

It was tough enough running The Golden Bowl restaurant, The Bakery & Sweet Shop, and the prepared food business. On top of all that, I was being encouraged to become a spokesperson and media personality. Today I was supposed to be hosting my first show. Debbie and her business partner were to be my first guests. I'd convinced myself I'd be able to do it.

Ellen sat between the rock star and me, her pretty freckled face always smiling. Paulo was a sweet, shy boy, half my age, and his brilliant mind was usually focused on his newest music composition. He was acclaimed as a musical genius the world over. There wasn't an instrument he couldn't play. On top of that, his strong, distinctive tenor could make you swoon. For a kid who did so much singing, he usually had precious little to say. I guess his message was in his music, and that was more than enough.

His family and his music meant everything to him. I knew I'd have to lure him into conversation along those lines. I swallowed the massive lump growing in my throat. How would I do it? Ice cream?

"Ice cream, huh?" My thought came out loud.

Ellen giggled. "He's never eaten as much ice cream in his life as he has since we met you, Annie."

I watched his smile disappear into a kiss to the top of her head.

My staff was incredible. Karen, my confections manager, and Gerald, the food prep facility manager, had everything ready to go when we arrived.

Once the cameras started, Paulo calmed down, and Ellen joined in to keep the conversation flowing. As a trained nurse, she was knowledgeable about nutrition, and she was American, so she was comfortable to talk to. Paulo was born of Spanish parents and raised in Salzburg, Austria. Sometimes—like when I was nervous—I'd miss a word here and there.

But I needn't have worried. I was getting used to my European extended family, and the half hour show was over in an instant. Really, it was barely enough time to discuss and demonstrate Paulo's favorite flavors, blueberry and chocolate chip. A voiceover at the end of the show would tell fans and potential customers how to order from The Golden Bowl website or toll-free number.

Joe Harris, our super agent, and Buck Wynn, a consultant to the restaurant and food service industry, had thought of every detail. The staff had everything at my fingertips. Despite my nerves, I knew my job was not hard. Thank God, today I didn't make it harder than it had to be. I was grateful to have the first show under my belt. Now my second show should be a piece of cake.

As Paulo and Ellen popped blueberries, I dug a spoon into the blueberry ice cream. "This really is the best stuff." I sighed as it slid slowly down my throat, relaxing me.

Ellen's giggle pulled me out of my daze.

I took another spoonful, planning my retort. "Well, it has fresh Maine blueberries, full of antioxidants and phytonutrients." I waved the empty spoon in the air and back to the bowl. "Fresh cream. Dairy—from local organic farmers—has nutritional benefits." I noticed Paulo's vivid eyes and polite smile. The cameras were still on. I panicked. Ice cream went down the wrong way. *Choking on camera—great way to start my career*. Paulo handed me a glass of water.

Then my sister Debbie appeared with her business partner, Glori, and their entourage. I felt truly humbled.

My sister came to my rescue with a new outfit, and soon I was in the chair for hair and makeup. Nerves came out as impatience. "How many times do we need to do this?"

"How did you get blueberry in your hair?" the stylist asked. "Your hair's so light and fine—maybe we should leave it."

I bit my lip.

By the time the stylist was done, I was almost in tears. The final blow came when my script disappeared. No one would admit to taking it. Nerves turned my brain into mush.

Glori Coulson Dusseault, pop icon and CEO of Glori, the international fashion empire, the definition of head-to-toe glamour, approached me. "Hon, I love your hair. Never saw you streak it before. The blue is awesome."

Paulo couldn't hold it in another second. "It's in honor of the Maine blueberry."

The rest of the family and onlookers burst out laughing, louder and louder as my face grew redder and redder. My sister Debbie mirrored my red face, her hand covering her mouth to shield the smile.

I decided I had to go with it. I curtsied. "The Maine blueberry should be honored here. Apparently, I'm the one to do it."

Joe Harris pointed to my studio kitchen. "Then let's go do it. You don't need your script, Annie. You've got it memorized."

As I stood at my counter, the topic for the show eluded me. Luckily, I remembered my guests' names, and rambled through their introduction. I took a seat and stared blankly at my sister, world-renowned fashion designer Debbie Lambrecht, and her partner, pop star and fashion icon Glori Coulson Dusseault. There was silence.

Fortunately, Glori was incapable of being quiet for a second. "What are we cooking today, hon?"

I glanced at the ingredients in front of me and back at Glori. I had no idea what we were cooking. I must have had that deer in the headlights look. "Okay, I'll tell you about the blue streaks in my hair."

I noticed my sister's eyes were full of confusion. But Glori didn't miss a beat.

"Cool. I don't like cooking anyway. I stink at it."

The light bulb went on. We were supposed to be doing a show for busy women—or men—who don't have the time or inclination to cook. Tips and tricks. But I was committed to my hair.

And Glori was talking a blue streak. Literally. We learned all about the tips and tricks to streaking hair blue, or any color. I couldn't get a word in edgewise. It seemed like fifteen minutes later when she took a breath.

I jumped in. "Well, today my hair is streaked blue in honor of the Maine blueberry."

There was a simultaneous "oh" from Debbie and Glori.

I could feel my face heating to a bold shade of red. "Did you know that eighty-five percent of the world's supply of wild blueberries comes from Washington County? Just a stone's throw from our studio here in Hancock County." *How to segue*? "And today blueberries are high on my list for cooks who don't have time to cook."

"Really?" It looked like Glori believed me, at least.

I was hoping against hope to hear the producer's voice out of the darkness behind the bright lights. Why wasn't he yelling, "stop?" I had to keep going. I dumped everything blueberry at my guests, who gracefully asked simple questions wherever they could. When would this be over?

I realized Debbie had hardly made a peep, and time was, mercifully, growing short. I turned to her. "Debbie, with a husband and two miraculous sets of triplets, not to mention a demanding business, do you ever cook?"

Her shy smile soothed me. "Sometimes. I … I make simple meals … mostly vegetables and protein. Fruit for dessert. It's healthy and keeps me from sliding back into my eating disorder."

Glori let out a heavy sigh. "Hon, Debbie spent most of her life with anorexia. You didn't know her then, but she barely ate anything—and she'd go up and down the stairs—anything to burn off any calories she ate. She had another complication called bulimia. It really messed up her heart. And she's still at risk for it coming back. That's why we're always on her about eating, ya know."

Acid pumped up into my throat. This was a train out of control. Debbie's eating disorder was a continuous fascination in the media. I didn't want to go there, blazing another light on her one shortcoming. She was my sweet, dear little sister. I was supposed to be supportive.

I stood up and leaned over the counter, stretching toward the blackness beyond the lights. I forgot the producer's name. "Sorry. I've really messed up this show. Let's cut this off now, and I'll regroup. I'll get it right next time. I promise."

~ *Buck* ~

I woke up to midday sunshine and a sea breeze streaming in the one window in my fourth floor turret in Annie's old mansion. Staring at blue sky and treetops, I felt peace for the first time in months. I recognized the words running through my head as one of the prayers I'd pulled out of the bowl last night.

Come to me, all of you who are weary and carry heavy burdens, and I will give you rest. Take my yoke upon you. Let me teach you, because I am humble and gentle at heart, and you will find rest for your souls. For my yoke is easy to bear, and the burden I give you is light. Matt 11:28-30 NLT

Thoughts of Annie spurred me to come more to consciousness, but the prayer gave me an excuse to rest in the warmth of a gentle breeze. Annie was probably still at the studio, working on her first television show. I closed my eyes.

A tiny humming sound caught my ear. *A child?* I turned in the bed to face Annie's niece sitting on a wooden chair, drawing on a paper tablet in her lap. I hiked the sheet up around my chest. "Sabena!"

She looked up at me with Cat's deep blue magnetic eyes, yet she was Debbie's child. "Hi, Buck." She returned to her art.

I sat up in the bed, tugging at the sheet and quilt. "Does your mother know where you are?"

"I don't know. She's on a TV show. This is my art studio, but you can stay here. I don't let my brothers come in, but you can come in."

I couldn't help smiling. "That's very kind of you. And why can't your brothers come in?"

"Because they said I couldn't play with them."

"I see. Well, I'm sure working on your art is more fun than playing with them."

"Yes. They like to get into trouble. Nanny Shirlene says they roughhouse. Then I usually get hurt, and Papa gets angry with them. I think it's lunchtime, so I'm going downstairs now. Are you joining me for lunch? We can have a picnic."

"I'd be delighted to join you for lunch. Thank you. I'll be down soon."

"Okay!" She slid off the chair, left her supplies on a child-sized table, and let herself out.

I wondered how life would have been different if I'd met Annie as a teenager. Except for darker blue eyes, Sabena was the image of Annie. Wispy fine white hair she'd undoubtedly inherited from Annie's biological father, Dr. Craig Westcott, known to all as "Doc," and pale skin seemed to be the family heritage.

A vague ache I decided was regret lingered in my chest. My fiftieth birthday was five months away. *Still time to turn things around.* Today was a new day.

When I pushed through the swinging door, I saw Cat and Cisco at the kitchen table, their infant son asleep in Cisco's arms. "Good to see you, Buck," he said.

As I took a seat by the bay window, Cat poured me some tea. "Sabena said you'd join her for a picnic lunch."

"That was the plan. I didn't know I was sleeping in her art studio."

We shared a laugh as I noticed the children racing around the back garden with Doc. It gave me pause. "I don't think I'm Doc's favorite person these days."

Cisco faced me. "He's a little overprotective of Annie. You can't blame him. It's only a year since Annie and Debbie found out he's their father. They need time to get all the baggage straightened out."

"I suppose so." I swallowed my tea. "Annie's still at the studio?"

Cisco smirked. "They got all hung up on Maine blueberries according to Joe. So they're re-doing the show."

"How does one get hung up on blueberries?" My question met with laughter. I remembered the artwork I'd torn from Sabena's tablet and took the page from my pocket. "I couldn't help noticing how advanced this child is—for a six-year-old. Her drawing is fantastic. And since it's obviously The Golden Bowl, and it has my name on it, I felt justified in taking it." I handed it to Cat.

"Hmm. Sabena's a wonderful artist. She's as talented as her mother and great-grandmother, I believe."

"Indeed. But what is this Supernatural Diet she has at the top? And this list of names?"

Cisco leaned over to see. "You made the top of the list, Buck."

"Rather insulting, considering I've worked with a personal trainer for years, so I don't need to diet."

Cat and Cisco burst into laughter. I recalled seeing the names of fashion icons and Special Forces on the list, along with Annie, who was quite slim as well. How did I let myself get sucked into a six-year-old's drawing? Perhaps my breakdown was not over.

The screen door slammed, and Sabena appeared barefoot and clutching an apple. "Auntie! Do apples come from Maine or just blueberries?"

Cat summoned her with outstretched arms. "Apples can come from Maine, too."

Sabena climbed up. Cat hiked up her oversized red shorts and sat her in her lap. She took a bite of her apple as she surveyed her artwork. "Auntie, I have all the invitations ready to go. I was just waiting for Buck to come."

Cat kissed the back of her head. "Tell us what this is all about."

"It's our new club."

Cisco chuckled. "I didn't make the list."

Sabena made a face. "You can come if you want to. You can be a teacher with Auntie."

"Oh, Auntie is the teacher? Auntie Annie? She's a nutritionist."

"No. This is a *supernatural* diet club. Auntie Cat is the teacher."

Cisco turned to his wife. "Okay, Auntie Cat, tell us the purpose of The Supernatural Diet Club."

Cat smirked at him then at me. Her eyes bored into mine. "Receive the kingdom of God like a little child. The Supernatural Diet is as simple as this—a nourishing way of life as led by God."

I forced a grin. I was a charter member of The Supernatural Diet Club. *God help me.*

Sabena sat on the kitchen table reading her list of chosen ones when Annie came through the door with the crowd of extended family who'd accompanied her to the studio. I was instantly on my feet and relieved that she was in my arms. It had been weeks since I'd last seen her, and things had been unclear, to put it mildly. I escorted her out the door, down the back lawn, past the preparations for a barbeque, and down the stairs to the beach.

We found a secluded spot in the sand behind a rocky wall. I kissed her, knowing full well we had only an illusion of privacy. Rhodes stood on the cliff above us, armed and dangerous.

"I've missed you, Buck. So much."

"Annie, what if I—" I hardly dared say it. "What if I take a holiday? Open-ended time off. What do you think?"

"What about your business? What about Paris? Did they put off the opening?"

"One of my partners can handle it. Not a problem. Who doesn't want to go to Paris?"

She laughed. "I suppose … when you put it that way." She tugged me toward the water. "Let's walk. It's been a wacky day, and I feel a little weird here with Mr. Rhodes practically on top of us. I need some air."

We walked along the water's edge, allowing the advancing tide to wash over our ankles. "Maybe we can go someplace where the water is actually warm. What do you think, Annie?"

"Sounds great, but I'm over my head as it is. Trying to do these TV shows on top of everything else. And I want to spend time with Debbie. Having the family here is a dream come true. Whatever time they can eek out for me, I want to be there."

"I understand. They'll be wrapping up their U.S. tour right after Thanksgiving. Why don't we take a week at the beginning of December? That should be perfect timing."

She stopped in her tracks and stared me in the eye. "Buck, that's sweet, but the holidays'll be madness this year. I can't fly off on vacation and leave everyone here to contend with The Golden Bowl. And *you* worked too hard to get everything organized and running to let things go. Maybe in January."

I took her by the shoulders, fear welling up with nausea. It was as though she was slipping through my fingertips. "Annie, I worked so hard to make sure you'd have a profitable business that would allow you time to yourself. So your staff would be capable of running things on a daily basis. The numbers show it's working. You needn't drive yourself into an early grave."

A high-pitched voice on the wind caught our attention. Tiny Sabena barreled up the beach, papers in her hands, a bag dangling at her side. Annie chuckled. "That girl's so skinny, she's always losing her shorts. Those knobby little knees … how adorable is she?"

She was a sight. I couldn't help smiling. Her parents strolled behind her, arm in arm, obviously just as amused. Could Annie and I ever have what Debbie and David have? Maybe this new thing Cat had signed me up for could bring that happiness. Maybe there was hope.

Sabena reached us, out of breath, extending our personal invitations to her Supernatural Diet Club.

Annie grabbed her up in her arms. "What's this?"

"You have to come to our first meeting. Okay?"

"Okay, honey. Buck, too?"

I flashed my invitation. "Me, too."

Debbie spoke as they approached. "We were invited, too."

Annie attempted to read hers, battling the wind while trying to hold the child. "Sounds like a very exclusive club."

"Yes. My brothers aren't invited, though."

"Really? Why not?"

"They're not old enough. They wouldn't understand."

Annie giggled. "I heard you're the youngest—by what? Five minutes?"

With that, Sabena's father, David, let out a laugh. He nodded at Annie as he took his daughter back. "We'll let you know when the first meeting is." He lifted the child so they were face to face. "Now let's let them enjoy the beach."

Sabena waved goodbye over her father's shoulder. Annie blew her a kiss. "She's the most incredible child. She weighed like a pound at birth, all these challenges—and she's smart as a whip. She's fluent in English and German, and her Spanish puts me to shame. You can tell she's going to be just as talented artistically as Debbie is. She seems to have most of scripture memorized. At six years old!"

I had to wonder. "God only knows what this Supernatural Diet Club is all about."

~ *Annie* ~

You'd think, doing cooking shows all day, that I would have eaten something. Aside from a few spoonsful of ice cream, no. The scent of barbeque drew me back down the beach, Buck in pursuit.

Really, I was too hungry and tired to consider his proposition. Things had been too jumbled for me to think or pray my way through all the feelings. The intensity in his steely eyes was too much today. I needed to keep things light.

"You didn't ask me about my blue hair."

"It looks stunning with your sundress."

I giggled. "I might be wearing a lot of blue. I'm not so sure it's going to wash out." I told him about the blueberry fiasco. By the time I'd related the story, we joined the family for a late lunch/early dinner on the beach.

Glori examined her invitation, commenting on the number of fit and thin members of the new club. I think she was a little miffed to be included.

Sabena stood on a pail and attracted everyone's attention. Quite a feat in this crowd. "I'm going to explain it, Auntie. The dictionary says diet means a way of living. It comes from the word, Deity. That's the purpose of my club. Auntie Cat says, the Supernatural Diet is a nourishing way of life as led by God. Do we all understand now?"

David turned reflexive laughter into a cough.

Glori stood up and waved at her. "Hon, I really don't."

Sabena was unfazed. "That's okay, Auntie. That's why you're in the club." That was it. The beach echoed with rollicking laughter.

It wasn't long after when Sabena and the rest of the kids conked out from a full day of constant activity. The adults sat by the fire on the beach, toasting marshmallows, making s'mores, and enjoying conversation. As the hours went by, couples drifted away. I woke up with my head on Buck's chest, noticed his Rolex, and checked the time. I sat up and wiped my eyes. The fire had long since petered out and moonlight shone on the water.

"Annie." He drew me to his lips.

The want was too overwhelming. "Buck, it's been a long day, and I need to get some sleep. I've got to be at The Golden Bowl in four and a half hours."

"You don't need to work, Annie." He was still half asleep.

~ *Buck* ~

By the time I climbed the stairs to my artist's turret, I was wide-awake. Perspective from that one window was certainly limited. I began to pace like a caged animal. Something needed to change.

After tossing in the bed for a while, I decided to shower, shave, and dress in a business suit. Perhaps it was a desire to take control over something. Anything. I went back downstairs to the kitchen for coffee. A fresh pot was brewing, but my attention went to the scene on the lawn outside the window. Annie and Rhodes sat in the Adirondack chairs enjoying sunrise, conversation, and a coffee. I spun on my heel and left.

Minutes later, I stood at the prayer bowl on the front porch of Annie's restaurant. It overflowed with paper. Something drew me to it, and I began to sweat. Nausea welled up at the thought of repeating the previous night. I read the sign. *Leave a prayer. Take a prayer.* I closed my eyes and took one. It was scrawled in purple—a child's handwriting.

The journey of the SUPERnatural Diet is not natural in our day.

"Sabena." I unlocked the front door as quickly as I could, ran to the restroom, and retched.

TWO

~ *Annie* ~

I decided to grab another cup of coffee before heading off to work at The Golden Bowl. Pushing through the kitchen door, I found Doc pouring his. "Annie! Care for a cup?"

"Yeah, we need to brew this by the barrel." I handed him my mug.

"Take a seat. I need to ask you about something." He led me to the kitchen table.

"Everything okay?"

He put his cup down and took out a pocket calendar. "Yeah. I need to ask you about inviting a friend up to stay for a weekend. Space is pretty tight, so I wanted to clear it with you."

"Okay." I took a seat. "We're pretty full up for the foreseeable future. Who's your friend?"

Doc looked a little confused as he ran his hand over a full head of gray hair. "He's one of my associates—from my practice in New York. Brilliant cardiologist, and he has a number of patents and a couple of very lucrative deals with some medical device companies. I think you'll like him."

A little alarm went off in my head. "Oh. How old is this guy, Doc?"

"Just about your age. Nice looking guy. Divorced two or three years ago now. You'd like him."

I smiled at my coffee. Doc was retired from medicine, but his mind was as sharp as ever. Unfortunately, it looked like his new vocation was matchmaking. "I'm sure he's very nice. But I'm pretty busy this summer, we've got plenty of company, and I'm not in any rush down the aisle. So if you're inviting him here to meet me—"

Doc looked at the ceiling. "I think we can work it out easily. I'll sleep downstairs in the bomb shelter." His eyes met mine. "He can take my room. I bet he'd enjoy Marberry. Did I mention he has a yacht?"

"No, you didn't mention that. Listen, Doc, I know you're not Buck's biggest fan—"

He leaned over and took my hand. "Annie, it's been well over a decade now since you lost Russ. I know there's no one in Marberry that's suitable. Let's face it. You're a beautiful—still young—woman with a master's degree. Most of the people you work with aren't even college-educated. It's difficult to find a suitable mate in a place like this. Marberry's a nice *family* town."

I spoke over him. "Look, I'm not in the market for a new husband right now. I have enough to do to get my business where it needs to be and fund my charities. I want to spend time with the family we just found—it's only been a year. You and I were *acquaintances* until a year ago. It takes time to sort out all the *stuff*. I'm not planning on adding a new husband to the mix any time soon."

Doc jostled my hand to get my attention. "That's fine. But I'm sure you feel a little twinge when all the couples show up, and you don't have Russ. I've heard you comment on how happy Debbie and David are—"

That little twinge touched a nerve all right. My voice escalated. "Doc, I know you're trying to help, but this isn't helping."

"I'll tell you who isn't helping, and that's Buck! Oh yeah, he looks and sounds like the proper British gent. Well educated, well spoken, smart, rich, but the guy's a player, Annie. He'll break your heart. And I'm not going to stand by and watch it happen."

I stood up. "Buck is a friend. A *friend*. He's done so much for The Golden Bowl—I don't know where we'd be without him. I can't tell you what the future holds, Doc, but it's my personal business. And I don't want to discuss it." I flung what was left of my coffee into the sink and put the cup in the dishwasher.

"Annie!"

I faced him. "You're welcome to invite your cardiologist friend anytime, as long as you can find room for him. Just remember, we're keeping all the family rooms through Thanksgiving, even if they're away for a few days here and there. This is their home away from home. We're keeping their rooms. I've got to get to work." I almost ran from the kitchen.

~ *Buck* ~

It was around 9:00 a.m. when Annie found me in the customer service area. "Buck, I thought you were taking some time off."

I led her into the private office and shut the door. "I wanted to make sure things were in order and run the numbers. No worries. Brianna and her crew left the place spotless. Sales are exploding with each stop of The Golden Bowl Tour." I noticed the papers in her hand. "More invitations?"

She chuckled. "Sabena wanted me to make sure and give them out today. I'm not sure why, but she's invited Lisa and her friend, Peg. And also Karen and Ashleigh. And she didn't say when the meeting is supposed to be. It's just the invitation to join her club."

My stomach was tumbling with acid. I attempted a smile. "Well, this is a six-year-old we're dealing with."

Annie's smile triggered too many feelings.

"That's hard to remember sometimes. Listen, I need to deliver these before I do anything else, but join me for breakfast. Say fifteen minutes. I'll have it delivered here. What would you like?"

I almost said I'd like her on the desk, but decorum reigned. "I'll have what you're having."

She left with a smile, and I dropped into the chair. *I can't do this.* I took my briefcase and walked out to the parking lot. The salty breeze should have been invigorating. But I was a sweaty mess. I tossed the case into the car and drove to New York.

My apartment was not comforting, or even comfortable, but I called it home. It had been decorated by one of the city's most exclusive designers and featured in celebrity magazines. I was proud of that. But looking at it now, it seemed sterile, cold, cavernous. A home for the imposter, Buckminster Wynn of Brooke, Lewis & Wynn with offices in New York and London. Almighty Buck. Charter member of The Supernatural Diet Club. Whatever that was.

I stood at the floor-to-ceiling windows overlooking Central Park. The vicious voice in my head told me I was one of the elite. I'd made it. I had everything. Everything but love, Cat said. She was so right.

This wasn't home anymore. I wasn't the mogul I thought I was.

I dropped the briefcase on a chair and headed to the hidden closet in my bedroom. The closet behind the walk-in closet, which was stuffed with neatly arranged clothing and shoes, all custom made.

I dragged out boxes of men's magazines—classic editions, I'd told myself—enough to fill the average American garage. I called the shredding service I used for my company. They were quick, efficient, and confidential.

When the boxes were hauled away, I stood in the middle of that space, thinking of nothing, really. I felt numb. I opened a box of jewelry I kept in case I needed a gift for a young woman. Invariably I'd learn of a birthday on the spur of the moment. I couldn't be bothered keeping them all straight. The jewelry was quite valuable. It kept my circle of acquaintances wide and willing. If I were to be seen with a woman, she would be a glamorous woman on my arm.

I pulled out an old watch, a joke gift from one of my partners years ago. It was a most unusual, bawdy antique worth thousands of dollars. I took it to the kitchen and laid it on the cutting board, then went to the tool kit under the sink. I smashed the watch to smithereens and tossed the debris into the trash.

I called my jeweler and mumbled something about an inheritance. He knew full well what I was talking about and appeared within an hour. He bought the box of jewelry for a very good price. I wrote out a check to Annie's charity for the full amount.

It was late when I sat down to check messages. Annie had called several times wondering where I was. I replayed her voicemail again and again. She could have been reciting the alphabet. I was transfixed.

But I couldn't call her. Instead, I called a young woman who was everything Annie was not.

~ Lisa ~

I was surprised to get an invitation to Annie's niece's new group and had no idea what The Supernatural Diet Club was all about. As a dishwasher at The Golden Bowl, I probably wasn't the brightest bulb, but my manager, Ashleigh, got one too, and she had no idea what was up. But, hey, we'd get to mingle with rock stars on the beach. I was in.

At break time I quickly put a brush through my brown hair and stifled the thought of how *average* I was. I went off to find Billy. Lately it was hard to tell the difference between the rock stars' mob of fans and his. Being a handsome ex-SEAL employed as a bodyguard for the rich and famous, well, his appeal to women was obvious.

I found him at the counter demonstrating how to eat a chocolate ice cream soda. Not surprising since he really was just an overgrown kid. A shock of sun-bleached hair and that fun-loving smile made him irresistible. Sabena and Glori's four-year-old daughter, Christina, were highly entertained. Cat and Glori were getting into it, too. Sure enough there were four other guards guarding them. Yeah, Billy was a rock star, too, and that made me sweat.

Since I always took dating advice from Ash, I sauntered over to the counter pretending to be nonchalant, whatever that exactly was. "Hi."

Billy interrupted his demo and gave me a squeeze. "Hey."

Cat and Glori smiled and said, "Hi, Lisa." *They remembered my name.*

Sabena announced, "It's girls' day out."

"Awesome," I said.

Christina nodded and waved her straw, dribbling chocolate all over her outfit. She giggled, but I dove for the straw and grabbed it away. Her dress was pinker than pink and sparklier than sparkly. It probably cost my month's wages.

Glori took it all in stride, dabbing at her with a damp napkin. "I'm thinking of having Debbie do some fancy aprons for kids. Ya know, it'd be a great thing to keep their party dresses clean and accessorize, too."

Cat let out a giggle, and Glori, just as overdressed as her daughter, turned to her like she was ready to hear what Cat really thought of that idea.

Cat winked at me. "It's such a blessing we have a boy."

Glori chuckled. "You're right about that, hon. Look at you in those old jeans. Do you ever take them off?"

Cat didn't seem insulted in the least. "Only when you force me to."

"That's the truth."

I was so into Glori's conversation, Mr. Rhodes startled me when he came between me and Billy and took his soda away from him. "I'm betting this is your third or fourth one." He didn't look too happy with Billy.

"Uh ... not sure."

"I need you to handle the chaos in the parking lot."

"Yes, Sir." Billy planted a quick kiss on the side of my head and left out the door.

Mr. Rhodes took a sip of Billy's soda. "Good stuff." He left it on the counter and went off to Annie's office.

Sabena took the opportunity to jump off her stool and come over to me. "Make sure to remember to come to our meeting tomorrow morning, Lisa. Okay?"

This kid was such a little politician. "I'll be there."

Glori rolled her famous green eyes. "I can't wait to hear about the Supernatural Diet. I swear I've tried every one."

Sabena giggled. "You'll be surprised, Auntie." Then she took off to talk to a white-haired old lady who caught her attention. The bodyguard was right on her heels.

I took a seat. "I need help with my diet, too. I need to lose some more. I mean Billy has all these pretty girls practically hanging on him every day. It's like Buck says—he's got an entourage. Never heard that word till Buck said it, but it's true. It's like a miracle he's still interested in me."

Glori finished wiping Christina's chocolate mustache. "Hon, I know you wash dishes and everything, but you've gotta dress better than jeans and t-shirts. At least for après work."

"What's après work? I know you're married to a French guy, but I never learned French."

Cat let out a giggle, and Glori joined her. "Neither did I, hon. Just a few strategic words. Christina speaks better French than me. But anyway, you need to dress better after you're done with the dishes."

"Well, I could never wear what you wear. First of all, I couldn't afford it. And second of all, I could never fit into those things."

"You've got totally different bone structure, hon."

"Yeah, I don't think it's the bones that's the problem. It's my butt. I could run the beach for a thousand years and never look like you."

~ *Buck* ~

When I came to I wondered why there was no sea breeze. The prayer was rolling in my head.

Come to me, all of you who are weary and carry heavy burdens, and I will give you rest. Take my yoke upon you. Let me teach you, because I am humble and gentle at heart, and you will find rest for your souls. For my yoke is easy to bear, and the burden I give you is light.

I opened my eyes, and the lights of the city reminded me I was in New York. I remembered how little comfort this dark-eyed beauty was the last time I enjoyed her company. I thanked her with double her usual fee, and ushered her out the door, agreeing she was the best I've ever had.

I was at a complete loss. I decided the solution was to get unconscious. I downed a sleeping pill with liquor.

The combination gave me a sense of bravado before knocking me out. I phoned Titan, a former Special Forces star and now celebrity trainer. He insisted there was no room in his schedule for another client, but the late hour and my perseverance wore him down. It didn't hurt that he'd consulted my firm regarding his intention to dabble in the restaurant business.

He finally agreed to fit me into his group class for celebrity jocks. No doubt I'd have a time trying to keep up. But I was determined. Seeing Rhodes' bloody face in my mind's eye would keep me motivated.

I hit the pillow content with my plan, such as it was.

Pounding on my door gave way to a familiar voice yelling curses, and I awoke from one of the most satisfying nightmares I've ever had, beating Rhodes to a pulp. I got out of bed and answered the door. "How did you get in the building?"

William Brooke, my business partner, pushed through and strode to the bar. "If they don't know me by now, there's no hope." He poured himself a scotch. "What in bloody blazes is wrong with you, Wynn? It's 2:00 in the afternoon, and Cisco Clemente's been trying to get hold of you since yesterday morning. I thought you must be dead. I got here as fast as I could. You're alive. How do you explain that? We don't snub Cisco Clemente."

I landed on my couch, wondering if a drink would ward off the headache that began to gnaw at me.

"Buck!" He waved the scotch in front of my face. "What's the matter? It's Anne Brewster, isn't it? The woman you came racing back from Tokyo for. Turned our firm upside down for. That's not like you."

Rubbing the sleep out of my eyes, I couldn't come up with a reply.

He took a seat in an ugly chair that was the epitome of style. "Look, The Golden Bowl is a massive success story for us. There's no denying that. You did an incredible job with that place. Now we've got our name out there with the likes of Cisco and Cat Clemente—and all the philanthropy they're involved with. It reflects well on us. We've booked more business this summer than *my* wildest dreams. As a matter of fact, our next partners' meeting is all about expansion. Brooke, Lewis & Wynn is a global name. Clients are clamoring. It's all good, Buck. But you've got to pull yourself together."

He put his glass down on an ugly table and writhed out of the seat. "Take a couple days off. But first make sure you're squared away with Clemente. Call him *now*. I'll see you Monday morning at the office. Be ready for that meeting."

He let himself out.

As I went for my phone, it buzzed. *Annie!* "Hello."

"Buck." It was a tiny voice.

"Sabena?"

"You have to come to our meeting. It's tomorrow at sunrise. Right here on the beach. Where are you?"

"I'm in New York. What are you doing with Annie's phone?"

"If you get in your car *now*, you can be here on time. It's very important. Are you in your car?"

I stretched back on the couch. "No."

"Auntie's been very sad since you left. She was crying. Are you in your car *now*?"

I rubbed my eyes. "I'm not in my car, Sabena."

"How long will it take? Auntie was crying, then Mama was crying. You have to come to our meeting. Are you in your car yet?"

I could hear Annie in the background. "Buck is on the phone, Auntie."

"Buck?" Annie's voice melted my heart. "Here, Sabena, sit with me. We'll talk to Buck." She returned to the phone. "Buck, are you there?"

"Hello, Annie."

"Are you okay?"

"I'm all right. You?"

She sounded exasperated. "Well, I have Sabena standing on the arm of my Adirondack chair. She's insisting you come to our little meeting tomorrow—" There was a momentary break as she addressed her niece. "Honey, you're gonna fall or scrape yourself on the wood. Sit here with me, and we'll talk to Buck." She sighed. "Sorry, Buck, she's determined. She wants to know if you're in your car now."

"No, I'm not in my car."

I heard Annie report to Sabena, and her sigh told me she was back. "Why? Why did you leave?" Her voice cracked. "Honey, you need to go eat dinner now. I'm talking to Buck. I'll make sure he knows the time, the place, and how important it is that he's there with us. Okay? Now go get some dinner—don't jump! Okay. Just go inside. And no more jumping off chairs."

I was aware of the heaviness in my chest, like it was made of mush.

I could hear Annie's heavy breath. "Um … what happened, Buck?" She was crying.

It was a cowardly reaction, and that revelation sank in. How could I explain it? "It was my fault, Annie. I saw you and Rhodes engrossed in each other's company, and it infuriated me. I decided I'd best leave."

"Engrossed?" I could tell she was trying to stop the tears. "I don't understand."

"Sunrise and coffee in the Adirondack chairs yesterday."

"Engrossed?" There was more of an edge. "I still don't understand."

"I think you can figure out the game he's playing."

There was frustration in her mournful breath. "I don't know what game he's playing. For that matter, I don't know what game *you're* playing. I do know I've been carrying your Valentine card with me for months. In case you don't remember, it says, 'For the first time in my life I want to come home.' I took that to mean home is *here*, Buck. Not New York. Not London. Obviously, I've been mistaken." There was a pause and muffled breath. "Anyway, I hope you'll be back by sunrise. Maybe we can sort some things out. Maybe not. At least you'll make Sabena a happy girl."

It felt like a massive weight on my chest. "I have some things to take care of. There's an important partners meeting on Monday. I'll see what I can do."

Her voice was breathless. "All right. Bye."

~ *Annie* ~

I ran down to the beach and along the water's edge. I wanted to toss my phone into the ocean. But that would do nothing but create a new hassle, another expense. My mind was a whirlwind. My body trembled with sadness—and yes, probably anger. He'd signed that Valentine card, "Love, Buck." As my friends all said, the "L" word. Neither one of us had ever said it aloud. Too scary, I guess. And really, I didn't know him well enough to say that, though in my heart, I felt it.

How did I end up in this mess?

Nathan approached. *Speak of the devil.*

"Annie, they have your first two shows edited. Your sister wants to sit down with you and the family in the parlor this evening to watch."

Thoughts of Valentine's Day fresh in my mind, I remembered that's when Nathan first called me, "Annie." It occurred to me he reserved "Annie" for the times we were alone together. With people around, it was always "Mrs. Brewster." Confused over the whole matter, not to mention my feelings for him, I continued to address him as "Mr. Rhodes."

I forced a smile. "Okay. Great. Thanks. No doubt, Sabena filled you in on the details of our new club meeting."

He smirked. "She was very insistent I be there. I have no idea what to expect."

My stomach knotted. "Whatever it is, I'm sure it'll be interesting."

Dread twisted the knots. Sabena was one thing, but Cat was certainly another. I could only imagine what she'd have to say to The Supernatural Diet Club.

THREE

~ *Annie* ~

It was the crack of dawn, and Sabena was in rare form. The Supernatural Diet Club assembled on the beach, coffees in hand. I served a blueberry and oat crisp with yogurt. With the breakfast, there was continued discussion from last evening on my first two episodes of *Recipes and Stories from The Golden Bowl*, and more compliments from my extended family. Since they were seasoned professionals in the entertainment industry, I was relieved when they praised it.

We took our seats on blankets and beach chairs, coffees refilled, and watched Sabena drag an old lobster trap as big as she was up on the sand.

I noticed her father watching her, smiling, shaking his head. By the time she reached the soft sand, it had become too much. He got up to help. "Where are you taking this?"

She pointed. He deposited the trap on the designated spot, and Debbie rushed over with a heavy beach mat. Sabena grabbed a notebook and marker from my blanket and climbed up on the cushioned trap, balancing quite nicely. She began the roll call for The Supernatural Diet Club. "Papa, Mama, Auntie Annie, Doc, Auntie Glori, Auntie Ellen, Lisa, Peg, Karen, Ashleigh, Billy, Nathan ..." She cast a worried glance up at the cliff behind us. "Where's Buck?"

My heart sank. I was hoping he wouldn't disappoint a sweet, enthusiastic six-year-old. I watched her march toward the stairs.

"Buck! You're late."

"I'm here with the teachers, Sabena. I needed a preparatory lesson."

I turned to see Buck descending the stairs with Cat and Cisco. He plucked her from the sand and kissed her forehead.

Her face was earnest in the dim light. "You had me worried, Buck."

The group broke into laughter.

"I couldn't miss the first meeting of The Supernatural Diet Club. I rearranged my schedule to be here. Shall we begin?"

He said his hellos as he walked amongst the blankets and chairs to deposit Sabena on the lobster trap. Then he took a seat beside me.

"Good morning, Annie."

"I'm glad you could make it." He accepted the thermos I offered and poured himself a coffee.

Cat and Cisco took their seats nearby.

Sabena called the meeting to order, just as the sun was lifting on the horizon. She dropped her notebook and pen and straightened up atop the rickety lobster trap, as though she was giving a speech to Congress. It was hard to keep a straight face watching her.

"Good morning everyone. God is doing a new thing. And we're calling it The Supernatural Diet Club.

Buck turned to me. "Hmm. I'm hoping to find out just what this 'new thing' is."

I smiled politely. "Me, too."

Sabena pointed. "If you ask Auntie Glori, she'll tell you diet is a four letter word. It's easier to sell that threadbare meaning. But it's way much better than that. The more sane usage is not heard these days. Time to revive it!"

I noticed David rubbing his chin, leaning into Debbie. His voice carried on the breeze. "Where did we get her?"

My sister giggled. I wasn't the only one choking back laughter.

Sabena didn't seem to notice her audience's amusement. "Diet is a four letter word. But there's a healthy, even sacred, meaning of the word. The dictionary defines diet as a way of *living*, *nourishment*, something *prescribed* for you … for *enjoyment*. It's a *journey*. And it comes from the word, *Deity*. These are all definitions that we'll be using. We'll be *living*."

Glori began the applause. I'm not sure what her motivation was. "Bravo, hon."

Sabena waved her arms. "I'm not finished yet, Auntie!"

We settled down.

Sabena resumed her oration. "The *journey* of the *Super*natural Diet is not natural. And we're taking this journey together, helping each other. Okay?"

"Okay!" was the unanimous response.

"I made some notes with Auntie, and she made copies for you, so we can use this to help us." She dove off the lobster trap and went for a folder on our blanket. "I'm giving everyone the notes, and now Auntie Cat is going to talk."

Cat covered the lobster trap with another fluffy towel and took a seat. "Thank you, Sabena. First, I want to tell you what a brilliant job you've done here. Your assessment of the word, diet, is exceptional. Truly food for thought."

Sabena let out a beguiling little giggle and settled into her father's arms.

Buck drew me close to him, a sudden movement that startled me. "Look how her hair is lit up in the sunlight. It's as though God is pouring light on her."

Cat's golden blonde hair was ablaze, magnifying her normally ethereal appearance. I said a silent prayer of gratitude. Those among us who did not usually pay attention to the spiritual side of life would undoubtedly be inspired today.

"I'm not quite sure when Sabena decided to organize this club, and how she arrived at the membership. But we've discussed the meanings of the terms, diet and supernatural. She asked me to give you my thoughts to start us off, and as we go along, we'll meet regularly and work together to help and encourage each other in whatever ways seem most beneficial. I hope the flexibility of this agenda does not let us take the importance of this adventure less seriously."

Cat surveyed the group, and each person agreed to give The Supernatural Diet Club a chance. "Wonderful!" She resumed her seat. "I'll leave you with a few thoughts. I think it's noteworthy that a young child created this group. Let's approach God as a little child. Believe and trust God as our good and loving parent. As we develop and deepen our relationship with God, we'll change our thinking, and from there, our lives. We'll be able to see ourselves from God's perspective, rest in his will for us. Science tells us now what scripture has said all along—belief in a benevolent God makes us happier and healthier. So that's why Sabena and I agreed The Supernatural Diet is as simple as this—a nourishing way of life as led by God."

Sabena led enthusiastic applause, and jumped out of David's lap. "Okay, now we need to talk about what we need help with. How to help each other. Okay?"

Lisa, a dishwasher at The Golden Bowl, was first to speak up. "Well, I lost forty-five pounds, and I need help keeping it off. I'm always into junk food, so I need to stop that. And Peg, here, she needs help quitting cigarettes."

Peg waved. "I'm in my late sixties, and I been a smoker all my life. But it's not good for the baby. I babysit Lisa's little Rosie, so I want to do the best I can for her."

Glori leaned forward in her beach chair. "Hon, I can help you with that. I quit smoking for my husband and my little girl. Also, I can give you help with dieting—the regular way. But if God could step in and make it easier, I'm all for it."

Karen, my confections manager, sat beside Glori. "I'll admit, I'm a sugar addict, and there's no getting away from it with my job. So it'll probably take a miracle for me to eat healthier and lose some weight."

Glori patted her hand. "You can do it, hon. We'll help. Do you have a family to cook for?"

Karen lowered her voice. "It's just me now. I've been divorced fifteen years. My kids'll be out of college this year."

Ashleigh volunteered next. "I manage first shift at The Golden Bowl, and it's crazy busy most of the time. So I tend to grab stuff. Usually sugar or something that's not healthy. And the stupid thing … we have healthy meals we serve to everyone else. Doc just did a program with The Marberry Girls to highlight all the healthy choices we have at the restaurant." She turned in his direction. "Thanks for all your help with that, Doc. Now that everyone knows the heart-healthy choices, it makes it easier."

Doc smiled and nodded. "Glad I could help, Ash."

Cat addressed Doc. "Is there something you would like to say regarding The Supernatural Diet?"

Doc blushed a bit, now that he was on the spot. The same reaction my sister and I had obviously inherited from him. "Well, Cat, most of my life, I've not been a church-goer. Once I met Annie's adoptive parents, Pastor Mike and Millie, well, I do enjoy attending their services in Ripple Lake on occasion. So I'm sure this club will be eye-opening for me." He nodded and held up the handout Cat had distributed. "Thank you."

"You're most welcome." Cat glanced at those of us who remained silent. "Well, Sabena, how about you?"

Sabena ran to Cat and leaned on her leg. "I pray that we have miracles in our group. And I pray that God keeps us all healthy and safe. And I pray for my brothers. Maybe someday they can be in our club."

Cat hugged her. "Thank you. We'll all pray those prayers, too."

Since the rest of us were not forthcoming in sharing our thoughts, Cat ended the meeting in a prayer she based on scripture. "Lord, we come to you, many of us weary and carrying heavy burdens. We trust that you will give us rest. We take your yoke upon us. We ask you to teach us to be humble and gentle at heart. We'll find rest for our souls. Your yoke is easy to bear, and the burden you give us is light … And let us be sure to remember, your yoke is easy when we're heading in the same direction you are."

"That's the trick," I said to the sky. "Heading in the same direction as God. Sometimes that direction is as clear as mud."

Buck's voice was low and clear. "Indeed."

After the meeting, we spent time milling around on the beach and catching up with everyone, with some discussion of how to proceed with individual needs. Those interested in a healthier lifestyle eventually came to the idea of creating an exercise group.

I turned to Buck. "Not for me. My walks on the beach are precious time alone with God. I don't mind the occasional walk with The Marberry Girls, but not another exercise group … even if they are the girls I work with."

"You're fine as you are, Annie. Fit, slim, healthy. No need to add more pressure to your day."

"Thanks. I know I've overdone the sweets lately, but that's just a matter of focusing on better nutrition."

He pulled me aside. "Perhaps we can help each other with that. Keep each other accountable. I've signed up with a new trainer. Maybe you've heard of Titan?"

My jaw dropped. "That Delta Forces guy that's always on all the gossip shows? He's a maniac."

"That's the one."

"Buck, he'll kill you."

"Kill me or cure me."

"Cure you of what?" Fear and anger surged coffee up into my throat.

"You probably wouldn't understand."

I noticed Nathan nearby, a grin on his face. *Smug.* He'd obviously overheard us. That's what this was all about. Some ridiculous rivalry.

There was something in me that only wanted to bolt. I turned, almost colliding with Billy and my brother-in-law. "David, Buck was just saying there should be an exercise group for the men. He was planning on starting with that guy, Titan, in New York."

David's smirk reminded me of Nathan. "You have Special Forces right here. Work out with us every morning. It won't cost you a dime."

Billy winked. "Maybe an arm and a leg, though."

I reacted without thinking. "Well, if you promise not to kill him, it's probably the best idea."

Buck's expression was cold. "Thanks for the offer."

Nathan appeared in front of me. "Mrs. Brewster, we're ready to take you to the restaurant when you are."

"Thank you."

He cast a scornful glance at Buck and headed up the stairs.

I stepped away from the group, hoping Buck would follow. He was in no rush. I knew I'd hammered his ego, but tact was difficult to come by lately. My feelings were hurt, too.

I took his hand, tugging him toward the water. "I'm sorry, Buck, I wasn't trying to be mean. These people make a profession out of being in top physical condition. Unless that's your profession, you can't compete. And you shouldn't. You've got a business to run.

People depend on you. A lot of people. You don't have time to compete with Navy SEALs and Delta Forces. You're healthy, you're in great shape, and you have more important things to do with your precious time."

"Indeed." Now he was sulking.

Frustration reached my boiling point. "What is it with you? One minute you're asking me to fly away with you, and the next, you can't drive away fast enough! Just tell me we're on or we're off, Buck. I can't take this stupidity."

He turned on his heel and walked off.

~ *Buck* ~

I traipsed up the beach then turned into the woods, thinking I'd locate the path where Annie and I had gone cross-country skiing only a few months ago. I succeeded only in becoming more lost. I belted at the brush in front of me, aggravated at myself for being so useless, hoping to forge a new path into the old and prove myself worthy. *To whom*?

I was almost ready to take out my phone when I saw David approaching.

"W-T-F!" I yelled.

His smirk broadened into a momentary smile.

I let out a string of curses, slamming my newfound walking stick against a tree. I didn't care that this world-class secret agent, assassin, and Special Forces sensation was doing all he could to keep from cracking up laughing at me. He finally let it go in a guffaw.

I turned to him in a rage. "How do I cope with this? How? We're grown adults. Successful business owners. How do I win her? How do I get through *two* fathers—one just as formidable as the other? Do I confront the Pastor? Or the holier-than-thou birth father that forgets he left a baby girl after he seduced her mother? They both think she's still their little girl. She's forty-eight years old!" The absurdity of that stopped me dead for a moment. The assassin's face was now unreadable.

Anger boiled again, and I stabbed the stick at the tree. "And once I get through that—there's Rhodes and SEAL Team Six! Bound and determined to keep her from me."

David put his hand up, probably to try and calm me down.

"But wait! There's more." I swung the stick against the tree. "We have the dead husband—her knight in shining armor. And family up the Wazoo. All new! All still bonding. And me? I'm lost in the woods, coming unglued."

He took a bottle of water from his rucksack and offered it to me. "You need to stay hydrated."

I plunged my walking stick into the ground, grabbed it, and gulped half in one swallow. Then I took a breath and wiped my mouth with the back of my hand. "I suppose insanity is one of the first signs of dehydration."

He grinned. "Or falling in love."

The very public scandal that unfortunately plagued his initial relationship with his wife Debbie crossed my mind. His behavior certainly could have been deemed insane. "I suppose you have some firsthand experience of that."

"Yes. You might find it's a permanent condition. It's not so bad."

I finished off the water, pondering my insanity over Annie.

He took my empty bottle and returned it to his knapsack.

"You are perfect. An assassin who recycles." It occurred to me that smart remark could get me killed.

He smirked. "Why don't we find the beach?"

It was an embarrassingly short trip. He led me out onto a ledge.

"On the rocks again?" My mind was back on the rocks by The Golden Bowl with Cat, the waves lashing at me.

"Again?"

"Never mind." I crept out to sit on a chair-like formation in stone. "Rather comfortable." At least the waves were relatively calm.

He handed me an apple.

"You certainly came prepared. What else do you have in that thing?"

Fortunately, he was amused. "When I saw you rush off, I decided I should catch up with you. I didn't want the children to get hold of the knife and the gun, so I took the rucksack with me." He took a bite of his apple.

I decided I needed to lose my attitude. "Thanks for saving me."

"No problem. After all, we're diet club partners." He didn't try and keep a straight face.

"The *Super*natural Diet Club. It's the supernatural part that scares the crap out of me. What does that mean?"

"You're better off asking Cat."

I took a bite of the apple. "How have you managed all this time? Your job is the opposite of the rest of your life, your family."

He shook his head. "I don't really know. Cat calls it grace and mercy. I guess that's what it is. Debbie is the most important thing in my life. So I figure out everything in relation to her. I put her first. I suppose it helps that she puts God first, so everything seems to fall into place from there. She's my connection to the divine. That's about as supernatural as I get."

It dawned on me that Annie could be the most important thing in my life. I wasn't positive she wanted me to be. And I wasn't positive I wanted her to be. Living for myself was all I ever focused on. The *Me* Diet. "Hmm."

David turned to me. "What?"

"I believe I've had a little epiphany. The Supernatural Diet means living for someone else—putting someone else ahead of self-interest."

He smirked. "I suppose."

"Do you think Rhodes is capable of that?"

"Yes."

Bad news for me. "Why do you say that?"

"He's a SEAL. That's why he ran to the school when the shooters showed up. That's why he dove into the ocean in February to save Annie's life."

"I suppose." I hated to think of Rhodes in any positive light.

"What is this feud you have going with Rhodes?"

"Isn't it obvious he's out to get Annie and rub my face in the dirt?"

"No. Why don't you tell me about that?"

"You were right there last month when he presented his case to Cisco—and you. Blackmail."

He rolled his eyes. "He was protecting Annie. That's his job."

"Protecting her from me."

"Truthfully, yes."

"I love Annie. Why would that be necessary? Haven't I demonstrated how much I care for her?"

"That's up to Annie to decide." He tossed the apple core into the ocean.

I raised my voice. "And how can she make a correct decision with Rhodes out to destroy me?"

He half snorted. "You're the one destroying yourself, Buck. If there was no damning evidence, Rhodes couldn't have found it."

"Of all people, you're not the one to point fingers." I realized my error in pushing the assassin who'd had his sordid life paraded in front of the worldwide media.

He grabbed me by my shirt. "You're here today precisely because I understand. I'm willing to give you the benefit of the doubt. Don't try my patience. Treat Annie with respect. If and when she's ready to be with you, I'll be making quite sure you're ready to be with her." He let go, and I slumped back onto the rock. "Understood?"

"Understood."

By the time I made it back to the fourth floor turret, I was exhausted and exasperated. Annie had gone to work at The Golden Bowl. I took a long shower, then collapsed on the bed.

I was falling perfectly into Rhodes' trap, and now realized Cisco and David were likely behind the whole thing. They had the capabilities to uncover anything about anyone on the planet. My secrets were not so secret. I'd flaunted my casual relationships with beautiful young women. My salacious interests would not have been difficult to discover.

I pulled a pile of pillows under me and half-sat in the bed, staring out my window. It occurred to me that Annie's birth father, Doc, had lived no more than a block away from me in Manhattan before he'd retired to Maine. I gagged with the certainty that Doc knew whatever Rhodes did. Annie's closest relatives opposed me. I'd have to fight for her, if I truly wanted her.

I did. That much I knew.

FOUR

~ *Lisa* ~

I took a break to eat some lunch downstairs in the staff lounge. It was a comfortable room with a wall full of windows that overlooked the water. Our manager, Ashleigh, waved me over to her table.

She had a big smile for me. "So what do you think of the Supernatural Diet Club?"

I giggled. "I can't believe they asked me. I mean I'm a dishwasher. And they're rock stars. But I guess Annie's family is as amazing as she is. It's like livin' a dream here."

Ash blew bubbles into her strawberry shake, the hair from her ponytail bouncing around her head. "I've never heard a dishwasher say she was living her dream. But I guess you're right. I met Paulo Clemente in person—again! And his wife is in the same club as me. *That's* supernatural all right."

"I know. Right?" I took a bite of my turkey sandwich and wiped away the cranberry sauce that oozed onto my lip.

"Well, I've been thinking we need to be really prepared for the next meeting. And a lot of us are concerned about being healthier. I highlighted the definition of diet here on the notes. It talks about a diet as a journey, a way of living, and it can even be an enjoyable prescription."

"I guess. But it wasn't an enjoyable prescription getting forty-something pounds off. If it wasn't for Billy, I never could've done it.

I mean, having him as a boyfriend. Wow. That's motivation. I'd never do all that exercise without him to inspire me. Ya know?"

She laughed. "I guess there's nothing like a Navy SEAL to get you to exercise."

"Yep."

"So what do you think of starting a healthy eating club as a part of the Supernatural Diet Club? I mean Doc and Annie already did the tough work of putting together the menu. We can encourage people to stick together and support each other and make more business for The Golden Bowl by promoting the menu. People can order the club meals for the day, and it's like a sense of community, because we're all getting healthier together. I know it'll be a cinch to get The Marberry Girls on board."

The cranberries were getting the better of me, and I wiped my chin. "Sounds good to me. Then I wouldn't have to think about what to eat. I wouldn't have to cook. It could already be planned out every day. All of Marberry could do it. I bet it'd make money for Annie, too."

Ash was excited. "It sure will. Even if we just start with supper. Just to get it going. And supper is the toughest meal of the day. You want something yummy, but not a million calories. And you're tired by the end of the day, so you don't want to cook. Like, three quarters of the time, I take something home from here for dinner. I think it's a no-brainer."

"Yeah."

"I know Annie and Buck'll let me run with it. We already offer the meals. They just need to be presented as part of the club. Between eat-in and take-out, it'll be huge. I know it. Think how many moms want to stay on a good diet, and it's tough with the rest of the family wanting the regular stuff. This way they can order the club meal and not feel like they're on a diet. I bet the motels go big for it, too."

"Yeah, this could be huge."

Ash jumped out of her seat. "Okay, I'm gonna run this by Annie. Can you make a poster for us? You're so good at that stuff."

"Okay." I guess that came from coloring with Rosie. Ash ran upstairs to find Annie, and I took the poster board and supplies from the closet. I laid out the poster on my table and wrote out the best invitation I could think of.

Want to eat healthier? Don't want to cook? Join our Super Club!

I left it by the daily specials board and went back to work. By the time I took my afternoon break we had more than a couple hundred members. Names and contact information were scribbled all over the poster filling every inch of space. Ash was beaming like the sun.

"How did that happen?"

She grabbed my arm. "Everyone loves the name—Super Club! Everyone wants to join, even the kids who aren't on a diet. You're a marketing genius, Lisa."

I didn't tell her I was a marketing genius who couldn't spell to save my life.

~*Buck* ~

I arrived at The Golden Bowl in time for the lunch rush. I intended to focus on the wait staff's performance, but spent more time observing Annie wowing her customers. People were drawn to her, and she engaged them in meaningful conversation. It was obvious they loved her, and she loved them. No one came away without a smile.

There wasn't a seat to be had in the restaurant or in The Bakery & Sweet Shop. The grounds were crowded with people of all ages, waiting to be seated, or enjoying the afternoon sunshine after their meal. There were lines at the take-out windows, with most every kid leaving with blueberry ice cream in some form or another. Annie's business was a gold mine.

I ordered a blueberry smoothie and headed toward the beach, wondering what to say to Annie when I'd finally have the opportunity to speak to her. As I passed the front porch of the restaurant, I felt compelled to take another prayer from the bowl. I ambled down the back stairs, crumpling the ivory paper in my hand. I knew it was another from Cat. I'd purposely scrounged through the bowl feeling for that distinctive paper. Curiosity tinged with fear.

By chance, there was an empty bench overlooking the water. I stretched out comfortably, hoping to keep the bench to myself. Putting the smoothie aside, I focused on the prayer. *But seek first his kingdom and his righteousness, and all these things will be given to you as well. Matt. 6:33*

I supposed this was God's way of warning me to shape up. Perhaps if I cleaned myself up, I'd win Annie's heart.

I closed my eyes and let the sun warm my face. The sounds of the sea soothed me. The prayer verse rolled through my head. I had no idea in the world how to "seek first his kingdom," or even what that was.

I remembered my conversation with David out on that ledge. I'd concluded the Supernatural Diet means living for someone else—putting someone else ahead of self-interest. David had said he put Debbie first and she put God first. Obviously, Annie did the same. As for God, I had no idea how to put him first. Not sure I wanted to. It became clear to me I needed to do a better job of putting Annie first.

Someone dared take the seat at the far end of my bench. I opened my eyes, ready to challenge the intruder.

"Hi, Buck. I'm sorry I offended you this morning. I shouldn't have stuck my nose in where it didn't belong. You're an adult. You make your own decisions."

"Annie, I'm sorry. I behaved childishly. Forgive me."

She smiled tentatively. "You're forgiven."

I slid over to her, drew her in a hug, and went for the kiss.

She looked up at me. "Buck, there are paparazzi everywhere."

I let go. "Sorry. I suppose you wouldn't want your picture taken with me—in a compromising position."

I heard her sigh on the sea breeze. "That's not it. They just don't want to give the media anything to blow out of proportion. I don't want to do anything that would give my sister an ounce of trouble."

"I understand."

She smiled, and I believe I heard my heart sing. Her voice was melodic. "Why don't we start over? Let's have some lunch."

I sensed a faint growl from my stomach. "I do have a craving for a cheeseburger."

She took my hand, bounced up from her seat, and tugged playfully. "Coming right up."

~ Annie ~

I wasn't sure if the way to Buck's heart was through his stomach, but the right cheeseburger certainly improved his mood. He was so cheerful, it took very little convincing for him to lure me out of the restaurant and down Miller's Way, heading toward our private beach.

Midafternoon sun beat down on us, but the heat felt good tempered by the sea breeze. I'd remembered to bring my hat and sunglasses for protection. Nathan and one of his men followed us at a safe distance. As we approached my property line, privacy improved.

I got caught up in the feel of the sun and breeze on my skin, the feel of my hand in his. Quiet contentment.

"Well, Annie, you said we could start over, so I'll begin with that holiday I've been thinking about. I won't pressure you as to the time. But is that something you'd care to do?"

"Sure, Buck, someday. A couple days vacation would be nice."

"Good. One of the islands, perhaps."

Uneasiness washed over me. "Um ... Buck?"

"Yes?" He twirled me by the waist, and I was facing him.

I purposely stared into his steel gray eyes, his handsome face, aware my sunglasses shielded me from this bold move. "Since I'm ... your client ... well, you probably know a whole lot more about me than I know about you. To be honest, I feel like I don't know you well enough to go on vacation together ... I know that sounds a little weird."

He remained polished. "Well, let's fix that."

"Okay. Spoken like a true business consultant."

His smile was mischievous. "How shall we fix it?"

We were getting dangerously close to a kiss that wouldn't solve much. I pulled back. "We should do a Q&A."

"Sounds reasonable. You first."

"Okay ... What's your favorite color?"

He responded immediately. "It used to be black."

"I almost guessed that. But then I thought you'd say green because it's the color of money."

He chuckled. "Good guess. You know me better than you think. At one time I would have said that."

"Hmm. So what is it now?"

His expression softened. "The most beautiful shade of blue I've ever seen—the color of your eyes."

I was grateful the sunglasses blocked his view of an automatic tear. But he took them off my face and kissed me. My hat fell to the ground. I didn't want him to stop. "Um ... Buck ... this is ... supposed to be ... Q&A ..."

We were still nose-to-nose. "Okay," he said.

"Okay, your turn to ask a question."

He lifted his head and stared out to sea, but he kept me against him. I looked up at him wondering if he ever intended to let me go.

"All right, here's a burning question. Has anyone ever called your brother-in-law Dave?"

I burst out laughing and almost choked. "You mean, has anyone ever called David, *Dave*, and lived?"

"Precisely."

"I doubt it."

"That's what I thought." Then he went into a monologue on how people might have slipped up, calling him Dave and adding the "id" just before he shot them. It was a good thing Buck held me up during this little performance. Otherwise I'd have fallen over laughing.

There was no doubt Buck was charming company, and a fellow foodie, but I had to get some real information. He was expert at making superficial conversation out of thin air. My sides were paining me I was laughing so hard. I broke away from him like a drunken sailor and retrieved my hat. I rubbed the glaze of tears that fogged my vision, and he handed me my sunglasses. I jammed them on my face and blustered through the remnants of laughter. "Okay, Buck, I need to know about your family."

"I told you all about them ages ago."

Laughter continued. "All about them? You told me like five sentences." I shook my head and tried to compose myself. "You told me your parents are in good health and living in London. Your mother is American, and your father is English. Your younger brother and wife and three kids and a dog live in Portland, Oregon where he has a tech business. And you weren't sure about the dog. That's it."

He looked at me. "Truly, I'm not sure about the children either."

The sound that came out of me was part gasp, part sigh, part laughter. "Close knit family, huh?"

"Not exactly." He led me off the path down to the beach. We landed on warm dry sand and took our shoes off.

"Well, I have all day to hear about your family. Your parents must get along well to stay married this long."

Buck made a face and nodded. "Let's just say my parents stayed together for the sake of the—money."

"Oh." My heart sank a little. "Is … is that why you never married?"

"I suppose."

~ *Lisa* ~

Karen, our confections manager and the one in charge at The Bakery & Sweet Shop, got all upset even before the Super Club was official. People were clamoring for dietetic desserts, and Doc had never discussed the heart healthy desserts for the menu. Karen raised a big stink with Annie, so she called an emergency meeting of The Supernatural Diet Club.

Ash said Annie'd been so preoccupied with Buck, that she didn't have time to have a staff meeting during business hours. So she'd make it a Supernatural Diet Club meeting to make sure everyone would be happy. I thought Ash was right. Annie and Buck looked pretty cozy. I don't think they spent all their time on business.

Ash and I weren't upset to have it on a Saturday after work. We'd get to hang with rock stars and be treated to a lobster bake afterward. Sounded like a good deal to me. I drove Peg and Ash over to Annie's, and we giggled as we went through security at the front gate. There were some paparazzi around shooting pictures of us from a distance.

Billy met us at the door and told us Annie'd be ten or fifteen minutes late. He pointed us to the kitchen. Peg took my little Rosie upstairs to the nursery to hang with rock star babies.

Ash and I found Karen in the kitchen with Doc. I wasn't surprised she was complaining. "The demand is crazy already. Gerald needs to know what to order for packaging. We have no idea what we're gonna need. Are we doing smaller sized desserts? Are we adding new low calorie items?"

Doc was taking everything in stride, sitting there sipping coffee. "Annie needs to make that decision, Karen. She owns the place, and she's a licensed nutritionist. I can give my stamp of approval, but Annie needs to make the final decision."

Ash jumped right into the conversation. "Annie's always had that healthier choice label on all the dessert menus. Why all the fuss? We can just go with those at least for a while."

Karen took off her glasses and rubbed her eyes. It looked like she'd had it up to here. "Are we doing calorie counts for the desserts? Up to now we haven't done that. If we're going to do a diet product, it should have the calorie label."

Little Sabena busted through the screen door. "We're ready! Come to the beach."

Doc scooped her up. "What's this mustache you're sporting?" Sabena giggled as he scrubbed his finger across the top of her lip. "Hmm. Looks like you're wearing more squash than you ate, young lady."

We followed them to the beach.

Annie and Buck took chairs in a little circle with Karen, Ash, and me, while Sabena supervised everyone else in arranging her lobster trap and meeting chairs a ways down the beach. Annie poured us lemonade from a large pitcher. "I'm really sorry I've been out of touch on all this. Karen, I know I caused a lot of confusion for you. I'm sorry."

Karen looked Annie right in the eye. "It's okay. I probably overreacted. We've been crazy busy and now another new thing. I need to learn to take things more in stride."

It looked like Annie relaxed a little. "Tell me what's going on."

Karen let out a big sigh. "We're getting slammed. Everyone's asking about Super Club desserts, and I don't even know if there are any. All the questions … it's holding up the lines. So I've been telling my staff to point people to the healthy choice desserts, but I don't know if that's what you want. I thought we'd need some calorie counts, some special packaging … portion control."

Annie made a face. "I guess I never considered the dessert menu for Super Club, but I don't know why not. It makes sense people would want diet desserts. It's only been a couple of days since Ash and Lisa brought it up. I'm sorry, Karen, I'm just not staying on top of things."

Buck took Annie's hand, and Ash and I grinned at each other.

He looked at Karen. "You make some excellent points, Karen. Confusion is never a good thing. Communication should have been better. I'm very glad you brought this to our attention so quickly.

Long lines are an issue, and we've worked hard to deal with that. Customer experience is paramount."

Annie nodded. "True."

Karen took off her glasses and rubbed her eyes. I think she was getting emotional. "Thanks."

Buck took out his binder and went to work. "Perhaps ... if we set the Super Club apart, it will allow us to test various products and make promotion simpler as well. I'm thinking some old fashioned carts—like a dessert truck. We can do separate carts for Super Club meals and desserts. It makes it simpler to test, adds to the festive atmosphere, focuses the spotlight on the program, and it will help reduce the lines at your shop."

Annie's face was bright pink. "Buck, that's fantastic."

Karen and Ash nodded. "Sounds perfect," Karen said. "How long before we can get that going?"

Buck looked up from his tablet. "No time like the present. Summer is our peak season here. The carts will allow us more sales stations without the need to build or expand our current buildings. Late in the fall, when the crowds diminish, we can close the carts. By then we'll know what meals and desserts will be packaged for sale nationally."

Karen looked confused. "But it'll take time to get the carts ... and the packaging. What about the packaging? What desserts do you want, Annie?"

I had to chime in. "You have to have blueberry smoothies for one of the choices. Everybody loves those. And something chocolate."

Annie chuckled. "Okay."

Karen still looked worried. "But ..."

Buck looked straight at Karen. "We'll have the dessert carts ready to go this Tuesday at noon. Annie will have two or three desserts and three to five frozen dessert choices finalized by tomorrow morning. Gerald will have appropriate containers, and we'll have his people package the products. We'll generate the necessary labels in small quantities. That will allow us to get the products out quickly. If an item doesn't sell, it's not a big problem. We learn and move on."

Karen was stunned. "Tuesday noon?"

Buck was all business. "Dessert carts ready to roll Tuesday, noon. The meal carts will launch Wednesday, noon. Ash, Lisa, perhaps you can confer with Annie on some meal choices. I suggest three choices.

Gerald will do the packaging and labeling. My team will make sure the signage is compelling."

"Wednesday noon?" Karen could hardly believe it.

"Yes." Buck closed his binder. "Life is uncertain. Eat dessert first. Tuesday we launch Super Club desserts. Wednesday we launch Super Club meals. I'm sure testing at The Golden Bowl will go well. Then we'll be ready to roll out the prepared foods in time for January slimming season."

"Awesome!" Ash and I said at once. Karen was smiling.

I could see Annie turning to each of us, getting more excited the more we smiled. She turned to Buck. "So all we have to do is make a few choices on what meals to offer?"

"Yes."

"Well, that's simple, Buck. We just look at the reports and pick our best sellers on the healthy menu and figure portions and calorie counts."

Buck winked at her. "You're catching on, my dear. Aren't you glad you have reports to refer to?"

She laughed. Ash and I winked at each other. Karen picked up on our shenanigans and shook her head.

The smell of food lured us down the beach.

I heard Annie's voice behind me. "Buck, you're a genius."

As we took our seats, Sabena ran around handing each of us Cat's notes. With a last burst of energy, she landed on the lobster trap, and Cat grabbed her before she lost her balance. Thank goodness Cat remembered to put a towel there. Otherwise she could've gotten a nasty splinter.

"Welcome to The Supernatural Diet Club. Today is our second meeting, and we're focusing on the most important thing we all need to know. God is love. Perfect love. And God loves us—all of us. Auntie says God's love is unconditional, and that's the way we need to love God and each other. Okay, Auntie is going to speak now."

Cat assisted Sabena to a seat beside her on the lobster trap. "Thank you, Sabena. What an excellent introduction." She planted a kiss on her forehead, and Sabena giggled. She was pleased with herself.

I couldn't take my eyes off Cat. She was pretty and petite, but it was like a glow that came out of her that made her like a magnet. I remembered her talk on stage at the Christmas concert I saw on TV.

She invited everyone to be a light. Just like God, I guess. And that's what I saw when I looked at her. Didn't matter that she wore cut-offs and a tee shirt. She was a gold light.

Cat turned to us. "Sabena has said it all, really. The truth sets us free. God loves each one of us completely and totally—unconditionally. He meets us wherever we are in life. Scripture says he knocks and will come in if we open to him. God never forces us. We have free choice to answer that call or not. If we ignore the call, don't be surprised if God knocks again. I challenge you to answer that call. Open your heart to God. You'll find true love and true freedom."

She gave Sabena a squeeze and another kiss. "This week, let's focus on loving God and loving each other."

Sabena nodded. "That's the most important thing. In the end, there's faith, hope and love. And the greatest of these is love." Cat gave her another hug, and I could tell Sabena basked in the feeling.

Cat pointed down the beach and Sabena followed her hand. "It looks like Danny is having some fun in the tide pool. Why don't you go and give your brother some unconditional love?"

Sabena turned to her, red-faced. "I … I don't think he wants to hear about The Supernatural Diet Club. He thinks it's stupid."

Cat smiled. "God is meeting Danny in that tidal pool right now—showing him his creations and having fun right where Danny is. Might you do the same?"

Tears started down Sabena's face and mine too, I think. She ran down the beach to her brother. Next thing you know, he took her by the hand and pointed to something in the pool.

Ash grabbed my hand. "Aw … that's so sweet."

~ *Annie* ~

Buck and I remained on the beach after everyone else, except our ever-present bodyguards, retired for the night. We were cozy and comfortable snuggled in a blanket in front of a fire. Conversation had been intermittent and casual, but my feelings for Buck were becoming clearer, at least to me. I suppose my outward behavior was the same.

Probably part of that strengthening attachment was due to his business acumen. Deep down, I knew he'd always have my back when it came to The Golden Bowl. I didn't have to hold the entire business together myself. That was a huge relief.

I thought about how he'd treated Karen so well, acknowledging her concerns and treating them seriously. She felt listened to. She went from almost distraught to smiling. Just because he took the time to really listen and make her feel appreciated. "Thanks, Buck."

"For what?"

"For taking my employees seriously, for respecting them and listening. For coming up with genius ideas. And making it look so easy."

"Any time, Annie."

"Thanks for taking care of me."

He kissed the side of my face. "My pleasure."

"Um … Buck?"

"Yes?"

"What do you think about what Cat said about unconditional love?"

"I think it sounds lovely."

I laughed into his chest. "Such a diplomat."

He exhaled a loud breath. "It's all very nice, but when it comes right down to it, we live in a conditional world. If … then. If you make my business succeed, then you get paid. Then I'll recommend you. Then I'll like you. If you behave according to my arbitrary standards, then I won't beat you. If you give me this, then I'll give you that. Cat has the good fortune to be married to a billionaire who's smitten with her. She can well afford unconditional love … with the right people in the right circumstances. And God, I suppose."

If you behave according to my arbitrary standards, then I won't beat you. That was buried nice and neatly in the middle of the tirade. "Um … Buck?"

"Yes?"

"I'm guessing your father wasn't demonstrative with his kids."

"As a matter of fact, he was too demonstrative. I was happiest when he was away on business."

I lifted my head up to face him. "Demonstrative, how?"

"Violence, rage … I really don't want to waste a perfectly wonderful evening discussing him."

I put my hand to his face and watched flickers of fire reflected in his eyes. He took my hand and kissed it. "I'm sorry, Annie, I know you want to know me better, but my childhood angst is not worth discussing. I'd much rather talk about moving forward—with you."

"Okay. But my dad is a minister, so you have to know God is gonna fit in with us somehow, right?"

"Yes, I've been contemplating all this, and I assure you, the truth will set us free. Somehow."

I laughed in his face. "Okay. Your assurances don't sound too assuring. I'd love to hear your contemplations, Buck."

There was hesitation. "About the truth setting us free?"

"Yes."

"Well, Cat says that all the time, so I suppose it will. I really don't know what she means by that. It *is* a popular expression, though." He took me by the shoulders before I could respond. "But I have thought a good deal about you, about us. And I realize the Supernatural Diet means putting you first in my life. Absolutely first. And that's what I'm trying to do."

I thought I'd melt into his arms. Despite the darkness on the beach, I was sure there was light in his eyes. But Doc's words popped into my head. *The guy's a player, Annie. He'll break your heart.* Buck certainly had some smooth talk.

FIVE

~ Buck ~

By late Sunday night, I'd wrapped up every detail of the launch of the new Super Club products. Certain that the project would go as planned, I headed out to make my partners meeting in New York the following morning.

An overwhelming urge drew me back to The Golden Bowl before leaving Marberry. The grounds were deserted, but I knew security cameras were filming my every move. Nevertheless, I plunged my hand into the mass of papers overflowing the bowl. The feel of my chosen slip told me it had to be another one of Cat's prayers. Relief began to erase my desperation. Maybe it was really God who was in charge of all this. Or perhaps, I merely had a new addiction.

I sat in my car and read it.

Heart-shattered lives ready for love don't for a moment escape God's notice. From Psalm 51, The Message

The same sweaty fear I'd experienced on the ledge with Cat returned. Struggling to breathe, I careened out of the driveway hellbent for the Maine Turnpike.

When I reached my apartment, it was early morning in the city that never sleeps. I tossed my bag on the floor, fell back on the bed, and stared at the ceiling. I knew what I had to do. I couldn't do it. The magazines, the jewelry—that was relatively simple. My eyes fogged. I loved Annie. There was no question. I'd do anything for her. But I didn't know how to deal with this situation without making it worse. Whatever I did, I knew I'd make it worse.

Heart-shattered lives ready for love don't for a moment escape God's notice.

I spoke to the ceiling. "All right, prove you're real. Prove you've noticed me. Fix this."

My phone insisted I answer. "Yes?"

It was Will Brooke. "Just making sure you're in New York, Buck. Make sure you're on time this morning."

"I'll be there." I threw the phone down and headed to the shower. A glimpse in the mirror reminded me driving all night before an important meeting was not the best idea. I'd need to do something about the bags under my eyes.

By the time I emerged from my dressing room, I was the image of a high-powered executive in a dark suit and red tie. I tossed my briefcase on the bed to make sure I had everything I'd need for the day. A tangle of paper, the mashed up, straightened out prayers I'd sweated over on the rocks by The Golden Bowl was a reminder I did not need today. I threw the pile on my bed, locked the case, and set off for my meeting.

The day went smoothly. I was the center of attention since I was the reason Brooke, Lewis & Wynn was on track to double our business this year. I gloated over that fact and announced to my partners that they had no reason to gripe over my relationship with Annie. If not for the attention from all the publicity surrounding The Golden Bowl, we surely wouldn't have the explosion of new clients we'd seen of late. They had to agree. I basked in the glory.

We celebrated with cocktails and dinner at one of New York's finest restaurants—one of our clients, of course—not far from our office. I wasn't especially surprised when I noticed my administrative assistant barreling toward our table.

I raised my glass in her direction. "Janice! Come join us."

She stood over me. A furrowed face and frown took the edge off my high. "Buck, I'm sorry to disturb you here, but your phone is off."

"Really, can't I have a dinner in peace? I'll be back to business as usual tomorrow. Problems can wait."

Janice dropped into a chair the waiter seamlessly aimed at her backside. My partners leaned in to hear what she had to say. "I'm sorry, Buck, it can't wait. Your apartment has burned down."

"What?"

"The fire marshal is there. He told me the building is perfectly fine. It's just your apartment that burned."

"My ... my apartment?"

She nodded. "Everything inside."

"Ever-everything?"

"'Hotter than Hades,' he said. A total loss."

"Total?"

She nodded. "I'm sorry. If you leave now, you can probably catch him. I think he really wants to talk to you. I'll book a hotel room for you tonight."

It seemed that was the thing to do. *Go talk to the fire marshal.* Unfortunately, I was not able to stand up.

Leaving the elevator, I noticed everything looked perfectly fine. There was only a hint of smoke in the hall. The fire marshal greeted me and held up a small plastic bag. "I'm very sorry, Mr. Wynn. The apartment and contents are a total loss. This is the only thing that survived the fire. It's not even charred. I don't understand why, because it was in the middle of the bed. And that was completely burned. How could that happen?"

I took the plastic bag and realized it was one of Cat's prayers that I'd dumped on the bed before I left. I read aloud. "He makes winds his messengers, flames of fire his servants. Psalm 104:4" I remember a whiff of salt air before I passed out.

I woke up in the concierge's office, laid out on a couch. His spectacles reflected the bright light of the high intensity lamp over my head. The fire marshal stood over him, a perplexed look on his face.

I realized I was still clutching that plastic bag as I tried to sit up. "I need to see my apartment."

The concierge held my arm. "I'm not sure that's a good idea, Mr. Wynn. Everything's gone. Everything."

I pulled myself up to sit and face him, the glare of the light aggravating me more. "I need to see it."

His horrified expression made me want to retch. "The art collection is destroyed. A total loss. I'm so sorry. Insurance people are on the way. Arson investigators. They'll get to the bottom of it, and I'm sure you'll get a very good settlement."

Yes, I'd had a few drinks, and yes, I'd salvaged a very strange prayer from the ashes, but I couldn't have been that out of it. Sometimes people did have difficulty with my accent. I made sure to enunciate. "I need to see my apartment."

The fire marshal dutifully escorted me back upstairs. The open door led us into complete blackness—everything charred, floor to ceiling. The smell nauseated me.

A crew of investigators milled about. One of them approached us. "Looks like the fire started in the wall between the bed and the … uh … gallery. I hear a handyman installed lighting for a painting this morning. Not a licensed electrician. Probably caused an electrical fire. We need some time to figure out exactly what happened. Good thing no one was here. Once it got going, it destroyed the place in minutes."

Soot and emotion blocked my throat. There were no words anyway. I wiped my watery eyes and made my way to the room that had at one time been my pride and joy. Now it was waterlogged ashes. *God's way of fixing things.*

I stared at the remains of the newest and most precious painting of all, the one that had been highlighted with new light fixtures, and I wept.

My assistant had comfortable new clothes, shoes, and two business suits delivered to my hotel room. My sodden shoes and smelly suit disappeared. Room service arrived with food and drink. The vodka was all I needed. I sat in a comfortable chair in my dark room, stared at the lights of the city, and wondered what I'd say to Annie. I didn't have the wherewithal to turn on my phone. Tonight I only wanted to crawl into a hole and die.

I'd instructed my partners and coworkers not to breathe a word to anyone in Maine. But I knew word would leak somehow. There were too many gossips who knew the real me.

As the first sign of daylight appeared in my window, it occurred to me. Nathan Rhodes could well have been behind the whole thing. If he was involved, surely David and Cisco were giving the orders.

My alcohol-addled mind spun back to the day, about a month ago, when I was brought before the three of them for a "meeting." Rhodes had broken into my apartment while I was in Florida on business. He searched the place and sent photos of his findings to David. Until I saw them, I had no idea he'd set foot on my property.

David had warned me, in no uncertain terms, that he'd protect Annie from the likes of me. "It takes one to know one," I'd said. His only response was a smirk.

The glass fell from my hand and bounced on the floor. I was a weepy drunk. Annie's face was front and center in my mind's eye. That painting, the one her God destroyed, was commissioned by me. I'd given the artist a photo of us at the New Year's party at the White House. She was in my arms in an intimate dance, a highlight of my life, of *our life* together. It was perfect. It deserved the place of honor in my gallery. It deserved perfect lighting.

He makes winds his messengers, flames of fire his servants. I was back on the rocky ledge near The Golden Bowl, the wind whipping at me. It was all too much to fathom. *My only chance is Cat.* If I had any chance at all with Annie, it would be through Cat. I'd call Cat. But first I'd need to sober up.

I'd no sooner turned the phone on when it chimed with one of Paulo Clemente's songs. "Annie! I was just about to call."

"Buck, are you in your car?" The tiny voice tore at my heartstrings, but I let my impatience show.

"Sabena, what are you doing with Annie's phone?"

"Are you in your car now? We have a meeting today. It's important. Don't worry about the painting. Mama can do a new one for you."

My breath caught. My voice rose in a squeak. "Painting?" *What's going on?*

"Mama is an excellent artist. She can do one that's even better. You mustn't worry. I think she's working on it now. Just come home, Buck."

I forced myself to take a cleansing breath. It seemed I hadn't held my liquor. This child was precocious, but I was astute, even when drunk. My voice projected the calm I intended. "Sabena, I really don't know what painting you're referring to."

"It's the painting of Auntie ... Auntie Annie and you. Your faces melted on the wall. But don't you worry, Mama can make you a new one."

I nearly retched, right there in the easy chair. A quick push of the lever propelled me to the bathroom. I ran cold water on a washcloth.

"Buck, are you in your car yet?"

Beads of sweat formed on my forehead. I put the phone on speaker and applied the washcloth.

"Buck?"

The image of the remains of my painting would not leave my mind. I could smell the soot. My knees began to give out. "Sabena, where did you get the idea of a painting melting on the wall?"

"In my dream."

I attempted a chuckle. "Well, that was quite a dream. I assure you, all is well." I reached into my briefcase for a bottle of painkillers.

"I'll ask Papa to send a helicopter for you. Our meeting is at 5:00. Then we'll have a lobster bake. I'll go ask Papa now."

I choked on the pills. "No! No ... Sabena. No need to talk to Papa. No need for a helicopter." I slugged more water. "Just ... just put Annie on the phone. We'll work it all out." I wrung the washcloth in more cold water, took the phone, and headed back to the easy chair. "Sabena? Did you find Annie?"

"She's right outside in her chair with Auntie Cat. I can see them from the window. I'm sitting at the kitchen table."

"Okay. Very good."

"I've been making a sketch of your painting, but Mama can do it better. I'll give her this one to show her."

I slammed my head against the headrest. "No need! Just ... just put Annie on the phone. *Now*, Sabena." I waited in the dead air.

~ *Annie* ~

I couldn't help a smile as Sabena handed me my phone. She knew she wasn't supposed to have it, but those huge blue eyes and wisps of white hair atop an angel face meant she got away with most anything.

"Buck's on the phone, Auntie."

"Thank you."

She dropped onto the grass in front of Cat and me. "Remember to remind him about our meeting."

"I will."

Cat rose and ushered Sabena to the beach.

"Buck? How did your partners meeting go?"

"Very well, Annie, I couldn't be more pleased about the business."

Something was a little bit off. A big push behind the voice, and then a pause.

"Buck, are you okay?"

"A bit too much to drink last night. Too much celebrating. But I'm fine. Looking forward to our Diet Club meeting today."

"Oh, good! We were hoping you'd make it. The topic is sacred partnership. Cat and I were just having a conversation about it."

There was a strange noise in the background. "*So* looking forward to it."

"Okay."

"Annie, I need to get going if I'm to be on time. See you soon."

Strange. I stashed the phone in my pocket, and Nathan took the empty seat beside me. He had a bemused look on his face. "Mr. Rhodes?"

"Buck Wynn's apartment burned yesterday—a total loss. Everything. Toast."

I almost slid out of the chair.

The shock of learning about Buck's apartment brought me down to the beach in search of Cat. Sabena had run off to wade in the water with the other kids. Cat stood at the water's edge staring off into the sky.

I think I startled her. "Buck's apartment burned down, Cat. He says he's driving up today, but I think he's in shock."

She took me by the hands. "Let's pray for Buck." Something in the tone of her voice scared me to death.

But Cat's demeanor was perfectly calm. She led me in prayer, then let go of me. "We need to get over to The Golden Bowl. I hear your new product launch is happening at noon."

I took a breath. "How can you be so calm?"

The look on her face was priceless.

I chuckled. "Okay, I get it. God's in charge."

She smiled. "I believe this product line will be one of your most successful."

My response was automatic. "From your lips to God's ears." *This is Cat I'm talking to.* I broke up laughing.

~ *Buck* ~

It was after 10:00 p.m. when I arrived in Marberry, and it took all that I had to pass The Golden Bowl without stopping for another prayer. In spite of a sense of impending doom, I only wanted to find another prayerful slip of advice or fortunetelling from Cat. *Heart-shattered lives ready for love don't for a moment escape God's notice.* Repeating that little gem kept me driving. I resolved to speak with Cat personally in the morning.

As to The Supernatural Diet Club meeting, I was grateful that I'd missed it. I didn't look forward to Sabena's recap on sacred partnership, whatever that was.

Annie met me in the foyer with kisses and sympathy—exactly what I needed. The questions, I didn't need.

"I'm exhausted, Annie. I'll tell you all about this little disaster tomorrow. But do tell me how the dessert cart launch went."

She tightened her hug. "It couldn't have been better. People loved the cart, loved the desserts. The lines were crazy … and just as crazy in The Sweet Shop. But Karen was still thrilled. We all are. Thanks, Buck, it's an awesome idea, and you get the credit. I learned my lesson, once again, that reports are my friend." Her giggle made me smile.

The house was quiet, except for the ever-present sound of the surf. I descended from my fourth floor turret to Debbie's second floor art studio. It was 2:00 a.m. and I was wide-awake, my mind spinning. I had to see if Debbie had done a painting of Annie and me. The flashlight guided my silent steps. The door was open, as it often was. I stepped inside and surveyed the room.

Immediately, my attention was drawn to Debbie's easel. My heart pounded with the shock. My painting faced me.

I walked to it with leaden legs and shone my light on it. Every detail was the same, save the artist's signature. How could this be? I sat in the artist's chair, dumbfounded. It occurred to me this rendition included the modification of the original photo I'd asked my artist to make. He had effectively altered the neckline of her gown enhancing her cleavage. Embarrassment overtook my confusion.

I shone the light around the area looking for a copy of the photo I'd given to my artist. Although it was apparent Debbie's materials were still at hand, there was no sign of a photo. I noticed, in fact, Annie's face was even more beautiful, more expressive, than the version my artist had done.

There has to be a photo. I puttered over her supplies to find it. She'd obviously worked on this canvas recently, but there was no photo to be found.

The light slipped in my hand, directing my attention to a pile of canvases on the floor. Surprise spurred tingling fear, head to foot, and drove me to the stack. Sweat poured as I knelt over them. They were portraits—duplicates of only the faces in my gallery. Their names were neatly printed where the artist's signature would be. I flipped through them again and again. *How can this be?*

An overhead light came on, and I landed on my backside. I looked up to see David standing in the doorway, a faint grin on his face.

"If you're considering marrying into this family, Buck, you'll want to know there's no getting away with anything. No matter how smart you think you are."

I rolled to my knees then lumbered into a nearby chair. "How?"

He pulled a chair over and smirked. "I believe it has something to do with sacred partnership." He took a seat.

I took a moment to stew. "What?"

He almost smiled. "Who might be a better question. You know by now Cat seems to have a direct line to the divine. Since I've known

Debbie, I've seen her artistic skill in the form of clues and prophecies. And our children—I'd say five out of the six are reasonably normal. You've seen Sabena. I think she's a blend of Debbie and Cat. More frightening than all five of our boys put together."

"Indeed." I put my head in my hands. There was no sorting this out. When I dared look up, he'd taken a portrait from the top of the pile. My face must have looked to be one big question mark.

"Debbie started painting these before Rhodes took those photos of your art collection. She has no idea they're your conquests."

"Before?"

"Debbie has enough difficulties. Her health is fragile. She has no need to know your secrets, Buck."

My head was spinning. "So … so *you* sent Rhodes to break into my apartment. You … you knew you'd find these portraits before you sent him there?"

His eyes were all business. "Yes, I was fairly certain. Though, I must say, the extent of your collection was … impressive."

It dawned on me as acid gnawed at my throat. "*You*? You're the one who sent the electrician to burn my apartment."

He grinned. "That was truly an act of God. I didn't have to lift a finger."

I sat motionless, dripping with sweat, for a while. My brain filled with images and words, somehow processing the nightmare my life had become. David busied himself admiring his wife's artwork.

I turned to him. "Annie … doesn't seem to be … psychic."

The grin was still there. "Looks like the more sane side of the family, Buck. Congratulations."

I rubbed the sweat off my brow. *Heart-shattered lives ready for love don't for a moment escape God's notice.* "And there's that small matter of God to contend with."

It was mid-morning when I awoke from a fitful sleep. Annie had gone to work, and most of the family had gone off to the beach. I found Cat and Cisco settled in the Adirondack chairs, their baby boy asleep in Cisco's arms.

"May I join you?"

"Of course." Cat smiled up at me. Cisco nodded.

I dragged another chair to face them, and sat with my second cup of coffee. All the words I'd rehearsed eluded me.

Cisco's bright blue eyes locked on mine. "We're very sorry to hear about your apartment, Buck. I'm sure it's still a shock to you. I hope you'll be able to stay here with us until you can get everything resolved."

I cleared my throat. "That's very kind of you."

"May I ask why you didn't tell us about it?"

My eyes began to burn. "I … I simply couldn't summon the wherewithal to tell you … to tell Annie. I was too upset. I didn't want to upset her."

He looked at his wife and back at me. "I understand. If there's anything we can do, please don't hesitate to ask."

"Thank you."

He grinned. "I have a feeling you and Cat have some things to discuss. Jack and I are going to make some phone calls, if you'll excuse us."

My stomach slung the coffee upward, but I returned the smile. This was beyond strange, but to be expected after my experience in the art studio last night. With a nod, Cisco and his son disappeared through the kitchen door.

I reflexively leaned forward in my seat and the question was out of my mouth before I realized it. "How does Francisco Clemente—the third—end up with a firstborn son named Jack?"

Cat's giggle put my mind more at ease. "Even Cisco agrees there are too many Franciscos now, and since my father was John Francis, he agreed we should name our son in his honor. Everyone called my father, Jack. So now we have Jack."

"That makes sense." I couldn't bring myself to delve into the topic that brought me here. "So … your mother was Austrian."

"Yes. She and David's mother were sisters, and they were quite close. When my parents died, David's parents raised me as their own. I lived in Salzburg until I went to university in England."

"I see."

She smiled, but it was the intensity of those eyes that mesmerized me. "Is there something you want to discuss, Buck?"

SIX

~ *Buck* ~

"Yes." The certainty in my voice clashed with the confusion in my mind. I put the coffee on the arm of the chair. "I … I really don't know where to begin."

"You've been through a terrible stress. Perhaps you need to be still for a bit."

"That's exactly it, Cat. I don't have time to be still. Time waits for no man. Annie is slipping through my fingers as we speak."

"Why do you say that?"

"It's true. Rhodes will do anything to keep her from me." Scorching heat watered my eyes and brought that horrific prayer back at me. "*He makes winds his messengers, flames of fire his servants.* That was the only thing that survived that fire—a slip of paper from you. That's how your God fixes things."

"God's ways are not our ways."

"Well, amen to that, sister." I lifted the coffee to my lips.

Cat's giggle stopped me. "You still have your sense of humor, Buck."

"I feel particularly humorless right now. And I have no idea how to cope with all this. No idea."

As she opened her mouth, I had to say it. "Don't tell me it's sacred partnership. First of all, I have no idea what that really means. Second of all, *God* burned my apartment to *cinders*. I must say I'm concerned the next spontaneous combustion will be *me*."

Cat's eyes fixed on mine and silenced me. Her voice was soft and certain. "Buck, there's a battle for your mind, your soul, and it's happening now. You've made a decision, but Satan is persistent. He won't give up easily. Know that God is at work in you, and also through you. It takes time, time to renew your mind and trust God for what he wants for you, not what you want for you."

I rubbed my weary eyes. "Frankly, Cat, that doesn't sound like much fun."

Her eyes remained on mine. "That's sacred partnership, Buck. It's the way to reach your heart's desire."

"My heart's desire?" I took a deliberate gulp of coffee. Did I dare lay the truth out to Cat? I had no choice. "My heart's desire is Annie. Plain and simple. Yet, your God—and now mine, I suppose—is the very thing keeping her from me."

Her expression was serious. "Buck, sometimes God's answer is not a simple yes or no. Sometimes it's not yet. Have you considered that the very best thing for both of you could be waiting until the time is right? Have you considered that you might have some preparation to do?"

I couldn't resist a sardonic reply. "Of course. Why, I said to God just the other day, go ahead and fix things. Burn down this apartment. Whatever fixes things even better than I've fixed them so far. Just burn millions of dollars. No problem."

"Trust is the key to your sacred partnership. Trust God to work everything out for good. You'll recover the money from your insurance company. Your art collection is insured as well. And now you're free of it."

A lump congealed in my throat. "Art ... art collection?"

Her gaze didn't waver. "Yes."

"How ... how do you know about my art collection?" I should not have been so stunned. It was indeed obvious Cat had a connection to the divine—as well as to Cisco and David who had photos. I needed to hear her explanation.

Her smirk was reminiscent of David. "Debbie began painting those portraits some time ago. When she showed me the first, God put it on my heart. I didn't tell her that I knew why she was painting them. I think it would have upset her."

I could feel no sympathy for Debbie. "Were you the one who told Cisco and David about my art collection?"

"No. I told no one. But David is perceptive. He knows most of Debbie's paintings have a deeper meaning. And your reputation precedes you, Buck. It was simple enough for him to conclude there was a reason to send Nathan to New York to confirm his suspicions."

I heard the kitchen door snap closed. Debbie descended the stairs shaking herself off, the sea breeze ruffling her hair and her very feminine pink cotton dress. She took Cisco's vacant seat.

A strange sense of embarrassment welled up, but I managed to say "Good morning."

Her sweet smile penetrated a serious face. "I hope I'm not disturbing you. I just need a break."

Cat reached over and squeezed her hand. "What's wrong?"

She let out a sigh. "Oh, it's that portrait of Annie and Buck. Every time I try and fix her gown, I mess it up. I know her chest is out of proportion. I just can't get it right. It's aggravating."

As I gurgled coffee, I noticed Cat turned a reflexive smile away from the frustrated artist.

She resumed her concerned demeanor and patted her hand. "You mustn't worry, Debbie. I'm sure it's beautiful."

The wind blew Debbie's hair, revealing a streak of purple paint across her forehead. "No. Not yet." She smudged the purple with the back of her hand. "I want to give the painting to you, Buck. I hope it makes you feel better after losing your apartment in the fire. But I'm not sure when it'll be ready." She noticed the paint on her hand and set to work removing it with a tissue she found in her pocket.

I pointed to her forehead. "You have some smudged, too."

Cat rifled through her beach bag, came up with a moistened baby towel, and wiped away the purple. "Sabena does the same thing."

That job done, Debbie looked to Cat. "Annie called, and she's going to take all those portraits for a charity auction. It'll help clear out my studio, and she said they'd get maybe a half-million dollars for them. She said people are excited to buy my work."

I fought to keep the coffee down. "Portraits?"

Cat gave me a knowing look. "Debbie's done quite a few recently. She works so quickly and precisely. It amazes me to watch her. In the limited time she has, she can produce three or four a day."

"Well, they all have names, but I don't know them. I thought it can't do any harm to donate them to charity. The names are just first names, and they sound like a lot of nicknames. So I'll let Annie sell them." Debbie affirmed her plan with a nod. "But right now, I need a little break. I'm going to take a walk on the beach. Want to come?"

Cat shook her head. "Buck and I were almost finished with our discussion on sacred partnership. Then I'm going to find Cisco and Jack."

"Okay." Debbie smiled her goodbyes and headed toward the beach.

I turned right around in my seat following her, anxiety spiraling. As she disappeared down the stairs, I spun back to face Cat. "How much is it going to cost me to get out of this mess? Will she take five hundred thousand for those paintings?"

"You'll have to ask Annie."

I struggled back up the stairs to my fourth floor turret, the melted faces of my sin weighing me down. God was surely having a belly laugh over this one. Another half-million or more to redeem myself. Maybe that was his grand plan. Make Annie's charities rich and me poor. Take everything away from me. But would he give me Annie in the end?

I concocted a story as I showered, dressed, and headed over to The Golden Bowl. Shore Road was lined with cars, the parking lot packed. Billy, the ex-SEAL surfer security guard, waved me over with a friendly smile. A crowd of young women flocked around him. "Cool car, Buck. Your space is reserved for you."

I parked in my designated spot in full view of security cameras. Some of the women admired my Lamborghini and then followed me into the restaurant. Although Annie was not in her office under the staircase, I slipped inside and shut the door. I took a moment to decompress, fighting an urge to visit the prayer bowl again. Had I let go of all logic and reason?

When the coast was clear, I ascertained Annie was in her office in the customer service building. I took a fresh cup of coffee and my briefcase and strolled the path to the barn, inhaling warm salt air, admiring colorful flowers, appreciating the crowds of tourists all spending their money at The Golden Bowl. The new carts were perfect, and hordes of customers surrounded them. Employees were doing a fine job of promoting the products.

Logic and reason hadn't gone out the window. I puffed up with pride. Almighty Buck Wynn was largely responsible for this grand and profitable transformation.

I gave a quick knock on the office door and opened it in time to catch Annie's melodious laughter.

Rhodes stood in front of her desk. "I've got a meeting with David. See you later, Annie." He acknowledged me with a nod, and brushed past me.

I thought my blood pressure would explode. *How dare he call her Annie?* I tried to keep the door from slamming and my voice in check. "Hello, Annie."

She rose from her seat and walked around the desk. "Hi, Buck. How are you feeling today?"

"Much better, thanks." I drew her in for a hug and kiss. Relief at her willing response took the edge off my anger at Rhodes.

~ *Annie* ~

Despite my concerns over that terrible fire in Buck's apartment, my day had been quite productive. The launch of our new Super Club went off without a hitch. I'd had relative peace in my office in the customer service area of the converted barn. I'd completed all my ordering, checked in with most of my charities, written another script for my show, and arranged a charity auction to raise funds with artwork donated by my sister.

Buck's kisses took my mind off business, until he tossed his briefcase on the desk and pointed me toward the couch. "Um, Buck, I need to keep things professional at work."

His eyes told me what he wanted. "Your face is a brilliant shade of magenta, my dear."

I took a breath and a step back. "I'm not surprised. You have that effect on me." I wiped the hair out of my face.

There was something going on behind that smile, but I couldn't tell exactly what. Time to change the subject. "Tracey came by a few minutes ago with her report. Want to see it? It looks like people are buying the small-sized portions at the dessert cart and then going to The Bakery & Sweet Shop for larger sizes. Karen's already saying we need additional carts."

He grabbed me by the waist, and we both landed on the couch, his arm around me. "Let's discuss that—in a bit. Right now I need to discuss Debbie's portraits. I have a client who wants them all. He asked me to ship them tomorrow morning. Debbie thought five hundred thousand is more than reasonable. That goes to your charities. Is that agreeable?"

"Buck! That's fantastic. But I already arranged the auction."

"I'm sure Debbie will be doing more paintings. Move the date. A bird in the hand, so to speak."

"Well, I suppose, but maybe your client could just put in that bid, and we might do better. Joe Harris told me Debbie's artwork brings in a fortune. He thought we might get considerably more than that."

I could see his irritation, but he kept an even tone. "This client— well, I owe him a favor. I thought this would be a way to repay him. Maybe I can subsidize the difference?"

Embarrassment probably turned my face purple by this point. "I'm sorry to be greedy. We'll take the five hundred thousand. That can do a lot of good. Thanks."

"Are you sure?"

"Yes. You've done so much for us—for me. Tell your client they'll be on their way tomorrow."

~ *Buck* ~

With Rhodes now flaunting his first-name relationship with Annie, I didn't want to leave Maine for fear of losing her. I reluctantly returned to New York to deal with business issues and meet with the contractor who would be reconstructing my apartment. It took the better part of a day to straighten out the construction plans. I decided to head over to a client and check on their dinner operations.

My phone chimed as I left my building. "Yes, Janice."

"Buck, you have two massive boxes in your office. They're filled with paintings—some familiar faces. We really don't want that here, do we?"

I barked into the phone. "Why would you open boxes I sent to myself? Don't I have any privacy anymore?"

Janice was resolute. "I guess not. This is a place of business. Why don't you wait until you have your own place rebuilt before you start accumulating more smut?"

"For your information, those are—" I stopped myself before I put my foot in it. Telling anyone that Debbie Lambrecht painted them would lead to certain disaster.

Janice's voice rose. "Yeah, those are some pretty faces, Buck. But we both know what that leads to. I thought you have a real girlfriend now. What does she think of that stuff?"

My blood was boiling. "How dare you?"

She hung up on me. My secretary hung up on me. I probably should have dialed her back to fire her, or dialed a Twelve Step program, but I dialed Titan. Rhodes' blood-soaked face would be my consolation.

As luck would have it, Titan's class was that very evening. I joined in with all the enthusiasm I could muster. Rhodes was a goner. But by the end of the class, I was a puddle on the floor. Titan growled a motivational harangue at me. I couldn't move to get out of the way. I returned to my hotel room feeling like a total failure.

Fortunately, there was a well-stocked bar. I filled a large glass with vodka and a splash of fruit juice. That would make me feel like a jock.

I woke up in the recliner with one of Cat's verses on my lips. *"Heart-shattered lives ready for love don't for a moment escape God's notice."* Drunken laughter spewed out of me, and I rolled in the chair. I raised the half-empty bottle toward the ceiling. "You noticed, and you're squashing me like a bug. Like a heart-shattered bug." In my exuberance, I showered myself with the liquor, stinging my eyes. I laughed, and I wept.

I'm not sure how long that went on before my phone rang. I found it in the folds of the seat. "Annie?"

"Hi, Buck." It was the tiny voice of Sabena.

"Why don't you get your own phone, young lady?"

"Papa says I'm too young to have one. I think he's afraid of who I'll call."

I grunted. "He should be. What time is it?"

"Umm …" There was a pause. "It's 3:15 in the morning. I couldn't sleep because I'm worried you won't get here for our meeting."

I could feel the vodka wanting to come up. "No need, Sabena, I'm still practicing sacred partnership. That's a doozy. May take me quite a while to get that down. You go on without me."

I heard a tiny sigh. "Do you have any questions?"

"No. No questions. God and I are having a little drink. He's meeting me right where I am."

"Drink living water, Buck. Quench your thirst."

"I will. You tell Annie I'll be back very soon."

"In time for our meeting? It's all about grace."

"Grace who?" I cracked up at my own joke and dropped the phone.

It was after 10:00 AM when the phone jolted me out of my stupor. I fumbled around on the floor for it. My headache was blinding. "Yes?"

"Buck, we're in New York. Cisco thought you might like to join us for lunch and the flight back to Maine." It was David.

New York? Too many questions fired through my hung-over brain. "Uh … Yeah … Okay." I spilled my bottle of painkillers over the chair and the floor. "Where?" My mouth was dry as the desert, but I stuffed a couple of them in. I found a bottle of water and gulped them down. I was only remotely aware of too much silence on the other end.

"Buck, are you all right?"

"Fine, fine!" I closed my eyes and lay back on the bed. The spinning sensation slowed me down. "Why are you in the city? Where shall I meet you?"

"Cisco's doing some interviews for the business network— financial shows. There was a change in the schedule, so he wanted to fit it in this morning. He said you know the people we're meeting for lunch. Maybe a good business connection for you. We'll meet you at your hotel. I'll call when we're ready to leave."

After a pot of coffee, a shower, and a shave, I was as ready as I could be to face David and Cisco. I flipped on the television to watch as I dressed. Turning to the business network, there was Cisco's authoritative face, wowing a panel of interviewers. Not surprisingly, he'd made a fortune in the past day or so due to some fluctuation in currencies. Another big victory for Clemente Asset Management. Another day in the miraculous life of Cisco with the miraculous wife.

Since we both shared the same alma mater, I was well aware that he was a financial genius long before he married Cat. I suspect having a prophet on your side didn't do any harm either.

It dawned on me. I was a client of his. Perhaps this latest boon would benefit me as well. I stifled an urge to celebrate with a drink. My headache was just starting to subside. The phone chimed another Clemente's hit song, and I realized there was no caller ID. "Yes?"

It was David. "We'll arrive at your hotel in twenty minutes."

"I'll be ready." I returned the phone to my pocket, vaguely electrified at the thought of my new association with an actual assassin. It added a bit of cachet to a mere restaurant consultant.

I went to the mirror to straighten my tie. A cut on my left cheekbone, courtesy of Titan's workout, made me smirk. I could have been a reasonable spy movie hero.

Lunch with David, Cisco, and clients was pleasant. One of the men was a majority shareholder in a restaurant conglomerate. We'd met before, and I was happy to remind him of my existence in the presence of such elite company. It didn't hurt that the owner of the establishment fawned over us and sang my praises.

Admittedly, I wasted too much of my energy resenting our bodyguard, Nathan Rhodes. But by dessert, I was completely sober, and I realized two things. First, if he was here in New York, he wasn't in Maine flirting with Annie. And second, he was the servant here. I was at the table with the rich and famous. Memories of the shellacking I took at the hands of Titan the evening before were gone.

Rhodes drove us to the airport in their usual black SUV, David riding shotgun. I was looking forward to a comfortable trip in Cisco's private jet when my assistant phoned. "Buck, Gary from The Birch Tree Inn is in a panic, said he needs you there stat."

I sighed into the phone. "What's his problem now?"

"The Secretary of State—the pressure of the wedding—Gary needs some handholding."

"It's days away." I looked at my watch, as though that would tell me something.

Janice's voice boomed. "It's the day after tomorrow. The family and guests are arriving tomorrow."

"Oh for pity's sakes, it's the fourth wedding for that family at the Birch Tree. You'd think they'd have it down by now."

"Well, Buck, the guy's the Secretary of State now. Before, he was only a senator. Seems to make a big difference to Gary. And Gary's one of our best clients … one of our *first* clients. Just go help the guy out. He begged me for you, bleepin' Almighty Buck. Not Brooke, not Lewis, Almighty Buck Wynn. Go figure."

I took satisfaction at being in such demand. It certainly would be another feather in my cap to handle another wedding for the Secretary of State. "Very well, I'll drive up to Maine tonight. I'll be in the Berkshires tomorrow morning sometime."

"Hot date in Marberry, huh? Okay, I'll let Gary know."

Janice hung up before I could reprimand her.

As I took notice of our surroundings, I could hear David on the phone with his daughter. "Yes, Buck knows our meeting is all about grace … Yes, he'll be there … Yes, I'm sure he's looking forward to it."

I turned to Cisco. "I'm afraid I have to be in the Berkshires tomorrow. The Secretary of State's daughter is getting married, and our client is hosting. He's in need of some assistance, so I'll drive out there tomorrow. I'll pick up my car and head to Maine this evening."

Mercifully, by the time I arrived at Annie's, the kids were all in bed, and the Supernatural Diet Club meeting had been rescheduled for the following morning. Peace and quiet made me smile.

It was a perfect evening for a stroll on the beach. Annie was agreeable. When she went for her sweater, she returned with a small binder and a mischievous smile. "Sabena wanted me to make sure you got this before our meeting tomorrow. It's Cat's handout explaining grace and mercy."

"Hmm. I guess it's obvious I'm in the extra help group." I threw the binder on the kitchen table and tugged Annie by the waist. "Maybe you can explain it all to me in the moonlight ..." I kissed her. "On the beach."

"Maybe." There was desire in her eyes.

~ *Annie* ~

"Um, Buck, did you get mugged in New York?" I had to remark on the cut on his face. "It looks like someone hit you."

He tightened his grip on my shoulder and guided me down the stairs to the beach. The roar of the ocean obliterated his voice. "No worries," I think he said.

We enjoyed the glow of starlight, walking the beach, dodging the waves crashing up on the sand. Conversation was sparse. I got the feeling that suited Buck just fine. His kisses grew more insistent.

As darkness deepened we returned to the back lawn and sat in the Adirondack chairs. Soft light from the house supplemented the glorious moon and stars. We weren't even settled before Doc appeared, dragging another chair to face us. The irritation on his face stopped me from requesting privacy. "Hi Doc. Are you okay?"

He stood behind the chair. "I just had a call from a friend I hear from every so often—Al Rosen."

"Oh. The cardiologist you worked with." I wondered what crisis was brewing now. Maybe he had another divorced doctor in need of a "still young" woman with a master's degree. But I noticed Doc didn't have his matchmaking face on.

"Yes. As a matter of fact, Buck, he lives in your building. Summers in the Hamptons."

Buck was on guard. "Dr. Rosen. Yes."

Doc leaned slightly over the chair, facing Buck. "He and his wife are always at one cocktail party or another. They met a nice young woman—a management consultant. Very smart, he said. His wife would go to lunch with her from time to time. They went to her wedding. She married a CEO."

I could see Buck's eyes starting to bulge the way they always did when he was aggravated. "And her name is Deidre Moore."

Doc raised his voice. "That's right! Her name is Deidre Moore. The woman you lived with for twenty years. The woman you cheated on—on a daily basis. *You* called it an open relationship."

Buck stood up to face him. "What possible business is that of yours?"

Doc came around the chair pointing an accusing finger. "You're all over the tabloids, all over the television with your filthy hands all over my daughter."

"Again, what possible business is that of yours?" Buck wouldn't back down.

I could see Doc's face was red, even in the dim light. I jumped out of my seat. "Wait! Doc, no one can help those pictures. The paparazzi are everywhere."

He turned to me, incredulous.

I spoke before he could. "And … and Buck told me he was in a … that relationship … a … casual relationship … before we ever … dated." *Dated*? Seemed like we still hadn't dated. We'd faced one crisis after another together, built a business and a charity together, over the course of the past year. Ours was a strange relationship. It never felt like dating.

Doc's jaw was hanging open. "Annie, don't get any more involved with him. Wake up. He's a user. He'll take your heart and mop the floor with it. You'll be at work, and he'll be out with some floozy. Don't fall for his smooth talk. Don't." Doc suddenly turned toward the kitchen door. "Aww … Sabena."

I swung around to see my niece, barefoot and clad in a pale nightgown, clutching some notebooks. She ran toward us. "Auntie, I have the notes for tomorrow." She handed one to Buck. "It's all about grace and forgiveness. Good stuff."

She ran to Doc and settled in the chair with him. "I can read all the definitions with you." As Doc shook his head, Sabena opened the notebook.

He kissed the top of her head. "It's way past your bedtime, young lady, and it's chilly out here. Does Nanny Shirlene know where you are?"

Sabena shook her head. "No." She focused on the page. "Grace is undeserved favor. It's the undeserved forgiveness, favor, and mercy that God gives us. It's his kindness."

Doc squinted at the book. "Are you really reading that? It's too dark out here."

She nodded with an impish smile. "Now I'll tell you about mercy. It's more of God's kindness. Mercy is favor and forgiveness, especially when God gives it to a person who doesn't deserve it." She swung around in Doc's arms and looked to Buck. "Aren't we lucky to have grace and mercy, Buck?"

He managed a smile. "Indeed."

I took him by the hand, and we returned to the house. Since the kitchen was empty, I tugged him toward the table. "I'll make us some coffee."

He put the notebook down and took a seat. "Sounds good, Annie." He rubbed his face.

I put the pot on and took the chair beside him. "Doc had no right to attack you like that, Buck. I'm sorry."

He reached for my hand. "No worries, I'm no prize. He knows that, and so do I. Up until now, I really didn't care. I've never loved anyone—*anyone*—in my life. Not until now. I love you, Annie. Regardless of what happens, I love you, and I always will. I know it in my heart, if I actually have one."

Tears welled up, and I popped up to get the coffee. I didn't want him to see me react like that. I wiped my face and bit my lip as I fought through anger and sadness that darkened the delight of his revelation. When I composed myself, I turned to see he had his head on the table, arms protectively cushioning.

I went to him and laid my hand on his arm. "Buck, why don't we take our coffees to the library. We'll have some peace and privacy there. I know we need to talk."

He looked at me with bloodshot eyes, silently took the cups, and escorted me to the library. We settled on a comfortable couch. I swept an abandoned board game into its box, clearing the coffee table. Buck sipped his coffee. "I don't know what to say, Annie. What Doc said is true."

I put my cup on the table and drew my legs up underneath me. "I know Doc is concerned for me. I think he's trying to cram a lifetime of missed fatherhood into a year. I can't blame him. But it was rude to confront you like that."

Buck nodded and took a gulp of his drink.

I decided I couldn't let him off the hook. If we were ever going to have a serious relationship, he'd need to be honest. "That said, I have the feeling I'm getting nowhere near the full story. That's okay if we're casual friends or business associates. But if you truly love me like you said you do, then I deserve complete honesty."

He met my eyes. "You're right, Annie."

The door cracked open and Doc lunged through, his face so purple, I thought he was having a heart attack. He loomed over the arm of the couch. "I don't care what business arrangement you have here, Wynn, I want you out of my daughter's life. You can have Brooke or Lewis call Cisco to keep the account going for all I care. But as for you—get out! And if I see your miserable face again, I swear, I'll kill you with my own hands."

The pit of my stomach was on fire, and Buck was motionless, glaring at Doc.

Doc pointed to the door. "Out! Out of here, *now*."

I found my voice. "Doc, please."

He plummeted over the arm of the couch and grabbed Buck by his collar. In one swift move, Buck was up and Doc was pinned against the wall.

"No!" I darted toward them.

Buck let him go. "I'm sorry, Annie."

He was out the front door before I could reach him. I stood immobile on the stair and watched the Lamborghini speed down the driveway.

Doc came up behind me in the doorway. "Good riddance."

My eyes filled, my entire body pins and needles. I think I stood on that front stair ten minutes before I could make it back inside and upstairs to my room.

I sprawled on my bed and had a good cry. Then I tried calling Buck about a dozen times. He never answered. I realized I was acting like a high school girl, but that didn't stop me from dialing again. Eventually, I fell into a restless sleep and dreamt of a little stick figure named Jonah running away from God. I came to consciousness watching his silver white shoes take a symbolic leap of faith off the boat.

SEVEN

~ *Buck* ~

Proceeding west on the Mass Pike, my mind was racing faster than my car. The road was clear. I was on automatic pilot, thinking of everything but where I was going.

I could let go of the whole thing. Let go of Annie. All the crazy foolishness with God and Cat and The Golden Bowl and all of them. That would be the simplest thing. Go back to my life-is-a-party philosophy. *Love is overrated. Love is too hard. I don't need it. Right now, I don't want it.*

I had said none of this to the sympathetic and shapely bartender at The Last Chance Saloon somewhere near Portland. With all the willpower I could muster, I'd taken one shot of their best vodka to take the edge off my pain. Then I'd left, headed for my next adventure with the Secretary of State at The Birch Tree Inn.

I was a mess, and it had nothing to do with the vodka or the Secretary of State. Buckminster Wynn of Brooke, Lewis & Wynn with offices in New York and London, world traveler, premiere consultant to the restaurant and food service industry, did not need love or family or anything to tie me down. Why did this repeat in my head? Why had I allowed these thoughts to assume cyclonic proportions since leaving Maine?

Heart-shattered lives ready for love don't for a moment escape God's notice. It was time to move on. Un-shatter my heart and move on. Bring back logic and reason.

I shifted to pass a slow moving car traveling in the left lane in front of me. An oil truck lumbered onto the road. There was nowhere to go and no time to stop. It felt as though a blast of wind swept up my car. I was airborne, and time stood still. I was in slow motion, and then upside down. There was no time for fear, only a longing for Annie. A strange longing for Annie. Disappointment at the way I'd lived my life.

I noticed some trees in the first moments of daylight, flying past me, yet strangely still. I was back in my fourth floor turret, contemplating whispering treetops. *Come to me, all of you who are weary and carry heavy burdens, and I will give you rest.*

The seatbelt cut into me. The car descended and hit water. I was upside down, but felt the sensation of a cushion around me—of a strange sense of peace. I was still alive, and water was pouring in. I opened the door almost effortlessly, mechanically, slowly. The seatbelt detached, and I made it out to the surface of the water. I was in the middle of a lake.

I looked for the shore and swam to it, dragging myself onto a muddy, leafy bank. I settled in the midst of twigs and shrubs and focused on my black Lamborghini as the black water swallowed it up. It was as though it was never there.

I looked up at the early morning sky, aglow in shades of pink and gold. *He makes winds his messengers, flames of fire his servants.* I began to shake. My body was fine. I was okay. How could I have survived that? There was no place to go. How did that happen?

Soft pine branches caught my attention as the sun highlighted the needles. Nearby saplings lit up with branches like threads of gold. The tips seemed suspended in midair. Fascinated, I traced the sunbeam across the water, sensing it would reach me.

A hot, humid breeze on my cheek woke me up. The wind was a messenger. The wind carried me to a safe landing. I was insane. I took my soggy phone from my suit pocket and laughed like a fool.

~ *Annie* ~

Since Buck never answered my phone calls, I tossed and turned all night, one weird dream after the other. Finally, I decided to make a special breakfast for everyone. *At least do something positive.* I threw on some clothes and headed down the hall and into my sister as she rushed out of her art studio. A streak of black paint across her face spiked my concern. "Sweetie, what are you doing painting at this hour?"

I noticed her hands shaking around a canvas. "I ... I need to see Cat."

I took the painting. "It's pretty." It looked like she'd done it quickly—just a pond with some trees and brush around it.

Tears dripped onto the black on her cheek, and the effect intrigued me. Debbie's high-pitched cry startled me. "There's a car under there. What happened?"

"Huh?"

She grabbed the painting and brushed past me, running to Cat's room. Cisco met her at the door. He didn't look surprised as he studied the canvas. "She won't wake up. I thought we were past this. But I can't get her to wake up."

Debbie melted. "There's a car under there. What happened?"

It wasn't long before David was there to comfort his wife, and Doc examined Cat. Her blood pressure was fine—everything fine. She just couldn't be roused. The family wasn't as panicked as I'd expect. Apparently every time something happened that concerned Cat, she fell into deep prayer. So deep, no one could wake her. She would always come out of it, eventually. But there was no telling how long that would take.

After half an hour of sitting around, I concluded I'd be most useful in the kitchen. With breakfast cooking, I decided to try Buck again. His phone went directly to voice mail. I made my voice as cheerful as I could and left a "thinking about you" message.

Doc came through the swinging door. "This is plain crazy. No wonder this family sticks together like this. Otherwise the men in the white coats would've come for Cat and Debbie long ago."

He poured himself some coffee. "All this rumor about Cat being a prophet—and Debbie, too. It's true. This God stuff is real. What other explanation is there?"

I shook my head and remembered the banana bread in the oven. "There is no other explanation, Doc. Can you see if we have cream cheese in the fridge?"

~ *Buck* ~

Traffic was sparse, moving along. Obviously, no one noticed my swan dive. I became enmeshed in confusion trying to retrace my car's path from the road. How had it avoided all those trees?

When the daze began to lift, I decided I could die here before anyone would find me, so it would be best to go find civilization. My phone was now a paperweight, much like my favorite car. I got to my feet and used branches to pull myself up the embankment. After slogging through some trees and brush, I entered what looked to be a cow pasture. A dilapidated barn in the distance beckoned me. Trudging along through the grass, the smell brought me back to the days of my youth on holiday in the English countryside.

Where did I go wrong? Did I go wrong? Yes. The self-centered life was fun for a while. But it got lonely fast. No matter how much money I made, it never did buy happiness. How cliché.

I only wanted to speak with Annie. To hold her. I needed to call my office, to get to the Berkshires to The Birch Tree Inn, to create the wedding of someone's dreams and assure the client this would be the event of the century. The Birch Tree would be legendary. Almighty Buck would save the day.

My foot caught in a hole, and I went down. Rolling over, I gaped at the morning sky and laughed like a fool, in the middle of a cow pasture. "Almighty Buck, you're an idiot." A heart-shattered idiot, shouting at the sky.

Eventually I sat up and raked pieces of dry grass from my hair. The heat of the sun felt better than I'd ever remembered. I recalled how happy I'd been last night when I realized my suitcase was in the car, and I needn't reappear in the house for another confrontation with Doc. I left as the hero. Laughter burst out of me. All my clothes were at the bottom of the lake.

After I'd exhausted myself cursing and laughing, I gathered myself up to carry on. Almighty Buck was an illusion, an imposter, the fake self I put on to face the world. I'd do best to leave him here in this field. I only wanted Annie and a life with her. But I was sure it was too late.

What would I have given Annie for a story—the truth she

wanted—had Doc not barged in? She did deserve the truth she asked for. Was I capable of giving it? Probably not.

I noticed a figure in the distance and marched on until I locked eyes with the wary farmer. I took out my sodden wallet and brushed away a leaf that clung to it. I removed a clump of hundred dollar bills and stretched my hand out to him. "You can have this if you let me use your phone."

"I'll call the police," he said.

"No police. I just need to call … my wife." My eyes filled.

He took an old-fashioned cell phone from his belt and handed it to me, then hesitantly took the money. His eyes popped as he pried the bills apart and counted it. "Where's your wife—the North Pole?"

I could barely see the phone to use it. "Maine. She's in Maine."

"That's not gonna cost nine hundred dollars. I don't need your money. Make your call. I'll go see if I can find you a towel." He handed me the money, turned, and headed toward the house.

I made the phone work.

~ *Annie* ~

After breakfast the kids poured out into the yard to play soccer. Cisco, Doc, Debbie, and David kept vigil over Cat. I needed some air, so I left instructions to call me when Cat was conscious and went to the beach. The water was calm and cool. I went in as far as my knees and walked along the shore. The warm sun soaked up my anxiety. My phone vibrated in my pocket. *Thank God, Cat's awake.* "Hello?"

"Annie, are you all right?"

"Buck!" He sounded a little strange. Was he still upset over Doc? Had he sensed something wrong with Cat? "Yeah, I'm okay. Cat's gonna be okay, too."

"Cat?"

"Um, yeah. She's in kind of a coma—a prayer trance, I think. Cisco says this happens when she's praying hard about something. I suppose all the stress with you and Doc sent her over the edge a bit. I know she thrives on peace and quiet and communion with God. Well, I guess we all do. Anyway, I know she'll wake up soon. I didn't mean to accuse you of causing her coma, Buck." Why was I rambling like this?

There was silence on the other end.

"I'm sorry, Buck. I know you've got your hands full with the Secretary of State and the wedding and all."

No comment.

"Well, I saw their website. The Birch Tree is gorgeous ... a credit to Brooke, Lewis & Wynn ... um ... Buck?"

"I love you, Annie." His voice was soft and strange and tender and tears flooded my eyes.

~ *Buck* ~

Perhaps it was pond scum blocking my voice. I could only hang on every word that Annie uttered. I wanted to proclaim my love. There was nothing else of importance today. Only Annie.

I saw the police car approach and turn up the dirt drive. I didn't want to upset her. "Annie, I need to go now. I'll call again soon ... I love you. Just know that, please." I dared not wait for her to reciprocate.

"Buck?"

I determined the correct button and clicked off the phone. The farmer appeared and spoke with the cop. They headed toward me. I rubbed my hand over my jacket and then through my hair in a futile effort to look human.

"Are you all right, Sir?" The officer was guarded but polite.

"I'm fine. I need to report an accident."

"What happened?"

"A truck cut me off, and somehow I ended up in the lake. I managed to get out of the car before it sank."

"Was anyone else with you?"

"No. Just me."

"What about the truck?"

"I have no idea. I imagine he kept going. When I made it to the embankment it looked as though traffic was proceeding normally. I don't think anyone saw my car leave the highway. It took me a while to make my way over to this gentleman. As you can see, my suit is ruined, and I'm expected at The Birch Tree Inn this morning on business. Can you help me get there?"

"The Birch Tree Inn?"

"Yes, the Secretary of State is due in shortly." I made a point to flash my Rolex. "Yes. I'm already three and a half hours late."

"You have some ID? You're part of that wedding?"

I fished through my soggy wallet. "Yes, I'm in charge of all the preparations for the Secretary of State—his daughter's wedding." I handed him my license.

"Buckminster Wynn. New York, New York."

"Yes."

"Okay, Mr. Wynn. You seem okay to me, but I think we should get you to a hospital to get checked out. I'm calling the EMTs."

"Not necessary, officer."

"You have a registration on you, by chance?"

"Yes." I dug through my wallet. "But I really can't spare the time to see a doctor right now. I assure you, I'm fine. God was with me." I chuckled a bit too heartily and handed him the registration. *Cat was praying for me.* "I do need to call my client and have him alert his tailor."

He smiled an amiable smile. "There's a Lamborghini in the lake?"

"I'm afraid so."

The farmer gave him a confused look. The officer shook his head, grimacing, and returned my registration. "That's gotta hurt."

I stuffed the soggy paper back into the wallet. "Indeed."

The entrance to the front garden of The Birch Tree Inn was a fragrant feast for the eyes. Flowers of every kind impeccably placed, the requisite birch trees precisely scattered. All prescribed and perfectly presented by Brooke, Lewis & Wynn, the experts in hospitality.

I slid out of the back seat of the patrol car, a large black plastic trash bag still clinging to my backside. Rolling it into a ball, I tossed it back into the car and thanked the officer profusely for the speedy ride to the inn, lights flashing. It was the best he could do for a soggy consultant to the Secretary of State.

Entering the courtyard, my eyes focused on a lovely plaque. *The heart has its reasons that reason knows nothing about. Blaise Pascal (1623-1662).* I stood still as a statue pondering how this explained my life. Blaise was insightful, his quote a remarkable legacy of his brief life.

Almighty Buck? What would he leave behind? Nothing, had he died in the sunken Lamborghini. Nothing worthwhile, save The Golden Bowl. And that was Annie's. I took a seat on a nearby bench and focused on the soft pink of the roses against a white trellis. It was the same shade that I loved on Annie. I supposed Debbie had recommended that color for her. She'd worn it more frequently of late.

I let myself think about Cat, in some kind of a trance, praying for me. That was the wind that guided my car. She'd called on the angels, no doubt. What else could it have been? I'd vaguely heard stories like that before. I'd never believed them.

"Buck! What are you doing out here?" Gary, chef and co-owner of The Birch Tree Inn stood over me, his considerable bulk all aflutter. "The truffles never arrived this morning. They were supposed to be on a flight from Oregon. What are we gonna do?"

My impulse was to laugh at him, but I mustered my best Almighty Buck authoritative expression. "That's the trouble with truffles, Gary." A picture of the wayward animated truffles, seated in the plane, captured my imagination. Giddiness consumed me, and I dissolved into foolish laughter. I didn't even care.

Gary fell to his knees, glaring at me eye to eye. "The Secretary of State is gonna be here in an hour!" Tears started down his puffy cheeks.

I noticed flakes of dried mud and pond scum falling from me to the classic marble bench. I pried a dirt-encrusted pine needle from my knee and composed myself, brushing dust and debris to the ground. "No worries, Gary, as long as you equip me with a new suit, dry shoes, and a phone, we'll be fine."

~ Annie ~

I brought some tea and a light meal to Cat's room and settled on the bed with Cat and Debbie. Sunlight and the sounds of the surf mixed with happy children streamed in the open windows. "I don't understand much about this coma you were in Cat, but a nice cup of tea and a sandwich ought to help revive you." I handed her the tea. "Just the way you like it—a touch of milk."

"Thanks, Annie. I'm fine. No need to worry about me."

Debbie refused my offer of food. "Cat has this happen when she needs to pray hard for someone." Her fingers caressed the dark water in her painting. "It was someone in this car, wasn't it? Did they survive?"

I stared at the painting again. "How do you know there's a car in there, Sweetie?"

I could see her throat spasm, and Cat reached for her with a calming touch. "I just know." Debbie's voice was barely audible.

Fright suddenly overwhelmed me, the blackness of that water resonating. "Buck?"

Cat quickly stashed her cup on a tray and grabbed my arm. "He's fine, Annie. You mustn't worry. The car is a loss. Buck is well."

In my panic, I wondered if I misunderstood her accent. *Buck, as well*? I exploded. "He's okay?"

"Yes." Her eyes were certain and comforting.

"This … this already happened?"

"Yes."

"What? When?"

"No one was hurt, but he was speeding and couldn't stop in time to avoid a crash. His car left the road and landed in a pond."

"They got him out?"

"He escaped and swam to shore."

Debbie let out a sigh of relief.

I was dumbfounded. "Why … why wouldn't he tell me? He sounded strange. He called me while you were still out cold. It must have happened before then. Why didn't he tell me?"

Cat patted my arm. "Perhaps he didn't want to upset you. And he needed to get to The Birch Tree Inn."

I didn't know who was dumber. Buck, for not telling me. Or me, for not realizing it was Buck in the lake the second I saw Debbie's painting.

~ *Lisa* ~

The Supernatural Diet Club meeting was moved to 6:00 p.m. That was fine with me. I needed time to review my notes on sacred partnership. I don't think I was doing that one very good. Billy told me it was tough for him to understand, too. But we took Cat's advice and started to pray together every day. It was an unbelievable feeling when Billy prayed out loud and asked God to bless me and Rosie and him and take care of us.

And things were going good.

I got a letter that everything was set for me to start my classes toward a nursing degree in September. Ellen made sure Paulo Clemente's foundation would pay my tuition, because she'd selected me to help them in underserved areas when I got my degree. And in the meantime, the hours worked out perfectly to keep my job at The Golden Bowl.

My friend Peg told God she wanted to do sacred partnership to quit smoking. So far she was smoke-free for almost a week. That's longer than she'd ever quit before.

I liked the evening meetings on the beach because Annie always fed us. Having dinner with rock stars was pretty cool.

While Ash and Peg and I set up some chairs near the lobster trap, Sabena ran around delivering little notebooks about grace and mercy. I wasn't sure my brain could hold another thing, but then I thought it'd be good practice for college. And maybe this would help us with that sacred partnership.

Cat came out of nowhere and rubbed her hand across my back. "Thank you, Lisa. We're all set to get started."

Sabena catapulted herself onto the lobster trap and started yelling and blowing her new whistle. I almost went to grab it from her, but then everyone filed onto the beach and took their seats.

Glori gave me a thumbs up. "Love your outfit, hon." I probably blushed. It was a brand new sundress I'd found on sale. Billy'd said he liked it, too.

Ash said, "I knew she'd like your dress. I bet she's pretty pleased with herself that you took her advice about dressing better."

"I guess. But I'm doin' it for Billy."

Ash giggled. "And he noticed."

I giggled. "Yeah." I was kind of embarrassed, so I changed the subject. "This is the second meeting Buck's missed. You think he dropped out?"

Ash made a face. "I don't know. I don't think so. He'd do anything for Annie. He's probably just traveling on business. Karen said he was doing something about a wedding for the Secretary of State. Maybe that's where he is."

"Wow."

Sabena did her intro then Cat asked everybody about their experience with sacred partnership so far. Peg chimed in about quitting cigarettes. And I told everyone how happy I was about school and how I started praying with Billy. Mr. Rhodes made a face like he was going to tease Billy about that. That got me a little bit mad, but I didn't say anything.

Cat picked up on it, though. She smiled at me. "Cisco and I pray together every morning. And we pray a blessing over our son, Jack. We dedicate our day to God, and God provides."

Glori chimed in. "It works, hon."

I turned to Mr. Rhodes. "Cool." I got a nod from him. Billy smirked at me.

Sabena read from her notebook about grace and mercy, and Cat told us how important it is for us to let go of resentments and forgive people. She said it's for our own good, not the people we forgive. When I thought about it, it made perfect sense.

Karen let out a loud "oh!"

Cat turned to her. "Tell us."

Karen looked a little embarrassed. "Well, it just occurred to me—today I had a surly customer. That's kind of a rarity at The Golden Bowl, but it happens. There wasn't anything we could do to please that man. After he finally left, I went into the back office with a big dish of chocolate ice cream. I thought I was making myself feel better, but I was just covering up the resentment I had toward him. And making myself even fatter."

She took off her glasses and rubbed her eyes. "I'm telling you now, I forgive that man. Like the notes say, I choose to forgive him. He's in God's hands. I'm not going to go home and eat another dish of ice cream over him."

Cat was beaming. "Thank you for sharing your story, Karen. I'm so glad for you. You're set free."

Then she asked us to use the notebook to write some names of people we needed to forgive. She said we could even list ourselves. Some people even listed God. I said I'd be too scared to do that, and everybody laughed. But they'd probably be just as scared.

I didn't need to think much before writing down Mr. Rhodes and all the women who were throwing themselves at Billy.

~ *Annie* ~

After our Supernatural Diet Club meeting adjourned, I stuffed my notebook deep into my beach bag and stashed that under my chair. I quickly took off down the beach. I was the opposite of Karen today. I was so upset I couldn't stomach the thought of dinner.

Doc had managed to reach the top of my resentment list. Buck was certainly there, but at least he seemed to be trying. He must have been in an awful state when his car went off the road into the water. And he had yet to return my calls. All I had from Buck since Doc's tirade was an "I love you." It was hard to put him on my list at all. I was worried sick about him.

Doc's voice on the sea breeze was insistent. "Annie!"

I stopped and turned, waiting for him. He was the last person I wanted to talk to, and he was red in the face when he finally caught up with me.

"Annie, I suppose you put me on your resentment list."

"I forgive you, Doc. Thank you for forgiving me."

"There's nothing to forgive you for. You're the victim here. You can't help it that Wynn hoodwinked you. He doesn't deserve your forgiveness. But if it helps *your* health, then fine."

"Okay." I couldn't utter another word without yelling, I was sure.

Doc put his arm around my shoulder, and we ambled forward. "Annie, I know I'm late to this fatherhood thing. I know you're a grown woman, but I love you, and I can't stand by and watch you make a terrible mistake."

I let out a heavy sigh. "I know your opinion, and I know I'm taking a risk. I could get my heart broken. But it happens to people every day, Doc. Hearts get broken. But sometimes it works out. Sometimes it's worth the pain, the risk. It's my decision whether or not it's worth the risk. I heard your opinion, and it's my right to make a decision that affects me. Just me. You need to bow out of it, Doc. It's not your place to ban Buck from my house."

He stopped and faced me. "It's my home, too, Annie."

Before he could say another word, I put my hand up. "You're right, and I suppose you have the right to ban anyone you want to. You shouldn't be uncomfortable in your own home. I get it."

"Good."

"Once the family leaves after Thanksgiving, I'll move back to my old apartment."

"What?"

"I lived on the third floor of The Golden Bowl for years. It's a cute apartment. The views are spectacular. It's a perfect solution. We both have our privacy."

I thought he'd explode. "That's ridiculous."

"Not at all. Can you think of a better solution?"

He sputtered at me. "Yes! Get rid of Buck."

I shook my head.

EIGHT

~ *Buck* ~

I'd been going nonstop for thirty-six hours when the Secretary of State assembled with the bride and groom and their guests in the back garden. As I wilted by the terrace door, I was drawn to the charming ceremony of planting a new birch tree to commemorate the wedding that would take place later that day.

A fine orator, Mr. Secretary took the opportunity to add his personal touch. His voice carried on a gentle breeze. "One of the reasons we love this inn so much—all these spectacular gardens and dazzling birch trees. All four of my girls will have been married here. This little tree will grow tall like the other three we've planted over the years. They remind me that the birch tree symbolizes new beginnings, purification, renewal. In German folklore, birch trees were used to make maypoles where lovers would dance. So the birch is a tree of life and love. This is a perfect specimen to remember my baby girl's special day." He threw a shovelful of dirt at the base of the tree.

New beginnings. I hoped it would be for me as well. The sunken Lamborghini would symbolize my old life of selfish ambition and dissipation. Here I stood, ready for a new beginning in my off-the-rack suit.

I walked back out to the front of the inn. *The plaque is mine.* "Blaise won't mind," I said to no one as I pulled it from its perch. *The heart has its reasons that reason knows nothing about.*

Gary appeared, handsomely attired, all smiles and nervous energy. I'd ordered him to get sleep twelve hours ago. His slap to my back might have decked me in my exhaustion.

I slipped the plaque under my arm, unapologetic. "Gary, you're completely capable of taking it from here. You've done this a million times. This is another flawless wedding exactly like the last one you hosted. You're rested. You're ready. I'm going to get some sleep. You may call me only if there's fire or blood."

He threw back his shoulders and set his jaw. "Okay, Buck, got it."

I retired to my room, put the plaque in my new suitcase, and went directly to the shower. The steam and hot water eased the aches I endured from head to toe. I noticed the remains of my trauma—an ugly stripe of black and blue where the seatbelt caught me. Crisp sheets and a soft bed never felt so good. I imagined Annie's sweet face to lull me to sleep.

"The truth will set you free." Cat's eyes were more intense than I'd ever seen them. The ocean below and the sky above us was fire. The rock I stood on was disintegrating with the waves. I feared they'd sweep me away.

My voice was strong, stronger than that morning on the rocky ledge in Maine. "Love does not delight in evil but rejoices with the truth." *I love Annie.* "The Supernatural Diet means living for someone else—putting someone else ahead of self-interest."

Cat's eyes were insistent. "The truth will set you free, Buck." She stood radiant on a solid rock, as mine crumbled to sand, fire swirling about me.

Sabena appeared beside me, her white hair and nightgown aglow. She tugged at my hand. "Aren't we lucky to have grace and mercy, Buck?"

I snatched her up to save her from the burning waves. "Forgive me, Annie."

I awoke staring into the bright light of the sun through my window yelling, "Forgive me, Annie." I sat up and threw off soaking sheets. *I need to tell her. Everything.*

The celebratory sounds of music and voices roused me in the evening. Once I'd made the decision to come clean with Annie, I'd fallen into a restful slumber. Now I sat in contemplation. How would I approach her? The truth might very well set me free—from Annie.

I decided to call Cat. I was rather surprised she took my call immediately. "Can you speak with me in confidence? Is there anyone else around you?" I could hear the roar of the ocean on the phone.

"I'm sitting alone on the rock, Buck. I couldn't miss this sunset— all fiery gold. We can speak confidentially. How are you?"

"I'm okay. I want to thank you for … for praying for me." Emotion clogged my voice. "I believe it helped … it saved me."

"God is good, Buck."

"I … I realized … I need to tell Annie … the truth."

"Yes."

A shot of heat blasted through me, watering my eyes. It was an effort to speak. "What do I say? I can't do this. How can I do this?"

"That's what sacred partnership is all about, Buck. You have God on your side. Trust him."

My eyes squeezed shut. "Hmm. The last time I tried that, he burnt down my apartment."

There was half a laugh. "It got your attention. Sometimes that's what it takes. We're only human, Buck."

Only human. Memories of Annie's Valentine's Day accident came in a jumble. That got my attention. "That's like the time Annie was swept out to sea. She told me that it got me back to Maine."

Cat's giggle told me she probably knew my punch line.

"I told her I'd have come with a phone call."

Her giggle turned to a joyful sound. "That's the way God is, Buck. You just need to *ask* him into your heart. A simple phone call, so to speak. But you chose the hard way. People often do."

One of my associates arrived at The Birch Tree Inn with my SUV, and then we headed to his next assignment in Boston. The drive was not nearly as fun as usual.

While he dozed in the passenger seat, I considered calling to order another Lamborghini. As I went for the phone, I noticed a blackish pond alongside the turnpike. I decided that was God's Spirit telling me to let the symbol of my former life remain at the bottom of the lake. I'd need to move on to a new life. When did I become so introspective? Perhaps Blaise was rubbing off on me. Or Cat.

In due time I dropped my associate at one of Boston's fine hotels and headed north to Maine. It took me a while to rehearse what I'd say to Annie. I picked up my phone and my mind went blank when I heard her sweet, "hello."

"Annie, I ... I've missed you so much."

Her emotional sigh went straight to my heart.

"Buck, are you okay?"

"Can I come home?"

"Yes."

"Then, I'm fine." I wiped mist from my eyes. "I'm heading north—almost to Portsmouth."

"Okay, I'll see you when you get here. And just a heads up ... Doc is off camping with the kids for a couple of days. So you don't have to worry about an altercation when you get here. He was still pretty steamed when he left, but hopefully time with the kids will improve his mood."

I smiled. "Did Sabena join him on this camping trip?"

Annie giggled. "She did."

"Good. She'll keep him occupied with Diet Club business."

She laughed. "I'm not sure that's a good thing at this point. We'll see. I've gotta run. I'm baking with my sister, and I think I need to rescue her from the flour bin."

I heard Debbie's laughter in the background as the phone clicked off.

When I arrived in Marberry, I felt compelled to make a stop at The Golden Bowl. I pulled into the parking lot and into my designated space. I reached for my notepad. For the first time, I wrote a prayer. "God, you know my heart and its reasons—better than I. Grant me my heart's desire." I assumed God knew that was Annie.

I cringed as I climbed the stairs and made my way through the crowd to the prayer bowl. *I should wait until dark.* I didn't want anyone to see me. As surreptitiously, as nonchalantly, as I could, I slipped the paper down along the inside of the bowl. I grabbed a paper and took a breath. No one was paying attention. A sigh of relief.

"Hey, Buck!"

Startled, I turned to see Billy.

"I like that SUV. Too bad about your Lamborghini."

We sat on the comfortable couch in the library, isolated from the rest of the house. I drew her into my arms. "Annie, I have a little present for you. Perhaps it will help me explain things."

"I have a present for you, too. I think it'll help explain some things, too."

Nerves began in my stomach as she handed me a package that was undoubtedly a painting. I tore the paper to reveal the lake where I nearly lost my life. "Well. Perhaps you know some of my story already."

She looked a bit surprised.

"I know about Debbie's prophetic paintings."

"Really?"

"David told me. Diet Club partners, you know."

She burst into laughter and snuggled into my side. I would have been happy to stay that way forever in the comfort of each other's arms, in the quiet of the evening. But instead, I'd have to begin a litany of awful truths about Almighty Buck Wynn. How could I risk it?

In that moment, I wondered how covering my tracks could be a bad thing. Annie would never have to find out. We could live together in ignorant bliss.

"Okay, I'll open your gift." She tore the paper and read the plaque, *"The heart has its reasons that reason knows nothing about. Blaise Pascal (1623-1662).* Wow." I could see a glaze of a tear in her eye.

"All my life I valued logic and reason. I considered myself superior to others—I had little patience for emotion. Money. Wealth. Success. Those were the things worth pursuing. It wasn't until I met you that my heart came to life."

She looked up at me, her eyes never more blue. "I thank God for you. You've done so much for me. I can't even begin to thank you. But you've touched my heart, too, in a way I never thought could happen again."

I thought my chest might explode. "Annie, I want to live my life with you, spend time with you, enjoy our lives together. I want to marry you."

Shock flashed across her face.

"I know, I know, you'll tell me we hardly know each other."

"Well … we … we probably need … more time … a little more time."

"Time is fine! Time is good. That's good." I'd broken out in a sweat from head to foot. "I just need to tell you the truth, first."

We sat in stunned silence. I couldn't believe I'd said that. I found a handkerchief and dabbed at my face and neck. Blood pounded in my ears. I took some cleansing breaths.

"Um … Buck?"

"Yes?"

"Truth is good. I'm ready when you are."

"Oh. Good." The handkerchief dropped to the floor, and I drew her to me as tightly as I could. "Well Annie, like Blaise said, the heart has its reasons, and I'm going to speak from my heart, and I'm not at all used to doing that. It will probably sound … bad."

I felt her laughter more than heard it. She drew away to face me. "I don't think your heart's as bad as you think it is. And my heart's strong enough to take anything you have to say to me—as long as it's the truth."

"Very well." I cleared my throat. "I've thought about this—what to say to you, how to say it to you—and I have no idea what I've planned to say. It's all a nervous blur right now."

"That's okay. Visit me when I'm taping a show, and you'll see a nervous blur, too. We're only human."

Only human. I was back on the rocks by The Golden Bowl with Cat. "Yes. You probably don't know—the day you first began your TV show—I'd spent most of the night out on the cliff by The Golden Bowl. Probably exactly the spot where that wave took you out to sea." My mind became a jumble of my memories and imaginings of Annie's terrible experience.

She caressed my hand, soothing me, and I continued. "Cat showed up about sunrise. I'd taken maybe fifty prayers out of that bowl during the course of the night, and most of them from Cat. I suppose I was having a breakdown of some sort. I was so afraid I'd lose you. Cat said God was convicting me. That's the way it felt. I sat on the ledge … the wind was whipping at me for hours on end. The waves were wild. Mist and blowing sand … I couldn't move. My head was spinning. I couldn't move from that spot."

Annie's eyes were fixed on mine. She gently rubbed my arm.

I let out a half a laugh. "When Cat arrived, the sea went calm. It was like a movie. The sun was starting to rise, and her hair was like a halo … the crazy things you think."

There was only a slight upturn to Annie's lip, an encouragement to continue.

"Cat prayed for me, and I remembered the blood pact I'd made with my business partners as a teenager. I believe I told you we met at university."

"Yes."

"Well, we agreed that money was the most important thing. Wealth, success, all the spoils, that's what we committed to. I know I admitted to you some time ago, half joking—money was my god. Cat basically said the same thing. So she led me in some prayers to make things right with God. The real God."

Annie's voice was emotional. "I'm so grateful she was there to help you, Buck, to help you invite God in. Your life is changing for the better, even though it may not feel like it yet. But you're here, and you're speaking the truth. Money's fine, Buck, but not when it becomes the main thing in life. Not when it becomes your god."

I snorted a laugh. "Money is a cold god when you're alone at night. You can't cuddle up with it. So I used it to buy people—to buy comfort. Things spiraled down from there. I liked Deidre, I really did. And she liked me and my money. For a while.

"I don't know who cheated on who first, but it doesn't matter. I had no intention of marrying her, no intention of giving her my hard-earned money in an inevitable divorce. We agreed to an open relationship. And for me—it was wide open. It was rather a relief when she moved out. I didn't have to consider logistics.

"That's why I was happy to move into my apartment in New York. It was a shrine—to me. I … I employed an artist to create a collection for my new gallery. I believe you've seen some of the faces who appeared in those works. My conquests, as David called them. All bought in one way or another, for one price or another."

I could see the realization in Annie's eyes.

I stumbled a bit. "Yes, my private gallery was my pride and joy, and I lied to you about a client wanting Debbie's versions of my paintings. I couldn't take the chance they'd fall into the hands of someone who would know who they were. Someone who knew the truth about me. I'm sorry, Annie."

Her voice was hesitant. "I understand, Buck."

"I hope you do, Annie, and I hope you can forgive me."

"I forgive you, Buck."

"You do? You don't have to think about it?"

She gave me a wary smile. "I choose to forgive you, Buck. But I have to say, I'll be thinking about it and working through some feelings. It's probably not going to be rosy overnight."

I wasn't exactly certain what she meant. "Very well. Tomorrow is fine then."

She laughed a bit sarcastically and shook her head.

I rubbed my eyes, exasperated, and well aware I was not done. "I need to tell you more, and you'll probably need to do more forgiving."

"Oh. Okay."

"I have a tendency to drink too much and watch … things I shouldn't watch … sometimes." I was sure I was the brilliant shade of red that Annie often turned, though now she was pale as a ghost.

"Adult entertainment."

"Exactly."

"Oh."

"You see why Doc was so against me. I'm quite sure Rhodes shared every detail with him. I suppose he had good reason."

"Um … Buck?" Her voice was barely audible.

"Yes?"

"That painting of you and me at the White House—the one Debbie is working on?"

An involuntary shudder went head to foot. "Yes."

"Was that one in your gallery, too?"

I was afraid I'd retch. Sweat dripped from my brow. "Yes, Annie, indeed it was."

"I understand." She looked to be shell-shocked.

I drew my sleeve across my eyes, now was not the time to weep. I tried to control my voice. "I … I hope you know it was my pride and joy. I'll never forget that dance, Annie. It was a highlight of my life. You're my life now."

Light dawned on me. "And I shouldn't have put it in that gallery. That's why he burned the apartment. That's why. It should never have been in that room. It was tainted." I was back on that ledge. I rested my head on the back of the couch. Roaring waves and winds, pounding heat enveloped me in a spinning vortex of confusion and realization. I pressed my forearm against my eyes to try and stop it.

Annie's voice penetrated the maelstrom. "Who burned your apartment?"

"It was God. I told him to fix things. I know I sound crazy, Annie. I'm sorry."

"You're not crazy, Buck."

I couldn't take my arm from my eyes. I drew purposeful breaths to calm myself. "That rogue wave—that morning with Cat—it came out of nowhere after we prayed for God to come in, for all the evil to leave. It doused me with water. Cat said it was a baptism of sorts, and then she told a Holy Spirit to come into me. Do you think it worked?"

I felt her head on my chest. "I know it worked, Buck."

I woke up on that couch, a pillow under my head and a blanket on top of me. Sun streamed in the windows adjacent to the fireplace. Annie was not there. I sat up and stretched away the kinks, then re-wrapped Debbie's black lake painting and tucked it under my arm. I managed to adjourn to my fourth floor turret without encountering anyone. A quick look in the bathroom mirror made me grateful for that. I looked worse than death.

Peering out the back window, I could see Annie seated in her Adirondack chair. I hastened to shower, shave, and dress, so I could speak to her alone. Would she ask me to leave, never to return?

~ *Annie* ~

I was grateful everyone left me alone to contemplate life, staring out to sea in my Adirondack chair. The thought that Cat probably issued the warning made me smile. It was nice to have a prophet in the family.

Really, at that point, all I could do was pray, and that was disjointed to say the least. I did choose to forgive Buck, but I knew it was a process. Who knew how long it would take? And I certainly would never forget. My feelings were raw.

I worried about him, too. I knew Buck was fond of some exclusive brand of vodka, but he'd never overindulged in my presence. His admission that he had threw up warning flags to say the least. What could I do about that now? I returned him to God's capable hands.

Stray purplish clouds reminded me of the gorgeous gown Debbie had created for me for my thrill of a lifetime New Year's Day party at the White House. Buck never looked more handsome, and I was practically unrecognizable with professionally done hair and makeup, a designer gown, and heels I could barely stand up in. Dancing with Buck made me feel like a princess. A fairy tale come true. He was my knight in shining armor, the second one to come along in my life.

I wasn't surprised his armor was a bit dented.

"Annie." His voice stirred my emotions.

I didn't turn around. "Mornin' Buck. Have a seat." I wondered how to relax the muscles in my face.

He dragged his chair closer to mine and took a seat. He cupped my hand in his, resting on the arm of my chair. I was surprised we sat quietly looking out to sea. At first his presence distracted me from my thoughts and prayers, but his continued silence became reassuring in a strange way.

I pondered how God works in incredible ways. There was no earthly way I could ever trust Buck enough to consider a marriage proposal. Despite what I'd told him about my heart being strong, I knew he had the power to smash it to pieces. And he had.

But God had taken the work of my sister's hands and created a message for me. A message of hope that Buck and I could make a life together.

I just didn't know when that could possibly be.

~ *Buck* ~

Holding Annie's hand, sitting in the warmth of the sun, listening to the sounds of the sea, watching seagulls soaring, I almost lulled myself into a sense that everything was okay. My mind returned to the last bitter cold days of winter after Annie's accident. *I would have come with a phone call.*

The two of us had sat here quietly enjoying each other's company and the scenery. At least Annie enjoyed the scenery—I was frozen in place. But we could simply sit peacefully together without needing witty repartee or much conversation at all. We were comfortable together. No need for Almighty Buck Wynn to impress. I could just be. Just be with her.

My eyes watered, and I tried to suck it in. Now I dreaded a word from her, terrified it would be good-bye.

"Buck?"

I thought it was Annie's voice, but it was so soft, it could have been the sea breeze.

She turned to me. "Last night you asked me if Cat's prayers worked for you—if Holy Spirit came to you—and I told you they worked."

"Yes." My voice was too loud, but I was fighting the lump in my throat. I squeezed her hand.

"I want you to know, Holy Spirit can be your conscience. Sometimes you'll have thoughts come through your mind, and they're from Holy Spirit. As time goes on, it gets easier to recognize that voice."

I remembered the little voice that told me now was not the time for a new car. "I see."

"Just so you know you're not crazy."

"Good."

Her expression softened a bit, and I thought I'd die for the need of her.

She stretched her free hand toward the sky, her body almost out of the seat and then back against the chair. "So Buck, I've been sitting here since before sunrise … thinking and praying. I cried a little. Okay—a lot. I've covered a lot of territory, a lot of feelings."

I followed her gaze up to an empty sky. I had no idea what to say to stop her from telling me to leave. "Yes."

"The same thought keeps popping into my head."

I couldn't bear to hear it.

She turned back to face me. "It's from scripture, and I don't remember exactly where. You'd have to ask Cat."

"Okay." Sweat began to pour.

"I will give you a new heart and put a new spirit in you."

"Okay ... I think you ... and Cat ... did that."

"God did that for you, Buck."

I began to shake. "Just ... just say you forgive me, Annie, that you want me in your life."

Her eyes were so beautiful. "I forgive you, Buck."

I could see the clouds forming in those blue eyes, the pain plain to see. I didn't know how much more I could take.

"I ... I just can't get that image out of my mind. All those women ... and me ... in your gallery. It's so creepy ... so sick. It makes my skin crawl." Tears poured down her face.

A groan came from deep inside.

She pulled her hand from my grip. "You need to go, Buck." She ran to the beach.

NINE

~ *Annie* ~

I thought I'd vomit. I ran to the water and landed on my knees in the waves. *What's the point?* God had sent me a sign I couldn't accept. Or was it a sign? Maybe I'd been hanging around Cat and Debbie too long. How could Buck and I go back to the way things were? It'd be impossible.

I heaved and sobbed, the waves lapping at me.

"Annie!" Debbie and Cat were beside me, hauling me to my feet. Nathan stood by, a weird look on his face. I caught a glimpse of Buck on the cliff above. We struggled out of the water, and all I could think was *don't let Buck see me like this.* Bedraggled wet hair, sand and vomit clinging to me. They lugged me up the stairs and across the lawn, past the empty Adirondack chairs to the kitchen door.

"Let's get you to your room," Cat said.

Nathan stepped forward. "Let me help."

I was mortified. "No!"

He picked me up and carried me upstairs, Debbie and Cat in pursuit.

Buck was gone.

I was showered and dressed in a clean lightweight flannel nightgown, propped on pillows in my bed with my sister. A perfect summer breeze tossed the curtains. The sounds of the surf were hypnotic. Cat came through the door with a bowl of chicken soup. Debbie instantly set up the tray.

Cat placed the bowl in front of me. "This will help you feel better. I've never had better chicken soup in all my travels."

"Thanks Cat, you're like my mother. She thinks chicken soup cures everything."

"It does." She handed me the spoon and sat on the bed cross-legged.

My head rolled back on the pillow. I was suddenly dancing at the White House, aware of Buck's arms around me. My eyes filled. "Is Doc right? Should I never see Buck again in my life?"

Debbie leaned over and kissed my cheek. Her eyes mirrored mine, blue and wet. I wiped my thumb under her eye. "I'm okay, Sweetie, don't cry."

She sat back a bit. "There was a time when I thought David and I wouldn't be together—after we were married, and I was pregnant. It was the hardest time of my life. I thought I'd die, except I was determined to have the babies. I was determined they'd be healthy and loved. But I didn't think David and I would be together. My heart felt like it was hardening to stone. I was so angry, but I don't even think I knew that at the time."

Cat handed her the tissue box.

Debbie blew her nose. "Well, we finally got everything talked through—and I made him read my journal, because sometimes I'm not so good at talking. And he understood my paintings. And I forgave him. And now he reads my journal all the time. And every day he asks to see my art, and we discuss it. But I'm much better at talking, too." She looked at me. "If that makes any sense."

Cat said, "It makes perfect sense."

I hugged her. "Yes."

She took more tissues. "Well, at first I didn't worry about all his girlfriends. But then, when Gwen showed up, it made me wonder." Her voice was getting waterlogged. "Well, I realized he probably ... had so many girlfriends ... because it made it easier to cope. You know, with his job. I think it must be very hard to shoot people all the time."

Debbie soaked another tissue. I bit my lip. My heart went out to her.

"Annie, I'm sorry to start crying on you. It's just that … I think Buck really loves you. And I think you really love him. So I hope you can work out whatever is the problem. I mean, if David and I could do it, I think you and Buck could do it."

I grabbed my sister in a hug and watched Cat's face. "I don't know, Sweetie, but please don't be upset. It'll all work out for the best, whatever that is."

Late that afternoon, I threw on some clothes and went downstairs to start dinner. Billy and the town florist intercepted me in the front hall.

"Hey, Annie." He held an expensive crystal vase, much like the one that had carried Valentine roses from Buck. "This is from Mr. Wynn, the business consultant. My wife said he insisted on roses this shade of pink. Here's the card he gave her to go with them."

"Thanks, Mitch." I took the heavy vase and envelope and headed back upstairs to my room. Billy escorted the florist out.

I put the arrangement on my bureau and sat on my bed. I recognized the luxurious stationery was the same as that from Brooke, Lewis & Wynn. The linen envelope was addressed to "Annie," and it was sealed with an old fashioned emblem. Emotion welled up again. Maybe this was Buck's form of closure.

I opened the envelope as carefully as I could and read the letter.

My Dearest, Annie,

I can't begin to put in words how very sorry I am for causing you so much pain. I only wish I could take it away, but I don't know how. The thought of not seeing you again is unbearable. But if seeing me would cause you the slightest discomfort, so be it. I will not contact you again. Of course, I would be ecstatic if you should ever feel the desire to contact me.

As to The Golden Bowl, I believe your business situation is well in hand. My partners and staff at Brooke, Lewis & Wynn will be delighted to continue to assist you and your staff with all your business needs.

I wish only the best for you and your lovely family.
Love,
Buck
A big fat teardrop landed on "Love, Buck."

The happy campers arrived home around 5:00 in the afternoon, and Doc immediately set to work on a barbeque. I was relieved I didn't have to cook.

I retreated to the kitchen to throw together a salad, heard the screen door slam, and turned to find Doc behind me. "The guys are taking care of the barbeque, Annie." He poured himself some coffee. "I heard about Buck."

I sighed. "Good news travels fast."

"Nathan was almost as happy as I am. He knows that guy is no good for you."

"Nathan? Well, knock me over with a feather."

The slamming screen door was followed by Sabena's high-pitched, "Auntie! We didn't even leave the property. Papa just told us. We thought we were going on a camping trip."

Doc lifted her above his head, the two of them laughing. "For your information, young lady, we did go on a camping trip."

I smiled at my niece, and forced enthusiasm. "Did you have fun?"

Sabena landed lightly on the kitchen floor. "Yes! We told stories by the campfire last night. And guess what? I told everyone all about The Supernatural Diet Club. They're all going to join next year."

I bent down and kissed the top of her head. "That's fantastic, honey."

"Yes, I'm calling a meeting for tomorrow at dinner. Can Buck come?"

"No, honey, he's travelling on business."

She looked crestfallen. "He's missed too many meetings, Auntie."

"I know, honey. It can't be helped."

"I can borrow your phone and call him. He might be having another drink with God."

Doc's coffee cup smashed on the floor.

~ *Buck* ~

A rustling by the door to my hotel suite roused me from my stupor. I remembered I was in New York and far too sober, though exhausted. The lights of the city were the only illumination in the room. I remained sprawled on the couch. A hushed voice began to concern me. A light went on. I sat up to face David and Cat.

Shock prompted my stupid question. "What are you doing here? How did you get in?"

David's sarcastic smirk promised an equally stupid answer. "I've trained my entire life for this moment." He deposited a credit card in his pocket, ushered his cousin into the room, and then flung the flimsy door closed.

Cat dropped a massive tote bag and put her hands on her hips. She gave him a look I'd never seen from her. I'd have fallen down laughing if I'd had the strength to get up.

David tried again. "Because we're Diet Club partners?"

Cat's expression was unchanged. "You're impossible." She glanced at me, a grinning wreck on the couch. "You're both impossible." She bent down and struggled to remove a pot from an insulated bag. David stepped in and freed the pot.

I watched with rapt attention. I suppose it was the most activity I'd seen in three days. "What's that?"

"Chicken soup," Cat said.

"From The Golden Bowl?"

"Yes." She took it to the kitchen.

My voice was pitiful. "Annie's chicken soup from The Golden Bowl. That's the best."

David found a bottle of water in the bag and tossed it to me. "Drink up."

I remembered our conversation about dehydration and insanity and falling in love. "Too late. I'm already insane. And hopelessly in love with Annie." I swallowed half the bottle. "What time is it?" I had no idea where I left my watch.

Cat reappeared. "It's half nine, Buck. I'm sorry it took us so long to get here."

"Not a problem. I've been a poor Diet Club partner myself." The amazement that they would even care to visit me penetrated my brain. My partners, my supposed friends, had not bothered to call since they learned what had happened.

I noticed the Rolex on the floor and reached for it. "Four days?"

Cat put her hand on my shoulder, then smoothed my hair. "We've been calling you and your office. Everyone's on holiday. When I finally spoke to someone, she said you were, too."

"Ah, yes. It's been a lovely holiday here on my couch. My rented couch. My partners decided to take that assignment in Paris off my hands."

"I'm sorry, Buck. I'll get you that soup."

I cleared the dining table of its papers and files, and Cat served the soup with warm whole grain bread and butter. A taste of Annie's soup stirred memories and feelings. My guests must have wondered if I was mad. I decided to take the bull by the horns, so to speak. "How is Annie?"

Cat's eyes were magnetic. "She misses you, Buck. She's quite upset."

I raised my water bottle in a toast. "That's better news than I expected."

Cat glanced at David, who was no help, and back at me. "How so?"

"At least her skin is no longer crawling."

David choked on the soup.

Cat didn't think that was funny. "Finish your soup, Buck, and we'll talk."

David leaned back in his chair, the smirk still in place. "How long has it been since you've had a drink?"

I swallowed hard. "Far … far too long, I'm afraid. Perhaps I should order a bottle of vodka."

I found my phone in the folds of my couch. Cat appeared and took it from me. "That won't be necessary, Buck. Liquor won't solve any problems. In your case, it could make them worse."

I landed back on my dining room chair. "Is this some sort of intervention?"

Cat resumed her seat and put my phone in front of her. "Some sort. Yes."

"I see." But I didn't. Did this mean I had some chance with Annie? I dared not ask. I couldn't let my fantasy be dashed.

After chitchat about the extended family and the upcoming concerts, we returned the dishes to the kitchen, and Cat removed a box of lemon bars from that tote bag. I couldn't help myself. "You're pregnant again? Congratulations."

She giggled as she piled them on a plate. "False alarm, Buck. But I lived on these when I was carrying Jack. I admit they're a weakness." She took one and handed me the plate. "Let's visit in your parlor. I'll get the pot of tea on the table."

David finished loading the bowls in the dishwasher and looked up grinning. "Enjoy your visit."

Cat had left the room, and I turned to him. "A trip to the woodshed, no doubt. I might rather help with the dishes." Who'd have thought I'd choose the assassin's company?

Cat stood at the window. "You have a remarkable view."

"Indeed. Central Park is right here. Good for walking and jogging. Not that I've walked or jogged in a while." I put the lemon bars on the table with the pot of tea and landed on the couch. I looked at my watch. "I've been right here for three days."

I wiped my hair back and stared at the floor. "It's been a difficult time to say the least. But I haven't had a drink since my car went into the drink, so to speak."

Cat ignored the various chairs and took a seat on the floor in front of the table, poured a cup of tea, and politely offered it to me. I waved a refusal, and she took a sip. "That's wonderful news, Buck. You're heading in the right direction."

"Just a matter of coincidence, really." I looked up at her. "When I arrived in New York after—" I cleared my throat. I couldn't say the word, "breakup."

Her eyes locked on mine. I couldn't move. "I'd had an uninspiring conversation with my business partners, and I was feeling quite distressed, actually. So I went to the University Club for a drink. I began scrolling through the news reports and saw the headline about a middle-aged woman found dead in her apartment a week after she'd expired. The bartender knew I'd … had a relationship with her years ago. He told me she'd died of cirrhosis at age forty-three. Then he left my favorite vodka in front of me. I took my phone and left the bar."

Cat didn't blink. "I'm sorry for your loss."

I squirmed in my seat. "That's just it. She wasn't my loss. She was a woman who was as alone as I am. As I've always been. A woman in the gallery. That's it. How sad. How very sad. And now I remember her as a deterrent to drink." I rubbed my eyes.

Cat's voice was soft. "She was a human being who deserved dignity. Whether or not you treated her with dignity, you know that now."

I could barely look her in the face. "I didn't treat her with dignity, did I? I suppose no one did, including herself. Yes, and now she's a deterrent to drink."

"You're not the same person you were before."

I hoped that was true. But I didn't know what to say, so I continued my story. "On my way out, I ran into my ex-girlfriend Deidre and her new husband. They were smiling and quite friendly. They even asked me to join them for dinner." I broke into laughter. "That certainly wasn't going to happen. Especially without a drink. All in all, a banner day. I returned to this suite, and haven't left since. Haven't had a drink since. Though I'm thinking now would be a good time."

Cat's lip turned up in a bit of a smile. "How's the construction going? When will your apartment be ready?"

Realizing my poor manners, I went to a chair across the room and retrieved a comfortable pillow. "Here, this will help." I handed it to her. "I've put my apartment on the market. My agent believes it will sell quickly. So many buyers enjoy building to suit their personal needs. As I did. And it worked out so well for me." I sat back down.

Cat ignored my sarcasm. "Where will you go?"

I poured myself some tea for something to focus on. "I have no plans. This is convenient to the office. I'll stay here when I'm in New York. When I'm not, I won't."

"Ah."

I looked her in the eye. "Believe it or not, it's best that I don't put down any semblance of roots right now. I'd only create another art collection. And that would make *my* skin crawl. This is simple. This is … nice." I swallowed an impending sob with a gulp of tea.

"Heart-shattered lives ready for love don't for a moment escape God's notice. Do you think God has forgotten you, Buck?"

I couldn't help a grin. "Oh, I don't think so. Once I get off this couch I'm bound to do something he can squash."

"Why do you think your life was spared?"

"I don't know. Do you?"

"Your Creator has a purpose for you. Find your purpose and your identity in God."

I tried to leave bitterness and impatience out of my voice. "I have no idea how to do that. I'm sure I've missed too many Diet Club meetings."

Cat's eyes bored into mine. "Be still and know. Find a quiet place and settle yourself. Take a few deep breaths. Quiet your mind. Listen. Pour out your heart to God. Listen. Know God loves you. You're precious to him. Trust that. Dedicate your day to God. Read scripture. Remember God is in charge. You'll find Holy Spirit will guide you along the right path." Her voice was almost hypnotic.

"Sounds lovely." *Was it Holy Spirit who put the specter of cirrhosis in front of the vodka the other day? Was it Holy Spirit who guided now-happily married Deidre to the University Club? Was it Holy Spirit who made me a different person?* Or was it all coincidence? It was too strange.

A sudden chorus of Paulo's latest hit blasted us out of the moment. Cat removed her phone from her jacket pocket and spoke with Joe Harris, her agent. When she finished her conversation, she looked up at me. "I'm afraid we need to get going. We're due in Chicago early tomorrow afternoon. And we have things to attend to before we leave Maine."

"Four sold-out shows, I hear."

"Yes, then many more after that. At least we can recuperate in Marberry in between times."

"Sounds perfect," I said.

Cat rose and returned the pillow to its chair. I watched her dig a business card out of her pocket. "Buck, I do hope you'll make an appointment. This counselor can help you work through your challenges, if you give it some effort."

I read the card and put it on the coffee table. "Thank you. I'll call."

"Good."

I followed her to the kitchen where David sat reading one of Sabena's notebooks.

He glanced up at me. "You should read this. It's quite helpful."

Cat shook her head. "David has no time to read the assignments either." She turned her sarcastic smile in his direction. "What will you have to say at the pearly gates?"

He didn't miss a beat. "I'll say I'm waiting for Debbie."

A sudden flood filled her eyes, and Cat ran off to the bathroom.

David's expression became concern.

"Is she all right?" I didn't know what to do.

He made a face. "I don't know. I'll talk to her. We've got to get going anyway." He stood up and handed me the notebook. "I know I give her a hard time. But I know this stuff is real. Deep down inside, you do, too."

Cat reappeared, red-eyed, but composed. "Buck, we love you." She reached for me, and we exchanged kisses on the cheek. "We'll stay in touch. Please don't hesitate to call me if you have any questions or you want to talk."

"Thank you, Cat. That's very kind of you."

She attempted a smirk and a toss of her head in David's direction. "Diet Club partners, you know." She took him by the hand. "We're off to Maine."

I followed them to the door. "What about the soup pot?"

She giggled. "Finish the soup, Buck. It's good for you."

David shook my hand and said, "See you later." I wondered if that was an indication that all was not lost with Annie.

I paced the floor, wondering at their generosity in flying to New York to bring me Annie's chicken soup. I returned to my couch with Sabena's notebook and became engrossed in the page titled "Promises of God." That sounded promising. Cat had typed it in plain language. "God is faithful … God will never leave us, will never forsake us."

I fell back on the couch in the quiet.

The next morning I finished off the chicken soup for breakfast, made an appointment with the counselor, and arranged for the incineration of Debbie's portraits, which had remained in boxes in my office. Due to the delicate nature of the project, and my concern that some of them could be stolen and make their way to public view, I personally oversaw the project. A half million dollars in ashes, but I felt only relief as I arrived at the counselor's office.

Now it was time to face life without addiction. Apparently the skin-crawling horror I'd already created for myself would not be enough deterrent. By the time I left the office, my electronic devices were equipped with sin-blocking software, and I had a sponsor willing to talk me out of the next drink. All the focus on such matters only made me want to stop at the first bar I could find. But it was a glimpse of the sky, the shade of Annie's blue eyes that stopped me at the door. Cat's visit had given me a tiny shred of hope.

I was sober and back at the office.

Fridays in summer meant the city lost most of its population to the Hamptons. My company had closed for a summer holiday. I stood at the large mahogany double door, *Brooke, Lewis & Wynn* etched there in gold. I put the key in the door, anticipating some quiet time to think and reflect.

"Mr. Wynn?"

I turned to face a comely brunette woman, probably in her thirties, fashionably dressed. Her smile was a bit shy and hesitant. She held her purse in front of her.

"Yes?"

She extended a hand. "I'm Lena Goodwin, and I've read all about what you did for The Golden Bowl up in Maine. I mean you took that place from a shack to millions of dollars in profits—and charity."

I cut her off. "How can I help you, Ms. Goodwin?"

"I'm *hoping* you can help me. I'm interested in purchasing a bed and breakfast."

I pushed the door open and welcomed her into the office. As I led her to my private office, a little voice told me that may not be the best idea. The entire floor was deserted. "Where is this bed and breakfast, Ms. Goodwin?"

"Please call me Lena." She took a seat in front of my desk. "It's on Cape Cod. It needs some work, but it has a great view of the water." She pushed a paper across the desk.

I took a seat and examined the details of the property. "It seems a reasonable location. What is your background, Ms. Goodwin?"

"Lena."

"Yes. Lena."

"Uh … well, I've got experience in retail."

"Retail?"

"Uh, yeah, I work in a little boutique. But I'm keeping my hairdresser's license … so I have that, too."

I'd often wished my well-appointed desk was equipped with an eject button. This was one of those times. "Impressive, Ms. Goodwin, but you must understand hospitality is a tough industry. Owning a bed and breakfast is grueling work unless you can afford a good staff. Even then, it's a challenge. I'm concerned your financial condition may not allow you to be successful in this endeavor."

"I have money, Mr. Wynn. I was hoping you could come up to Massachusetts and look at the place. Tell me what you think. I mean the owners are an elderly couple, and they've let the place go a little. But they still have customers. I think I can get a good deal on the place. I bet with your help, well, we could turn it into a great place. I have a lot of ideas."

"I'm sure you do." I took a folder, etched with the Brooke, Lewis & Wynn logo, out of my drawer, stood, and handed it to her. "Why don't you peruse this information at your leisure and contact us if we may be of service?"

She remained seated and opened the folder. Her manicured fingernail guided her down the page. "I'll give you my retainer now, Mr. Wynn. How soon can you get to Cape Cod?" She removed her checkbook from her purse. She must have read my mind. "Don't worry, the check'll clear. No problem."

"I'll check my schedule."

TEN

~ Buck ~

Since my schedule was pitifully open, I decided to drive up to Cape Cod the following morning. Traffic was heavy. I took a sip of a blueberry smoothie I'd purchased at one of New York's most popular shops—and a client of Brooke, Lewis & Wynn. I almost gagged. My eyes filled thinking about Annie and all my favorites from The Golden Bowl. Fortunately, my phone distracted me. "Yes?"

It was my partner, William Brooke. "Buck, what are you up to?"

"I'm stopped dead on the highway somewhere in Connecticut … on my way to check out a property for a new client … on Cape Cod."

"Can you get out to Chicago? Got a call from Skip Phillips. He's ready to do three more units in the Midwest. He wants you there yesterday."

"Of course."

"It's not like you've got vacation plans."

I silently cursed. "It's not like that at all."

"Okay, give him a call and set it up."

"I will."

Will was gone before I could ask how he was enjoying Paris. Since traffic was inching along, I had plenty of time to chat with Skip and make my travel reservations.

A brilliant idea occurred to me. I texted Cat and invited myself to their concert. She immediately returned with an invitation to join them backstage. Memories of their June 30th concert in Boston brought Annie back to me full force. Despite my rocky meeting with Cisco, David, and Rhodes, we'd had a great time together.

Thoughts of my time with Annie swirling, I played Paulo's latest inspirational album and sang and wept my way to the tiny, but busy, village of Osterville, Massachusetts. I'd given in to the heart-shattered Buck. Almighty Buck was dead somewhere in Titan's gym.

After removing all trace of emotion, I enjoyed lunch and a stroll through the village, bustling with well-heeled tourists. I returned to my SUV and drove around neighboring towns to get a sense of the area and the business climate. It was midafternoon when I pulled up to Bess & Bill's bed and breakfast. There were a fair number of cars in the parking lot, despite the fact that the sign dangled from its hinge, and the old homestead was badly in need of paint.

The front porch looked to be rickety, yet it was lined with elderly guests in rocking chairs. Some played checkers or chess. Some slept in the warm sun. It could have been mistaken for a nursing home. Perhaps Ms. Goodwin would get a good deal on the place.

I stepped back from the scene, suddenly horrified that this could be my future. A glimpse of the ocean sent me hiking toward the beckoning blue water and sky. Cat's words returned to me. *Be still and know. Find a quiet place and settle yourself. Take a few deep breaths. Quiet your mind. Listen. Pour out your heart to God. Listen. Know God loves you. You're precious to him. Trust that. Dedicate your day to God. Remember God is in charge. You'll find Holy Spirit will guide you along the right path.*

I sat amidst the dunes grateful that most of the inn's guests were not vital enough to use the beach. In relative privacy, I settled myself as best I could, though Annie was always there. I thought she would always be. I exhaled the emotion, but she wouldn't leave my mind. How could I ever contemplate sky and sea without her?

I took more deep breaths. I listened to the sounds of the wind and the waves, the gulls in the distance. I tried to remember God loves me. I laughed out loud. I didn't feel precious to anyone, never mind God. I was alone. I most always had been. But I dutifully told God this day was his. I told him I now understood he was in charge and could squash me like a bug on the windshield of life. So I consciously put my life in his hands. *For what it's worth.*

The wind picked up. I spoke aloud to the sky. "You're the one that said you're doing a new thing ... almost a year ago now." I looked at my watch as though that would tell me anything. I returned to my focus on the blue that was Annie's eyes. "Well, you do what you want, when you want. It's up to you. Last time I asked you to fix things, you burned my apartment. Frankly, I can't wait to see what's next." I reconsidered that position. "You know, I probably *can* wait to see what's next."

I took the salt air deep into my lungs. The warmth of the sun and sand soothed me. The blue of the sky mesmerized me. The breeze cradled me.

"Buck! You're here."

Her voice jarred me back to reality. I jumped up and brushed the sand off. "I'm here. I didn't expect to see you, Ms. Goodwin."

"Lena."

"Yes. Lena. Shall we go take a look at the inn?"

"Yeah. I'm staying here this weekend. I want to take a real close look before I buy. And now that I have you ... Wow ... I feel so much better. I wasn't so sure you could come right away."

"Well, here I am. Shall we?" I pointed her to the path.

With approval from Bess—who talked incessantly about Paulo Clemente and how thrilled I must be to know him as she followed us around the inn—I took photos of every room and defect. Really, there wasn't a square inch of that building that didn't need something done to it. The only thing of value was the postage stamp of sandy beach adjacent to it. Ms. Goodwin was not discouraged, despite Bess and Bill's wild valuation.

A vaguely musty smell permeated the inn, so I beat a hasty retreat. Ms. Goodwin grabbed my arm as I went for the exit. "Buck, join me for dinner. I want you to evaluate their restaurant, too."

Nausea welled up. "That won't be necessary. I'm sure we can negotiate a fine deal with my review of the premises. Their restaurant looks rather drab, I'm afraid. It adds no value that I can see. You'll be doing a complete renovation and starting from scratch with the restaurant … with all of it." I pushed through the door.

She landed somehow in front of me and placed her hands on my chest. "It could be fun."

I must have looked as shocked as I was.

"Please. You've come this far. I need your opinion on the food. I'm thinking of keeping their chef. I know the place isn't great, but he's a talented chef."

I headed down the stairs and busied myself taking photos of the exterior.

"Whatdaya say, Buck?"

"I say we can discuss the chef when the time comes. I'm not worried about finding a chef."

"Okay, if that's what you think."

"That's what I think." I came upon a particularly nasty crack in the foundation. "You may be better off razing the building."

"Oh." She wrapped herself around me to view the crevice. "Did you bring an overnight bag?"

"What?"

"Wouldn't it be fun to risk our lives together staying here overnight?"

Beads of sweat formed on my forehead. "Ms. Goodwin, I'm afraid that's not part of the client experience at Brooke, Lewis & Wynn."

"Too bad. Did you bring an overnight bag?"

I narrowed my eyes. "I always keep a bag packed in my car, Ms. Goodwin, as I travel a good deal, and I like to be prepared. I'm due in Chicago tomorrow morning."

She reached her arms around my neck, and I took her by the waist to push her away. It took some force to keep her from kissing me. "Ms. Goodwin, I'm afraid, somehow, you have the wrong idea. I'm going now to photograph the signage. Then I'm getting in my car to leave. After my return from Chicago, you'll receive my report and recommendations on this property. My associates and I would be happy to assist you, if you decide to proceed. Good day." I broke free of her grip.

She followed me to the dangling sign. "I'm thinking of calling this place *The Precipice*. Whatdaya think?"

"Perfect." I returned to the car, surprised and relieved she didn't follow me. I headed for a client's hotel near Logan Airport, consumed with thoughts of Annie and hope for some positivity from joining Cat and the extended family in Chicago. It occurred to me I thought of them more fondly than my own family.

I was at a stop light in Boston when it hit me. Almighty Buck Wynn would have taken full advantage of a beautiful and willing young woman. There was plenty of time to find a more comfortable hotel on the Cape. Annie was out of my life. I wondered what was wrong with me.

I will give you a new heart and put a new spirit in you. Annie had uttered these words right before she told me to go. Words of hope dashed in the next instant. I couldn't catch a breath.

~ *Annie* ~

The house was ridiculously quiet. Paulo's band was performing in the Midwest, and Debbie and Glori were visiting some of their buyers in Chicago. Doc was sailing with his cardiologist friend who'd appeared the minute my sister left town. We had an awkward cup of tea together, and I had to explain that Doc was an overzealous matchmaker. Nathan was entertained. I came away red-faced.

Now I settled in my Adirondack chair, positioned to take advantage of the colors of sunset. It'd been a long day at The Golden Bowl. Crowds grew larger by the day. My energy lessened by the day. Buck took up a big space in my head and my heart. I didn't sleep well. Invariably, I'd reach for his letter or stare at the plaque he'd given me just before we broke up. Both were covered with tear stains. Debbie and Cat called often to keep me on an even keel.

August sunsets can be spectacular in Maine, and this was no exception. I watched the show, comforted by sweeping color and the certainty that my Creator was in charge. The right shade of purple cloud dressed me in my gown, and I was dancing with Buck again.

Nathan silently took a seat beside me, rested his arms on his thighs, and stared in the direction of the sunset. I had nothing to say, but his presence disturbed me. I tried to refocus on the sky.

"Annie, I know you're going through a bad time. I kinda know how that feels. I'm sorry."

I turned to him. "Thanks, Mr. Rhodes."

He didn't face me. "I … uh … I was thinking a grilled cheese sandwich might help. You haven't eaten a thing today."

I couldn't help a half giggle. "Grilled cheese?"

"Yeah. It couldn't hurt."

"Are you hungry, Mr. Rhodes?"

"I had some dinner earlier. But I can make you a grilled cheese."

I half chuckled. "Thanks. That's very kind."

He stood and faced me. "Good. I make a mean grilled cheese, but that's about all I can make. You want it out here?"

I almost choked. "O—kay." I wasn't the least bit hungry, but as he rushed off to the kitchen, I realized I'd have a few more minutes of peace.

The heart has its reasons that reason knows nothing about. Waterworks began again. I wondered about Buck's heart and his reasons. He'd obviously come from a dysfunctional family. He'd obviously not received the love he needed from his parents.

Nathan appeared as moonlight glistened over the water. I watched him arrange sandwiches for both of us on a small table he placed in front of my chair. I thought about how he'd had a difficult childhood with a bitter mother. Cat had said Nathan had a hard time trusting anyone. *The heart has its reasons that reason knows nothing about.* He probably had no idea about his heart and its reasons, either.

He grinned at me. "I know you're gonna like this. It's as good as The Golden Bowl."

I couldn't help a smile.

The following morning I found Nathan, Doc, and his cardiologist friend sipping coffee at the kitchen table. "Good morning." I headed to the refrigerator for the eggs. "Breakfast is coming right up." I was as exhausted as I had been when I finally went to bed, so I didn't encourage conversation.

Doc headed to refill his cup, but it was obvious he wanted to talk to me. "Annie, how about taking some time off today? Things'll be fine at the restaurant. Come sailing with us. Nathan said he can show us some neat little islands and coves. It'll take your mind off things. You'll have some fun."

I took hold of Doc's arm and led him out the kitchen door. We stood at the bottom of the stair. "Is this another matchmaking session? Cuz, if it is, I'm not interested. He's very nice, but he's not for me. I'm sure he feels the same way."

Doc made a face. "He thinks you're sweet, Annie. He *is* interested."

I put my hands up and tried to keep my voice low. "It doesn't matter. I'm not!" My eyes began to sting. I only wanted to call Buck. But that was wrong, too. I was beginning to resent him for making me miss him so much.

I took a breath. "If you don't mind giving me peace and quiet—no getting-to-know-you conversation—I'll go with you. The boat's big enough to give me my own space. I need something different today, Doc, but it's not a new man. Time on the water … that could be nice. I don't want company. Can you do that? Can we do it my way today?"

He hugged me. "We can."

The yacht, *Fantasy NY*, was surely big enough to get lost in or on. I settled where Doc and his friend were not. Hat, sunglasses, and sunblock in place, I sat back and admired the sky. Eventually, I took Sabena's notebook out of my bag. I'd used Buck's Christmas card as a bookmark, and as I went to remove it, a small paper slipped out. My stomach fluttered. It was the first prayer Buck had taken from the bowl, and it had given me such hope. "God is doing a new thing," I announced to the sky. Unstoppable sobs came in spasms.

Tears were depleted, but my spastic innards didn't know. Seizures of grief continued. A large puffy white cloud etched in purple reminded me of a favorite verse from Psalm 108. *Every cloud's a flag to your faithfulness.* I controlled the spasms long enough to yell at the cloud. "God is faithful."

"I believe you, Annie." Nathan's voice made me jump.

I spun around to see him with a food cart. My voice didn't work. I watched him line up a table for two and place sandwiches in front of us. He emptied a bag of chips into a bowl and poured two glasses of iced tea. He returned the pitcher to the table and took a seat beside me. "It's grilled cheese again."

Spasms of laughter began. I quashed it with a tiny bite of a tasty grilled cheese.

Nathan was patiently quiet.

My first words were profound. "There must be a half stick of butter on this bread."

He smirked. "That's what makes it so good."

"Yep." I took another bite and decided to quit while the food stayed down. "So you've been through all this—crying fits and all? Any advice for the brokenhearted?"

He shrugged. "I guess you've just got to get through it the best you can. Run until you're drop-dead tired, I guess. Then you can finally sleep it off."

I took a sip of iced tea. "Hmm … I think I did that when I lost Russ. I didn't take the time to feel the feelings, like my sister always says."

He smirked. "It works for her, I guess."

I noticed a line of purple-tinged clouds and thoughts of dancing with Buck were back again, paining my head and heart. *This is getting old. It's not like it's been that long. It's not like we were married.* Tears returned. Memories of my husband Russ mingled with tattered hopes for a future with Buck.

Nathan's sympathetic gaze sent me to my bag for a tissue. I walked over to the rail to blow my nose without further embarrassment.

"Annie." Nathan was behind me. He put his hand on my shoulder, and I turned to face him. Sunlight caught the silver highlights of his salt and pepper hair. "This is a self-centered, selfish world we live in. I've never known anyone like you. You … and your … family … I mean you really care about people. You give up so much of your time and effort to help other people. It's staggering how much you give of yourself." The intensity in his deep brown eyes staggered me, strangely drawing me in and repelling me at the same time.

He paused for a second or two, looking me in the eye. I took a step back, and he took a step forward. "People are selfish. They go into marriages thinking of what they'll get out of it, not what they can do for the person they marry. You're better off knowing now who Buck really is. I found out the hard way who I was married to." He snorted. "Three times. And the last one was the worst."

Some combination of a laugh and a cry came out of me. "I'm sorry, Mr. Rhodes."

His face reddened. "Look, I know it was dumb to tell you to call me Mr. Rhodes. Can you call me Nathan? Everyone calls me Nathan."

I laughed so hard my stomach ached. The irony wasn't lost on him. When we'd first met, I'd said, "Everyone calls me Annie." And he'd insisted on Mrs. Brewster. I hung over the rail, letting the cool sea spray mist me. "Okay, Nathan." I'd said it out loud.

~ *Buck* ~

My time in the Midwest was brief, but uplifting. Cat and Debbie and family could not have been more gracious. The concert was phenomenal—musically and financially. I could feel the money pouring into The Golden Bowl and all its charities. The fans were as ravenous there as anywhere else. Cat's invitation to the crowd to implement prayer in their lives—to be salt and light—touched a chord with me. And with the rest of the audience, as far as I could tell.

My meetings with Skip Phillips were productive and efficient. All told, I'd spent only a bit more time with him than I had with Ms. Goodwin, yet my firm stood to make exponentially more money from that time. I returned to my New York office in a better frame of mind.

The mahogany doors swung open, and I nearly crashed headlong into a clerk. A ridiculously high stack of journals and papers in her arms lowered to reveal a familiar face. "Hi Buck! How was Chicago?"

"Ms. Goodwin?"

"Lena."

"Yes. Lena." A shockwave went through me. "What are you doing here?" I dropped my briefcase and took the unwieldy pile from her.

"Thanks, Buck, you're such a cutie. I'm taking these to the shredder. Right this way."

Cutie? Confusion spiraling, I followed her. "Ms. Goodwin?"

She pointed to the counter, and I dropped the stuff there. "I work here now. I'm the newest employee here at Brooke, Lewis & Wynn." Her smile was a dentist's dream.

She didn't wait for me to sputter another question. "I know the room's a mess now, but the shredding company'll be here tomorrow. They'll take everything. Then your offices'll look so much better!"

I tried again, but she forged on. "I decided you were right about *The Precipice*, Buck. You saved me from that one. I owe you big time. So here I am, your newest employee. Mr. Lewis hired me himself … personally. I'm getting the *employee* experience here at Brooke, Lewis & Wynn now." She smiled mischievously, smoothed her tight skirt, and sashayed out of the storage room. I was not the only one transfixed as she stooped to retrieve my briefcase and swung it playfully as she strolled on to my office.

It was probably forty seconds later when I barged into my partner's office and slammed the door behind me. "Are you mad?"

"Huh?" Carter Lewis looked up from his papers.

"This is a harassment lawsuit waiting to happen." A duel had begun brewing between Almighty Buck and Heart-shattered Buck. This was not good.

"What are you talkin' about?"

"I'm talking about Lena Goodwin, our *client*."

He chuckled. "She doesn't have two nickels to buy a bed and breakfast, and she knows it. But she wants to work in hospitality, and I have a feelin' she's good at it." He flashed a dirty smile. "She's a hard worker. She learns quick. Seems ambitious. Best of all, Janice loves her. That's the key, Buck. When Janice is happy, the office is happy."

I raised my brows. "I told you *and* Janice that I'd be interviewing for that position in the fall. You didn't even consult me before hiring my new clerk?"

His smile turned my stomach. "It happened in kind of a rush. You know how it is."

I returned to my office, slammed the door, and landed in my chair. Before I could take a calming breath, Janice knocked and entered with a stack of notes. "Welcome to New York, Buck. Thanks for removing those … uh … boxes. I'm sure the artwork will go great on your new apartment walls."

I glared at her.

She ignored me. "Lena is taking care of tidying up all the files. Mr. Brooke is due in from Paris tonight, and he'll be here for the photos tomorrow."

"Photos?"

"You didn't get the email?"

"Apparently not."

"Carter didn't tell you? You were just in with him."

I exhaled a breath. "Apparently it was not a pressing issue."

Carter hung on the open door frame. "Hey Buck, congrats on the cover of *Hospitality Today*."

"What?"

"Yeah, The Golden Bowl's on the cover, featuring your article … the one on the business model. Had a talk with the editor yesterday. He said it's a bit academic, but they'll fluff it up with photos. Joe Harris is all over it … sent them all the stuff they need. And they'll send a photographer here tomorrow to get our pictures, some candids, ya know."

"Fluff it up? I wrote a business paper."

"No problem, Buck, but they have an audience to please, and they thought they could get some mileage out of this. Golden Bowl is a hot commodity right now—thanks to you and Brooke, Lewis & Wynn."

I scratched my head. "This is a professional journal."

"Yeah, and their readers take vacations, too. Why not get all the publicity we can? For Golden Bowl and *for us*. Be ready for your pictures tomorrow." He straightened his tie and buttoned his jacket. "Okay, see you later. I'm taking Lena to lunch." His smile sickened me. I noticed Janice had a similar reaction.

I reached for my laptop. "Perhaps Carter will hire Ms. Goodwin as his assistant."

She leaned over my desk. "He's just as dirty an old man as you are. I feel sorry for that poor girl. All she wants is a good, well-paying job in a professional atmosphere. A day's work for a fair wage. And because she's so pretty … well, we'll see how long she lasts."

Janice deposited her notes on my desk and left to answer her phone.

I pondered the employer-employee experience at Brooke, Lewis & Wynn. Heart-shattering was as good a word as any to describe it.

Eleven

~ Buck ~

The office walls were closing in on me, and I found it difficult to get any work done. I decided to walk back to my hotel to work, but the green of Central Park lured me to a bench there. Summer sunshine and passersby created a much happier atmosphere. As I inhaled deeply, the scent of newly mown grass brought me back to Marberry. To Annie. I opened my briefcase and reviewed the promises in Sabena's notebook. *Holy Spirit will lead you into all truth.* What might that be?

Maybe it was the truth that I was done with this job. At least with this firm. Maybe I could find another position somewhere that would not be heart-shattering. It occurred to me that my business partners were as heart-shattered as I. Mired in the dirt. Did I have some obligation to try and help? I couldn't even help myself.

It was probably time for a change. Fifty was fast approaching. Perhaps I was already too old to start over. Mild panic brought my Alma Mater to mind. I'd certainly donated a fortune over the years. I had a record of excellence in my firm, and I'd written a number of business publications that were well received.

Academia could be the right avenue for me. This latest success with The Golden Bowl should assure a job of some status that could keep me entertained. No doubt I could negotiate a lucrative deal with my partners. Money wouldn't be an issue, unless of course, God decided to burn my savings and investments.

My phone interrupted my musings. *Annie*! My stomach flipped. "Annie?"

"Hi, Buck." It was Sabena. My eyes watered. Disappointment tore my gut, but the tiny voice brought relief. "We miss you, Buck. Are you coming to our meeting tomorrow?"

"I'm afraid I won't be able to make that one, Sabena. Does Auntie know you have her phone?"

"You need to get here soon, Buck. Auntie Annie is sick."

"Sick? What happened?" I was on the edge of my seat.

"I don't know, but Mama says she's heartsick. I think you could make her feel better. You make her laugh. Are you in your car, Buck?"

I only wished I could be. "No, I'm not. I'm at work now." My voice was hoarse. "Perhaps Auntie Cat could get her some chicken soup. Why don't you ask her?"

"Okay. When are you coming home, Buck? I'm going to plant a garden with Auntie … in the greenhouse."

I tried to clear my throat. "That sounds marvelous. You'll be a busy girl. That greenhouse looks to be a hundred years old."

"That's what Auntie says. They used it in the olden days. But we're going to fix it and grow corn."

I choked. "Corn in a greenhouse?"

"I have to go! See you soon." Sabena had likely been found out.

~ *Annie* ~

Having the family back home in Marberry was such a relief to me. They seemed energized by their concert series in the Midwest. Debbie and Glori had more orders than they knew what to do with, and the kids were full of stories. Sabena was determined to plant corn.

My days were best kept to routine, and one of my most treasured routines was early morning in my chair as the sun rose over the ocean. I was more pensive than prayerful today.

Sitting there in the quiet, I became fascinated as the sun shone on strands of my flyaway hair creating translucent tubes and rainbow nodes. The brilliance of it all reminded me of our call to be salt and light in the world, a point Cat stressed in every concert of the tour.

Such a simple, unexpected moment gave momentary relief from my thoughts and memories.

My phone jangled my last nerve. It was Gus, my maintenance manager. I barely had a chance to say hello. "Annie, I can't be mowin' lawns. I'm gettin' too old for that stuff."

"Okay, Gus, but I don't understand. Did someone ask you to mow the lawns?"

"Not straight out, but the landscaper's three days overdue, and when I called him this mornin' he said Lisa Quinn wrote him a letter to fire him. Said his work wasn't up to snuff. Don't come back. That wasn't a decent way to go about it. That was pretty shabby treatment."

I wondered if Gus was on drugs. "Lisa Quinn?"

"I don't know why you got a dishwasher involved with landscape decisions. I figured it has somethin' to do with that Super Club thing."

"No, Gus, Lisa has nothing to do with landscaping. That's your job. I can't imagine how the landscaper got such a letter. They've been doing a great job as far as I'm concerned. It must be a mistake. I'll try and look into it when I get to the office. But could you call the landscaper and apologize and get him over to mow the grounds as soon as possible?"

"Okay. Sorry for callin' you shabby."

"It's okay. I'm sure this has been pretty frustrating for you."

"Okay." He was gone.

Cat took the empty chair beside me and squeezed my hand. "I'm so happy to be back to our miraculous sunrise. How blessed we are here."

"We are." I smiled and tears welled up. It wasn't Gus and the landscaper.

"Do you want to talk?"

I wiped my eyes. "I know you've gone through some awful struggles, Cat, but sometimes I'm so envious of you. Sometimes it'd be nice to know the future. How come you know some things so clearly, but not others?"

"Whatever I know is to serve God's purposes. I don't always know how. It's up to God what he chooses for me to know and how that's to be used. That's all right with me because it's all right with him. Sometimes, by God's grace and mercy, I see things that help me understand … help me heal … or help others. It's a gift God gives me. As long as it makes him happy, it makes me happy."

I marveled at her willingness to give herself so totally to her Maker. I couldn't imagine having that gift, and then have it taken away without warning or explanation. But Cat was so dedicated, so selfless, I couldn't imagine God ever taking that gift away.

I gripped my stomach. This morning it wouldn't even take my usual coffee. "Wow. Right now, I wish I could have the ability to see the future. I wonder what the future would be if I call Buck. Maybe he's moved on by now. Or if he hasn't—if he still wants me—what if that's not the right thing? I keep praying, but it's all clear as mud."

Cat giggled. "It's all quite clear, Annie. I think you're afraid of the answer."

"Huh?"

"You wake up with the same thought every morning."

Light dawned. "I will give you a new heart and put a new spirit in you." A bubble in my throat blocked my voice. "Oh, Cat!" I nodded. "I do wake up with that verse in my mind. But then I remember the last line of The Prayer of Jabez: that you would keep me from evil."

I put my hands to my head hoping to block the pain of it all. "I thought it means to stay away from Buck. But maybe I'm wrong. God gave *Buck* a new heart and a new spirit. I made sure he understood that ... before I told him to go." I looked for a tissue in my beach bag.

Cat took my hand and my attention from the bag. "That's right, Annie, the evil isn't Buck."

Confusion mounted. "Then why do those verses come one right after the other every morning? How does a new heart and a new spirit relate to keeping me from evil? It's like a puzzle."

Cat's eyes were sympathetic. "My sense is that God is protecting Buck from evil, as he's a new person. A child of God."

"A new person? With a new heart and a new spirit."

She nodded.

"Then why am I pushing him away?" My voice and my body trembled.

"He's obviously done things that have hurt you deeply. You're afraid you can't trust him. You've learned he's had problems with addiction. All good reasons not to marry someone. Despite all that, you still love him."

I doubled over in pain. "I do."

Cat gently rubbed my back. "In the natural, it does make sense to avoid such a man."

A new heart and a new spirit lingered, bouncing in my brain. I sat up. "But in the supernatural … that's a whole other story."

Cat's little smirk confirmed that. "You must remember you're also a beloved child of God."

A wisp of a sea breeze on my face emphasized Cat's point. "I guess it boils down to extreme trust to live so much in the supernatural like you do."

Could I dare to take that chance? To trust that deep? The expression on Cat's face said it was worth the risk. Lisa called her a gold light. It was the light of pure joy that radiated from her.

"Have you been in touch with Buck?"

"Yes." Her eyes gave nothing away.

"Is he okay?"

"He's devastated, Annie, but to his credit, he's sought counseling and he's picking up the pieces. He's moving forward as best he can."

With my stomach in spasms, I couldn't bring myself to ask Cat exactly what moving forward meant.

I'd been scarce at The Golden Bowl lately, and there was a constant stream of people who wanted to speak with me. Karen and Gerald met me at the door to my office near the Customer Service area.

Gerald was talking as soon as he laid eyes on me. "Annie, our packaging supplier messed up the order for The Super Club." He opened my office door and ushered me in.

Karen was on my heels. "The demand's been growing every single day for our desserts. Gerald said we won't have the packaging before tomorrow. We'll probably run out today."

I fell into my chair. "Is there any place else we can get that packaging?"

Gerald looked distraught. "I've been on the phone all morning. It's like the world supply of dessert cups has been sucked up."

My mind was gone. "Okay, well, I guess it's not the end of the world. Most of the people end up buying the bigger sizes at The Sweet Shop anyway. We'll apologize to the customers and offer them something else once we're sold out."

Gerald's voice cracked. "I'm sorry. I know this is a big opportunity for us to get into the diet market."

"It's okay. One or two days won't make or break us."

When they finally left, I put my head down on the desk. Ten o'clock in the morning, and I was fried.

I woke up with Nathan's hand on my back. "Annie? Are you okay?"

Not another grilled cheese sandwich. The thought that I may have said that aloud popped me up in my chair. "Fine, I'm fine, Mr. Rhodes … Nathan." I noticed my head chef standing in the doorway. He wasted not a moment.

"Annie, I just got a delivery of twice the amount of carrots and potatoes I ordered and half the amount of onions. The guy insisted the order was right. So I called his boss. He said Lisa Quinn changed the order. Lisa says she has no idea what that was all about. So I called him back, and he emailed me the order. It said Lisa Quinn on there. I don't know what she's up to, but I think you need to fire her. So now we've got this extra food. You want it for your dad's food pantry?"

"Sure. That sounds great. Dad can always use more donations."

He had one foot out the door. "Okay, I'll get the stuff to your dad. Also, I told the guy that Lisa has nothing to do with the orders. So it better not happen again." He slammed the door shut.

I sighed.

"Are you sure you're all right, Annie?" Nathan's expression was real concern.

I leaned on the desk and rose from my seat. "Fine. It's nothing a butter pecan cone won't take care of."

"Uh … I tried to get you some. Karen said they ran out."

I headed over to the restaurant to find Lisa, not that I held out much hope she knew what was going on. But the walk woke me up a bit. I stopped at the bowl to explain Leave a Prayer/Take a Prayer to a crowd of women hovering around the sign. In the process, I took a slip of paper from the bowl and glanced at it. *Pride goes before the fall.* Then it proceeded to describe a prideful person who needed prayer. It wasn't written on Cat's paper, and it wasn't her handwriting, but I felt those five words in the pit of my stomach. I headed down the back stairs to the beach.

It hit me like a ton of bricks, and I dropped onto a bench along Miller's Way. A woman reading there never looked up from her book. I fell into my private little whirlwind. *A new heart and a new spirit … Buck is a new person … Why am I pushing him away? Why am I not there to support him as he moves forward?* Deep down, under the crawling skin, it was pride, and under that, it was fear.

How could I marry a guy who would associate with loose women? And immortalize them in an art gallery. With me.

How many people knew about that behavior? It felt like everyone but me. How embarrassing. What would people say? That's not the question, is it? What would God say? He'd spoken to me before Buck had ever left.

~ *Lisa* ~

Annie found me in the employee lounge on break. I had a feeling it wouldn't be long before she showed up. I was in the doghouse for something I didn't do. I gulped my blueberry smoothie. "Hi Annie. I didn't do anything. Gus was yelling at me about messing up the lawns, and the guys in the kitchen've been teasing me about getting into the ordering side of things, now that I'm such a big shot with Super Club."

She sat across the table from me. "I'm sorry, Lisa. Something strange is going on, and I need to find out what. I know you've been using the computer lately to get ready for school, and I'm wondering if somehow, something in a program has picked up your name and mixed everything all up. I can fit what I know about computers into a thimble. But it's really all I can think of."

Annie looked so dog-tired, I almost cried. "I'm sorry. I don't know much about computers either. Maybe that happened, but if it did, it was a mistake. I'd never do anything to make you mad. You're my boss and my friend."

She grinned. "I know, Diet Club partners, right?"

We giggled like a couple of little kids. Then she made the chef come and apologize to me.

TWELVE

~ *Buck* ~

I arrived at my office dressed in a dark suit and tie. The photographer was on time and professional. Things went smoothly until we lined up for a shot of the three partners with their entire staff. Needless to say, it took a while to position everyone. Janice and Lena were placed beside me. *Oh joy*. I concentrated on my appointment to speak by phone with the president of my Alma Mater later today. The two women insisted on relating Almighty Buck stories, to my detriment, I might add.

I drew my breaths deliberately and evenly so as to calm myself. At last the photographer was ready. We were to say cheese. Lena jumped up and planted a kiss on my surprised cheek. We did not need to say cheese for the next photo.

As soon as the ordeal was over, I returned to my hotel couch to discuss future possibilities in London.

~ *Annie* ~

The kids had boundless energy, and they cleaned up the old greenhouse in short order. I was summoned to assist them in planting some flowers and vegetables. Digging in the dirt was more therapeutic, and less caloric, than grilled cheese sandwiches. It wasn't long before we were all laughing. My sister had a severe case of the giggles, and it was contagious.

My phone set off automatic butterflies in my stomach. I couldn't take another thing. Wiping my hands on an old towel, I picked it up. It was Joe Harris. "Annie, we've got a cancellation for your show. Death in the family. So I have a great idea."

"Okay, Joe, tell me."

"With all the publicity coming up with Buck and his firm, it'd be interesting to have him on as your guest. Your public's become intrigued by you two, and he's a great promoter for The Golden Bowl. He can talk a little bit about that business model article he wrote and all the foodie stuff. With your chemistry, I think it'll make a great show."

My butterflies turned to killer bees. "I … I don't know if he can make it."

"I just got off the phone with his assistant. He's on vacation in London now, but she's scheduled him to do the show. She'll re-arrange his travel so he can fly into Boston and head right to Maine. No problem."

Who was Buck vacationing with? "Well, she needs to clear it with Buck. Let me know when she does."

"No worries, Annie, it's all set. Should be an easy show for you." Joe was gone before I could utter another sound.

The next call concerned yet another ordering snafu at the restaurant. Poor Lisa was blamed again.

I was worn out by the time The Supernatural Diet Club assembled on the beach. Sabena was on fire atop her lobster trap. "Come to the Throne of Grace!"

Cat subdued her with a kiss. "Thank you, Sabena. I think so many of us have a hard time believing grace is there for us. We have a hard time believing God loves us so very much, that he's our perfect father."

Lisa muttered, "Yeah, my father's a jerk. He abandoned me. I have a hard time remembering God's a perfect father. He's off in heaven somewhere. Why does he really care so much about me when my own father couldn't care less? But then I got to know Annie, and all these blessings happened, and I don't know why. Turns out it's God. There isn't any other explanation. Ever since I decided to be a gold light, things keep gettin' better. Until now."

Ashleigh laughed. "It's not like we believe you're really messing up all the ordering, Lisa. We're just teasing. But I'll be happy when Buck finally gets back here to take a look at things."

Karen chimed in. "Me, too. But don't let this get to you, Lisa. It's a resentment that's building up. Don't be like me and eat junk food and ice cream over it."

Glori was chomping at the bit. "That's exactly what happens hon. Look at Debbie. She spent her entire life with eating disorders cuz her father—Ol' George—was such a tyrant. She had to feel a whole lot of feelings with her shrink to get over all those resentments. Right, hon?" She turned to Debbie.

Debbie blushed and retreated into David's arms. "Yes, but now I know not to let resentments harden. I feel the feelings and let them go. And I forgave Daddy." She cast a glance at Doc and stumbled over her words. "And I let go of resentments about Doc, also. A long time ago."

I noticed Doc, beet red, sitting on the edge of the group. Cat did, too. She went over to him, put her hand on his and knelt down to face him. "God is your perfect father, too. You can vent all your frustrations to him, all your pain. Know that your heavenly father loves you, forgives you. Forgive yourself. Let go of resentment and bitterness. Accept perfect love and grace."

I could see Doc was trying hard to remain composed. He nodded. "Thanks, Cat."

Later that evening I found Doc at the kitchen table with Sabena's notebook and a bottle of beer. I poured myself a cup of tea and joined him. "Are you okay? Your eyes are all red."

He stretched in the seat. "I'm all right. Just thinking."

I sensed I was too tired for this conversation. "About?"

"I know about Debbie's near-death experience when she had that heart attack. She told me about it last Christmas." He rubbed his face. "A nineteen-year-old having a heart attack. Crazy. And the biggest part of the blame goes to me, if you take the time to think about it. I let her mother marry that guy. I let her stay with him, when I could see what he'd done to her. I let Debbie grow up in that. So at age nineteen she's in heaven talking with her grandmother. It's unbelievable."

I patted his hand. "It changed her life, and it changed so many others. Think what a difference she's making in the world. God worked everything out for good."

He shook his head. "When I saw that painting of the lake ... the black ... I knew Wynn was in there. I knew it in my gut. I mean I understood her paintings are prophetic. But that's when I knew it in my gut. It scared the crap out of me. Debbie has a real connection to God. God must be real."

My stomach twisted thinking how Buck could easily have been killed.

Doc took a gulp of beer. "So now I know for sure God is real. And I'm full of resentments and bitterness, like Cat says. I guess I have to start at square one."

"That's as good a place as any."

He faced me. "Annie, the biggest regret of my life is leaving your mother. I know we were just kids, and she was determined to marry money, but I could have done more. We could have been a family."

I rose from my seat and hugged him. "Hindsight is always 20/20, Doc. Don't beat yourself up over it. We all make mistakes, and if we're smart, we realize we have all God's grace, right there for us. We learn and move forward."

I thought I should take my own advice.

~ *Buck* ~

I rarely checked my phone over the past ten days in England—just the occasional skim to see if there was a message from Annie. Not that I expected one.

As I sat at lunch, looking for details of my return trip amidst Janice's messages, I saw I was due in Maine in five days to guest on Annie's show. I phoned her. "Janice, did Annie approve of me doing her show or was this Joe's idea?"

I heard a heavy sigh. "The show's scheduled, Buck. We're all adults here. Don't whine. Go and do the show. Your car and driver will be waiting for you at Logan, so all you have to do is sit there and sleep till you arrive in Marberry. Do the show. Come back to New York. Amanda James will be here at the office the following Tuesday to interview you. You're getting a lot of mileage out of that article you wrote."

I ignored the fact that I'd be interviewed on the world's most popular news magazine show. "You're fully aware of my agreement with Annie."

Janice snapped. "Annie's moved on. It's time for you to move on, too."

"Moved on?" I hated that I was giving Janice the satisfaction of knowing how crushed I was.

"Just emailed you the gossip rag. Nathan the SEAL is movie star gorgeous. Who wouldn't fall for a bodyguard like that? Gotta run, Buck. See you in New York." *The Weekly World Gossip* appeared on my screen, a photo of Annie and Rhodes with his arm at her back. I closed the laptop.

I resolved to accept the offer from one of the world's most prestigious universities. They'd give me free reign to develop and teach a program for graduate students. Somehow I'd get through the interview with Annie, wish her well, tie things up with my firm, and begin anew. I only wanted a shot— or a fifth—right now.

I strode to the balcony and took some deep breaths. The scent of the garden, the warm sun, did nothing to calm me. I picked up the house phone.

Room service arrived with my favorite vodka. No need for mixers today. My phone blasted another Paulo Clemente hit. I put the bottle on the table and picked up the phone. "Cat?"

"Hello, Buck. Are you enjoying London?"

My insides seized up. "Very much, thank you. Is everything all right?"

"Busy, we have a day of rehearsals ahead. We'll enjoy it. I wanted to tell you we missed you at our meeting. We discussed resentments, bitterness, and how God's grace is there for us. Always. Especially in dark, difficult moments."

I slumped into the chair. "I see."

"I want you to know that."

I realized once again, there'd be no outwitting Cat. I needed this drink. Just one would help me cope. Resentment rose. Cat had no right to interfere in my personal affairs.

As silence lingered, anger fired up. Anger at Cat, then at myself. I picked up the bottle and threw it. It crashed against the mantel, glass and vodka spraying across the room. *Be still and know*. I took a breath. "Thank you, Cat."

I dared not ask her about Annie. It was best to focus on this tiny victory. One more minute without alcohol.

~ *Lisa* ~

When I saw Annie's picture on the front of *The Weekly World Gossip* with Mr. Rhodes, I almost fell out of my seat. Karen and Ash had tears in their eyes. I quickly flipped through the pages, looking at the pictures first. The caption under the photo of Annie and Buck said a source close to the couple revealed they called it quits. Now it was Annie and Mr. Rhodes.

It'd been a long day at work with more problems with food and supply orders. Everything said it was my fault. Annie had called the computer expert at Brooke, Lewis & Wynn, and they said everything looked fine on their end. But they were checking into it extra carefully because The Golden Bowl was an extra special client. I sure wished they'd get it fixed right away.

So Karen and Ash and me sat like three ducks in a row on the rocks near The Golden Bowl eating hot fudge sundaes. Thank goodness we never ran out of them. "Uh ... I know we don't want to be reminded ... but we said we wouldn't eat over resentments and stuff." I needed to get that out there.

Ashleigh laughed her head off, and Karen kept eating.

Now I was feeling real guilty. "We could take a walk on the beach after."

Ashleigh put her bowl down long enough to peel her hair off her face and remake her ponytail. "Sure."

Karen kept eating.

"Did anyone talk to Annie about Buck ... or Mr. Rhodes?"

Ash cleared her throat like she was about to tell us something important. "Uh ... I heard her call him Nathan."

I almost fell off the rock. "Huh?"

"Five or six times."

Karen finally stopped swallowing. "Annie loves Buck. Something happened. I don't know what. She never told us. But I know by the way she's been acting. She's depressed, even though her entire family's staying with her. This gossip paper is wrong. They just make up stories to print."

"Well, Mr. Rhodes saved her life last winter when the wave whipped her right off this rock. I know they get along fine. But I really know that Annie and Buck should be together. Maybe he's too busy with his business."

Karen shook her head. "He's always busy with his business. And he *always* made time for Annie. Half the time I knocked on her door she was on the phone with him. And it wasn't all business. Something's wrong. Very wrong." She scraped the bottom of the cup to get the last of the fudge.

"Well, we're Diet Club partners. We should be able to ask her." I started to feel sick.

Ash pointed to the beach. "There's Annie … walking all alone. Mr. Rhodes is behind her, but she's not paying attention. He's just being a bodyguard."

It sounded like Karen inhaled tears. She pushed her glasses up on her head and mopped her eyes with a crumpled napkin. "There's something very wrong."

~ *Annie* ~

I didn't call Buck because I was afraid he'd be with another woman. I think that would have killed me. The fact that the gossip media was on fire with my supposed romance with Nathan perplexed me. Obviously it was simple to get photos of the two of us, since he was my director of security. But how did they manufacture that into a news story? Who'd even care? Apparently half the world.

I had to wonder who "the source close to the couple" was. And my wondering about what people would say—obviously they'd say anything, whether it was true or not. I shuddered to think what would happen if or when Buck's interest in art became news. Yes, that would ravage my pride, to say the least.

As I walked the beach, each step brought new questions, more emotions. I wondered how Buck was handling all the publicity. I remembered the terrible scandal my sister and family endured when David's exploits were exposed in that same rag, *The Weekly World Gossip*. I prayed this latest story would die an early death.

Joe Harris was well used to dealing with scandal. He graciously handled all communications with the media, including Amanda James. Since I considered her somewhat of a friend, I didn't want to get into a conversation I might regret.

Buck would be here tomorrow afternoon to do my show. I only wanted to call him. But what could I possibly say? I certainly had a good business reason. I knew he'd get the ordering mess straightened out immediately. His colleagues weren't nearly as smart or devoted to the clients. Buck would be tenacious in getting the issues resolved.

But if I called him, my reason would be personal, and I'd end up blurting something embarrassing. I can't wait to see you, but are you seeing anyone else? Just talk and I'll listen endlessly to your voice. You hurt me, and I forgive you, and I'm ready to love you forever.

It was too frightening. I couldn't be rejected again. I bet he'd never even think that what he did would make me feel rejected.

I hoped, when I saw his face, I'd know what to say.

Nathan had given instructions for Buck to meet us at The Golden Bowl in my office in the barn. Then security would escort us all to my studio. I sat shaking in my chair, obsessed with Buck, and listening to a litany of problems with the ordering and continued product shortages. Poor Lisa threatened to quit, since she'd received so many taunts about her presumed involvement.

Finally, I banished the unhappy mob and headed to my private bathroom. Standing in front of the mirror, my haggard face stared back. It didn't matter that I'd worn Debbie's recommended pale pink to perk up my skin tone. I tried some of Glori's makeup, then reworked my hair into its clip. Wisps escaped in a frenzy around my head. Any other day I wouldn't have cared. I drank a full glass of water, hoping that would give me a healthier look. No. I drank another. In that moment, I understood how people could take to alcohol or pills in hopes of making all their problems disappear.

I returned to my desk and bowed my head in prayer hoping to calm down before Buck's arrival. *God is doing a new thing.* I prayed God would give me the desire of my heart. It wasn't so long ago when I'd realized what that was. But there'd been a flood of water under the bridge. I stood silently at my window and waited.

Embarrassment welled up at the thought of all my selfish prayers. I renewed my request, asking for God's best for all concerned. I needed to trust God through this. What else could I do?

Buck's SUV pulled into the lot, and I ran downstairs and out the door to meet him.

First, I noticed the strange look on Nathan's face, and then I saw the beautiful brunette in the passenger seat. Buck exited the driver's door. He appeared tired, his bright white shirtsleeves rolled up, his eyes intense.

His eyes told me it was me he wanted. But my eyes decided he'd found someone new. I focused on not crying, but thought I'd drop through the gravel when I heard his voice. "Annie." He approached me.

Nathan spoke before I could find my voice. "What are you doing with my wife?"

Buck froze in place, eyes bulging. "Your *wife*?"

"Your *wife*?" I gulped.

"Ex," Nathan said.

Buck looked as though he was trying to process it all. "The woman is a *nightmare*."

She got out of the car and strode toward Nathan. "Let's go inside. You really wanna put on a show for the paparazzi?" She carried a briefcase and followed me up the stairs.

I entered the office, and Buck came up in front of her, slamming the door, and he leaned back against it. His eyes were bloodshot. "Annie, I understand this is merely a professional … visit." I could see him swallow hard. "Please forgive me. I promised I'd never pressure you. Forgive me."

The heart has its reasons. "Buck, I want you in my life." I stepped forward and into his arms.

Thirteen

~ *Buck* ~

I couldn't catch my breath. Something blocked my voice. Had I heard her correctly? I drew her to me, her face on my chest, and felt her arms tighten around me.

Elation lasted but a moment. Tracey yelled and pounded on the door. "Annie! Our website's been hacked."

I opened the door, refusing to let go of Annie. Tracey, the customer service manager, pushed into the office, followed by Rhodes and Lena. Tracey turned Annie's laptop in our direction. "No! It's down … what?" Her eyes were as wide as saucers. Photos appeared on the screen in place of The Golden Bowl website.

Annie let out her shock. "Ohhh!"

My heart pounded. A collage of pictures of Lena and I at the bed and breakfast, strategically photographed to make them as incriminating as possible, filled the screen. The largest one in the middle was the surprise kiss at the office photo shoot, deliberately cropped and positioned for maximum impact.

Rhodes was irate. "What's going on here?" He turned to his ex-wife, who was now in the doorway.

She was demure. "Okay, so I was a little jealous." She nodded at Annie. "But I don't know what you see in her. She's … old."

I was indignant. "She's perfect!" Annie's little squeeze encouraged me. "So that's what this madness is all about? Jealousy?"

I faced Rhodes. "How would she have reason to be jealous?"

Lena spoke up. "He told me he had a new woman that was light years better'n me." She turned to Rhodes. "You're losin' your marbles, honey."

Rhodes was red faced by now. "*Fix* the website."

"It'd be a shame to destroy Annie's business. But you know what I'm capable of." She took out her phone.

"*Fix* the website."

"Just one little touch of a button and their whole system is toast."

"Ms. Goodwin, exactly what is it that you want?" I tried to keep an even tone.

"Revenge." She held up the phone. The pit of my stomach knew all our hard work would be toast.

In the instant before anyone could speak, David was behind her and effortlessly relieved her of the phone. In the instant she realized what had happened, he tossed the phone to Rhodes and subdued her, tying her hands and putting her in a chair. Her brief case had fallen to the floor.

She focused on him, licking her lips. "You're good."

"Count on it." His eyes remained on her. "You have five minutes to delete the photos and restore the website, and five minutes more to rectify all the supply issues you've created. For a woman of your talent, that should be eight minutes more than you need. If you fail to accomplish those tasks in the allotted time, you'll sorely regret it."

She bit her lip. "Hmm … How sore will I be?"

"Don't try my patience, Miss Goodwin. You've interrupted my holiday, and that's making me unhappy."

"Oh. Okay, I guess you're a little too scary to be unhappy. But I need my hands free to work on my laptop. And once I finish the job—do I get to go?"

David allowed a faint grin. "Once Buck agrees everything is satisfactory, you may leave." He freed her hands and guided her to Annie's chair where she began work on her laptop.

Rhodes stood over her in a lather. Wide-eyed, Tracey observed from a corner, and David by the door. Annie and I settled on the couch, waiting. Ten minutes was almost up.

"Revenge." Rhodes spoke quietly and sarcastically. "What did I do to you?"

She looked up at David. "All set. You can send Buck over now." She turned to Rhodes. "Well, Nate, what didn't you do to me? Huh? Let's start with stealing my ring."

His jaw dropped. "*Stealing* your ring? You *threw* it at me and told me to get lost." He let loose with a string of curses. Then she did. Part of me was entertained. But mostly, I wanted this over so I could be with Annie. I felt her shudder against me, and I tightened my arm around her. Undoubtedly, she was not used to such language and unpleasantness.

David raised his voice and shut them both up. He summoned me to the computer and directed Rhodes and Lena to the couch. Silently, Annie came with me and took a chair beside me. I took the time to do a careful review of the site and the ordering capabilities. I ascertained that Lisa Quinn's name no longer came up on orders or communications. All the while Rhodes and his ex-wife bickered on the couch.

I looked to Annie, then David. "This seems fine. Of course, she could have planted some kind of bug or virus or something. I need my IT person to take another look. I happen to know he's off this weekend."

David addressed the couple on the couch. "Mr. Rhodes, there's a—two bedroom—apartment on the third floor of the restaurant that's been recently renovated. You'll make sure Miss Goodwin stays there until Buck's IT expert has a chance to take a close look. Enjoy your weekend together."

"That's kidnapping!" Lena's voice did not match her expression.

David's gaze was sarcastic. "Must we list the charges we have against you?"

She thought the better of it. "No."

Rhodes lifted her from her seat. "You've been trouble from the minute I laid eyes on you." He picked up her phone and briefcase. "Let's go."

She turned and blew me a kiss before she followed him out the door.

Annie took Tracey by the hand. "I'm so sorry for all this grief."

"No problem. I'm relieved all this is over, and we can get back to normal around here. Thanks, Buck." She turned to David as she left. "Thank you, Mr. Lambrecht."

~ *Annie* ~

After the room cleared, Buck closed the door and took me in his arms. Relief washed through me, and my knees began to buckle. We settled back on the couch before I collapsed. "I can't thank you enough, Buck. What a weight off my shoulders. Every day there was at least one new crisis. Now it's over ... finally." I shuddered. "I thought David'd break her in two."

Buck drew me to his side, and my head fell on his shoulder.

"Needless to say, we're not doing a TV show today."

His voice was soft. "You're trembling, Annie. Just rest. Relax." He kissed the top of my head and gently stroked my hair.

When I came to, I was still in his arms, and I felt better than I had all summer. "What time is it?"

"Almost 7:00." He wiped stray hair out of my face.

"I've been asleep ... more than two hours? Wow." I sat up. "I'm sorry I conked out on you."

His eyes locked on mine. "You can conk anytime." His kisses quashed my giggles.

I needed to slow things down. I pulled back, but he still clung to me. "Are you hungry?"

He made a face. "Of course."

"How about some dinner? What would you like?"

Twenty minutes later two cheeseburgers arrived at my office, and Buck locked the door behind the waitress. I had to tease. "Um ... I don't think anyone's coming to steal our burgers."

"They can have the food. I want you." He took a whiff. "Well, I haven't had a cheeseburger in far too long."

I laughed. "I can always distract you with a cheeseburger, Buck."

He plopped me on the couch. "Indeed." He positioned a tray in front of me, and I took a fry. I hadn't eaten in so long, I realized I was ravenous.

He settled beside me. "We need to catch up."

I'd already started on the burger. "I know. Nothing good's been going on here. How about you?"

"Nothing good?"

I could feel my face getting red. "Well, aside from my family being here. It's been tough when they leave to do concerts. Doc and I haven't been getting along too well."

"How so?"

I kind of regretted going down that path. "Um ... he's trying to navigate some rough waters. He's never been a father until this past year. Now he's got two grown daughters, and he's trying to be a parent. I think we had a little bit of a breakthrough when we were discussing grace and forgiveness and resentments in the Diet Club meeting. He took it to heart, finally, and I think it's made a difference."

"Interesting." Buck put his burger down. "I had a bit of a confrontation with my father, too."

I washed down my food with some water. "Really? What happened? Was this while you were in England this past week?"

"Yes. I told him I forgave him for his behavior, the way he treated me and my brother ... and my mother. He never acknowledged to me that he'd caused some terrible pain. Didn't seem to care that I forgave him. But a few days later I received a call from my mother. She told me he'd apologized to her. She was grateful and relieved. So that made me feel better." He looked into space. "I have no need to see him again. The bitterness is gone, at least for now."

"Wow." *Chalk one up for The Supernatural Diet Club.* "Sounds like progress to me."

He put his arm around me. "I have made some progress. I know you've been a good influence on me. And so has Cat. She's been very gracious."

My eyes filled. "I've missed you so much. I was afraid you'd moved on. And when I saw that woman—Lena? Well, I thought she was your new girlfriend."

He let out a loud breath. "There's no other woman for me, Annie. You're my heart. I love you. I've never said that before. To anyone." I could see emotion welling up. "When I saw that gossip rag—you and Rhodes—I couldn't bear it. But in the end, it's your happiness that's the important thing. I told myself I wouldn't interfere." He wiped my teary face with his napkin.

I could hardly speak. "Thanks." I took the napkin. "I know how it feels to see the one you love with someone else. And I know now how the media can make things look. It's not real. Nathan's my director of security. I like him as a person, a friend, but not more than that."

"Well, I can assure you, I can't remotely abide his ex-wife."

I shook my head. "She's a winner. How did you get involved with her?"

"It seems she did some research before she showed up at my office door. She posed as a client who wanted me to evaluate a business opportunity for her—a bed and breakfast on Cape Cod. I told her it would be grueling work and difficult financially. That didn't dissuade her. She wrote a check, and I went to the property. Surprise, surprise, she showed up and behaved inappropriately. You saw the resulting collage on the screen."

I coughed and managed to avoid choking. "That's crazy."

"Indeed. And when I returned from a business trip to Chicago, there she was—Brooke, Lewis & Wynn's latest employee."

"Wow. She must've really wanted revenge. That's when all our computer woes started, I bet."

"I'm certain of that," Buck said. "I'm very sorry."

"It's not your fault. The media didn't help. All that fuss over Nathan and me. It was nonsense. I couldn't believe so many people would care."

"I wouldn't be surprised if she instigated that as well."

I put down the last of my burger. "You're kidding. She leaked that?"

"Entirely possible. She had the means and the motive."

"Wow. Another one for the forgiveness list. She sure brought out the worst in Nathan."

Buck grinned. There was no love lost between those two.

"I believe that's the only thing I have in common with Rhodes. We both loathe his ex-wife."

~ *Buck* ~

It did give me a certain sense of satisfaction that Rhodes was now holed up with Lena for the weekend. No doubt she would torture him mercilessly, and I would have Annie in my arms. Whether or not Annie believed the media hype, I was convinced Rhodes did have feelings for Annie. Why else would he have told Lena he'd found a woman who was better than she?

Regardless, this was perfect for me. I'd have Annie all to myself.

"Oh, Buck ... um ... I want you to know I had the apartment on the third floor renovated a bit. I'm thinking of moving back there after Thanksgiving. I'm not positive yet. I told Doc, and it made him furious."

"Why would you move back there?"

Her face reddened. "For privacy. He's been pushing his matchmaking ideas. Maybe now that he understands forgiveness and resentments better he'll be easier to live with. But I'm not sure. So just in case, the apartment will be ready if I need it."

"Hmm ... I need to talk to you."

She drew back a bit. "Is everything okay?"

"Fine! I need your opinion."

She tugged at my sleeve. "Will you walk with me? Then maybe sit on the beach for a while?"

"Of course." I escorted her down the stairs.

"Hey, Buck, glad you're back." Billy waited, at the ready to drive us to Annie's.

"It's good to be back." I shook his hand.

Back at the homestead, we heard music and voices coming from the rehearsal room, but Annie was happy to spend private time with me. Without encountering Doc, we located her sweater and beach bag, then headed out. We laid a blanket on the sand, and walked to the water's edge. Annie was quiet. I tried to organize my thoughts. The ocean was calm, brightly lit by the full moon. I could still hear the distant music.

"Um ... Buck? What I told you before ... about forgiveness? It really is a process. It really does take time."

"Okay. I understand." I cleared my throat. "Just as long as you're in my life. I'll wait as long as it takes. I'll prove to you I've changed." Hand in hand, we worked our way through a rocky area and then through tidal pools and more sand.

She stopped and looked up at me. "I do believe, you. I believe you've changed. That night we ... we broke up ... I knew it then. I've tried to take a look at myself, too, to understand myself better. I've worked through a lot of feelings. I guess fear is at the bottom of it all. I felt rejected, and it hurt my pride to think my picture would end up in a gallery with prostitutes. Then when all this media hype started about Nathan … I realized they'll make stories out of thin air. What if they ever found out about … your life … you know … with those women?"

Her words were like tiny pins and needles stabbing at me. I swallowed my emotion. "All very good points, Annie. You saw what happened with Debbie and David. That was ugly. The media is still consumed with them, years later." I was not making a good case for myself. I cleared my throat. "I doubt the media would be that fascinated with me and my problems and shortcomings. But you're wise to consider that possibility. Being Debbie's sister and the owner of The Golden Bowl, it surely puts you at risk."

The moonlight on her face created an angelic glow that mesmerized me. She reached up and put her hand to my cheek. I could hardly hear her over the sounds of the sea. "I've decided that's a risk I'm willing to take. I know in my heart that you love me. I know we're all broken—nobody's perfect. And I believe you want to change and have changed. It took courage for you to tell me the truth."

I had no words. I couldn't move. I wanted to kiss her, but I stood staring at her face. Her hand skimmed down over my shoulder and arm.

"I was letting self-pity and fear and pride run me, Buck. I was worried what people would think. It doesn't matter what the world thinks. Like Cat always says, we have an audience of one. And I know what He thinks. God's doing a new thing, right? So let's move forward and learn from our mistakes—and never repeat them."

I didn't think it possible to love a person more.

~ *Annie* ~

It was so late sunrise was beginning, and we sat comfortably wrapped in our blanket near the stairs to the back lawn. My mind flooded with thoughts of what our future together might be. I wondered about the logistics of our careers—and living with or near Doc. I couldn't imagine Buck would be satisfied with my third floor apartment over the restaurant.

I looked up to see him focused on the water inching toward us. "Buck?"

He tightened his grip on me and brushed me with a kiss. "We need to talk."

Uh-oh. "Is something wrong?"

"Nothing is wrong. Everything is right. I need your opinion."

"Okay."

"I went to England to speak with the powers-that-be at my Alma Mater. Long story short, they offered me a position. Having seen a photo of you and Rhodes together, I jumped to conclusions about your relationship. So I accepted the position."

"In England?"

"Yes. They're giving me free reign to put together and teach a graduate level course."

My heart sank. "Oh wow." I realized I was reverting to self-pity and consciously tried to change my attitude. This was an honor for Buck, and I needed to put my selfishness aside. I managed a cheerier, "Congratulations!"

He faced me. "Annie, I need to get away from my firm. It's not a healthy place for me. I haven't uttered a word to anyone. But I do have an exit strategy. My partners will buy me out. As you know, Brooke, Lewis & Wynn is a leader in the hospitality and food service industry, so the income from that sale will be considerable. I've been the driving force behind our company since it's inception. I'll be well compensated. We'll be free to do whatever we like, live wherever we wish."

"Oh."

"Actually, we can do that now. I have investments and considerable savings tucked away. What's mine is yours."

His generosity and thoughtfulness touched me. But did he intend to leave Marberry? I'd never considered it. "Buck, that's so very sweet. But how can I leave The Golden Bowl?" I tried to swallow the lump in my throat.

His sigh became a laugh. "You don't have to leave, unless you want to. I'm still hoping we can spend some time someplace warmer. I promise you we can get your business working so that you can take time off without worry."

"So we can still live here in Marberry?"

He smirked. "How could we ever leave Marberry?"

~ *Buck* ~

In order to avoid an altercation with Doc, I insisted on staying at the hotel my assistant had booked. It was midday on Saturday when I finally went to the room to drop off my suitcase, shower, and dress for Annie's television program.

When we arrived at the studio, we learned Lena Goodwin had been responsible for canceling Annie's scheduled celebrity guest due to a supposed death in the family. Her lies and manipulation worked perfectly. Joe Harris did her bidding without knowing until we arrived with a bang.

Joe took it all in stride, handling the situation with aplomb and rescheduling the celebrity. I silently thanked God that Lena's stab at revenge on Rhodes worked out so well for me. If I hadn't been given the chance to guest on her show, Annie and I might never have reconciled.

The interview went quickly and splendidly. Then we took the meal we'd produced to a picnic table behind the building. We enjoyed lunch and conversation with a view of the Atlantic through the trees.

I took a seat on the bench beside Annie. "I have a new fondness for pine trees."

She giggled. "Really?"

"Yes, I never had a chance to tell you that. When I landed in the lake and swam to shore, it was sunrise, and the light on the branches, well, it was quite beautiful."

"Sunrise, huh?" She planted a soft kiss on my cheek. "That was a tough day all around. I'm glad you had some moment of beauty in it."

I felt too much emotion overtaking me. "Well, let's dig in before this gets too cold."

Annie demonstrated a healthy appetite. "I love lobster as much as any other Mainer, but this is *the best evah*. Your secret herb butter is no secret anymore."

"I'm happy to let the secret out to benefit The Golden Bowl. Perhaps we'll add it to our prepared foods menu."

Annie's shocked face turned to a bright smile. "I bet it'll be a best seller to all the millionaires in New York and California."

"No doubt."

She threw her head back, beaming at the sky. "Gerald's already shipping three times as much lobster as I ever dreamed we could. We can add this and sell the herb mix and recipes besides. Cisco's gonna be amazed. Think how much we'll raise for our charities."

I grabbed her. "You have a one-track mind, my dear. Let me give you a buttery kiss." I did.

She was still smiling. "You did a good job changing my track."

Annie and I spent most of the weekend on the beach, in conversation or quietly enjoying each other's company. Fortunately, Doc and the rest of the family gave us privacy.

Monday morning my IT person was on the case, and he found no problem with the website or any of the systems at The Golden Bowl. Supplies and communications were back to normal. His parting words to me, "Why don't you hire her on here?"

The old saying about keeping your enemies close went through my mind, as Annie and I sat on the office couch. I could feel her sigh of relief.

"Um… Buck?"

I brushed a kiss over her forehead. "Yes?"

"What happens to Lena now?"

I'd purposely avoided Rhodes and his ex-wife all weekend. "I suppose we need to pay them a visit. What do you think of having her remain in the employ of Brooke, Lewis & Wynn?"

Her wide-eyed shock made me smile. "Aren't you afraid she'd make even more trouble?"

Trouble for Brooke and Lewis might not be a bad thing.

With that thought, my phone lit up, and I could see it was my assistant. "Yes, Janice."

"Buck, I know you've had some challenges at The Golden Bowl, but you remember Amanda James is flying in to New York to interview you tomorrow morning."

"I'm sorry, Janice, I did forget. Please let her know I can't make that interview."

"Ah… Buck… this is Amanda James we're talking about."

"I understand. I don't know when I'll be back in New York. I'll keep you posted."

"You do this interview and Almighty Buck is gonna be center stage this time, not just Annie's consultant in the background. You'll be a household name. You can't blow it off. I'll book your flight from Bangor."

I exhaled a frustrated breath. "Janice, I told you I don't know when I'll be back in New York. I'll let you know as soon as I do. Then we can contact her. Thank you." I disconnected the call knowing full well Carter would be on the line next. I shut the phone off.

"Um… Buck? Is everything okay?" Her voice melted the rest of the world away.

"Everything is fine, my dear." It suddenly felt good knowing Almighty Buck was still dead on Titan's gym floor. I didn't need to worry—about anything.

FOURTEEN

~ *Buck* ~

Billy alerted Rhodes, and Annie and I began our climb to the third floor apartment atop the restaurant. I could not envision living here, despite the magnificent ocean view from the hallway. Rhodes admitted us to the apartment and offered us coffee. Beverages in hand, we joined Lena at the kitchen table.

She was direct. "When can I leave?"

"You're quite confident our experts found nothing wrong, Ms. Goodwin."

"Lena."

"Yes. Lena."

She smiled and leaned my way. "You're lucky I fixed some of the messes they made on my way out."

Annie choked on her coffee, and I came to her aid. "I'm fine, Buck."

I turned back to Lena. "They did mention how very talented you are."

She snickered. "I'd say my finest moment was when I shut down dessert cup manufacturing and transportation for the entire East Coast. Pretty good, huh?"

Annie gasped. "You did that?"

Lena threw her head back with glee. "Uh huh."

I patted Annie lightly on the back to calm her and noticed Rhodes shaking his head. I turned to Lena. "Nevertheless, our IT department may well have a position for you."

She laughed, then patted my hand. "Buck, you're such a cutie!"

"Indeed." I watched Rhodes, propped on the kitchen counter, silently steaming.

Lena quickly became serious. "How much does it pay?"

"I can assure you—far better than the clerk's position, the boutique, or even your hairdressing."

She tipped back in her seat. "Hmm. And the Carter Lewis experience?"

"Optional."

Annie blushed pink.

Lena nodded. "You just might have a deal, Buck. I'll think numbers and get back to you."

"Very well."

"Okay. I'm packing up. Nate's arranged for a car. I'm heading back to New York. I'll give you a buzz when I decide about the job." She winked at me, and Rhodes caught it. He was not happy.

Lena rose from the table and faced him. "Nate, I want a decent meal before I leave. I bet you've got an expense account at The Golden Bowl."

He rolled his eyes.

~ *Annie* ~

I didn't know what to make of Lena Goodwin or Buck's offer to let her work at his firm. I didn't have much time to ponder. As soon as we arrived downstairs, we saw Cat and Cisco with baby Jack, mobbed by tourists in the parking lot. I remembered the Monday afternoon concerts Paulo and his group had been doing this summer when they weren't on the road. We'd never advertised them, or the crowds would have been completely out of hand.

I took little Jack into my arms, and we all headed to the back lawn where everything was set to go. Paulo and the rest of the band were waiting, signing autographs and chatting with fans. Fortunately, people were understanding and grateful for a free concert, so there was minimal pushing and jostling for position. Our security team kept everyone well in hand.

Buck and I took our seats. I couldn't stop smiling with little Jack nestled in my lap, Buck beside me, and my favorite musicians in the world playing for The Golden Bowl. *The desire of my heart.*

After an hour of music, we headed to the restaurant for cold drinks and late lunch. Cisco had relieved me of the baby, and I headed to the kitchen to make sure the family would get what they wanted. I noticed Lena going out the front door, Cat following her. I went after Cat. "Is everything okay?"

Cat nodded, but I'm certain she was shuddering as she stood waiting by the door. When I caught up to her, she whispered, "Pray for Lena."

"Okay." I wondered how Cat even knew her. I pushed through the door in time to see Lena toss a blue paper into the bowl.

"Bye, Annie." She half-waved at me and descended the stairs to meet Nathan in the parking lot. I watched her speak with him briefly, and then she drove off.

I turned to see Cat had plucked Lena's prayer from the bowl. She handed me an old ticket stub and went back inside. It read: *God help me.* Twinges in my stomach acknowledged Lena's brokenness and pain. Only God knew what that was all about. As I put the ticket in my pocket, gratitude overrode the pain. Lena Goodwin was reaching out to her Creator. *Thank you, God.* Maybe I'd played a tiny part in a new beginning.

~ *Buck* ~

Monday evening we assembled on the beach for a Diet Club meeting. I had no idea how many I'd missed. Sabena was nowhere in sight. Her parents arrived on the beach and announced she'd had a long and busy day playing with her brothers and all their little friends. Sabena was sound asleep. Cat remarked that her fourth floor art studio had been abandoned for some time.

Debbie giggled. "She's finally getting along with her brothers. I think she's taking some of her own advice."

David smirked. "Grace and mercy—for us."

Cat sat on the edge of the lobster trap. "Well, since our little leader is indisposed, I think our plan to separate into groups today will work out well. The women will join me in the library. The men will enjoy the beach. The topic: keep your eyes on God. Cisco will lead."

As I reluctantly kissed Annie good-bye, I noticed Billy bounding down the stairs, a keg on his shoulder. Cisco laughed. "This should be good." He lifted his wife to stand on the lobster trap, his arms protectively encircling her. "We'll do all our lessons first."

She kissed him. "I don't believe you."

While the men congregated around food and beer, I settled into my chair with mineral water and a very real pain in my stomach at the thought of facing Doc—sober. Rhodes would be no picnic either. *Keep my eyes on God.* How? Hopefully, he'd be doing a new thing. Something good this time. Again.

Doc took a seat beside Rhodes, and Billy landed on the other side. Cisco passed around the new additions to our notebooks. David took a seat by me, and I breathed a sigh of relief. I didn't want to face a panel of superheroes and Doc.

Cisco pulled up his chair. "Any news?"

Rhodes rubbed his chin. "Yeah, in case you didn't notice, my ex-wife showed up in Marberry, almost destroyed the entire workings of The Golden Bowl. Now she's thinkin' she'll take an IT job at Brooke, Lewis & Wynn."

Billy let out a guffaw, then quickly stifled it.

David smirked. "Interesting. At least you'll be able to keep an eye on her." He flipped through his notebook.

Rhodes stared at him. "I'm not so sure I want to."

David smirked at the notebook. Billy grinned ear to ear.

Rhodes turned to him. "What's so funny?"

Billy took a swig of beer. "You still love her."

"Love her? She drives me crazy." Rhodes was red in the face.

"Yeah. You love her." Billy nodded. "You may as well admit it."

Rhodes threw his notebook in the sand and went for a beer.

Billy was all smiles. "He's crazy about her."

I was delighted that all attention was focused on Rhodes and his plight.

Unfortunately, Doc had his own ideas. His notebook was open to some appropriate page, no doubt. "And speaking of crazy love, and resentments, and whatever it is God is up to these days—I'm voting to expel Wynn from this family, The Golden Bowl, and the entire state of Maine."

David looked up from his notebook, the smirk still in place. "The entire state of Maine?"

"Yes." He pointed at me. "I've had more than enough of you seducing my daughter. You've made her life miserable."

Billy was starting on his third beer. "Doc, I saw her with Buck this afternoon. She looked *really* happy."

David and Cisco burst out laughing. I tried to keep a straight face.

Rhodes resumed his seat and handed Doc a beer. "Sorry to say it, Doc, but you're the one making Annie miserable. I guess she got over whatever resentments she had. Now it's your turn."

I couldn't believe my ears.

In spite of losing Rhodes as his ally, Doc continued his complaints. I believe I was not the only one who was tired of it. David yawned in his face. Billy made a sandwich for himself and drank another beer.

Cisco apparently had had enough, as well. "Okay, Doc, thanks for letting us know your thoughts." He opened his notebook. "Cat wants us to make sure to keep our focus on God here." He flipped a page.

Doc interrupted. "That's all well and good, but let's face it, your wife is extraordinary. She has no problem hearing from God."

Billy spoke over Doc. "Yeah, maybe we could all do better if we just *listen*." He put a finger to his lips. "Sshhh."

It took everything I had not to fall down laughing. Watching David's shoulders shaking did it. I cracked up.

Doc was out of his chair. David intercepted him before he slugged me with his notebook.

Cisco raised his voice. "Look! We've got to accomplish something positive here. So I'll read this verse, and you can go about your business and read the rest of the notes and connect with God on your own time."

Doc was in his seat, David standing behind him with his hands on his shoulders, keeping him from popping up again. "All right, David, I get it. You can let go now. Buck'll live another day."

David returned to his seat. Cisco read the verse. "This is from Second Corinthians 1:22… *and he has identified us as his own by placing the Holy Spirit in our hearts as the first installment that guarantees everything he has promised us.*"

Doc looked at David. "Okay, it looks like I have more resentments to get over. Can I get up now?"

"Of course. Be nice to Buck."

"Right." Doc struggled out of the chair and headed for the house.

Relief washed over me, and I watched Billy pour two more beers. He handed one to Rhodes and took his seat beside him. "I'm gonna ask Lisa to marry me. You think she'll say yes?"

Rhodes looked stunned. "Uh… congratulations."

"Thanks. If she says yes, I'm gonna ask you to be best man. We need a witness."

Rhodes was matter of fact. "Yeah. I'm familiar with the procedure."

Before the rest of us could offer congratulations, Doc's blood-curdling yell echoed on the beach. "David! Quick! David!"

We were all out of our seats sprinting up the stairs after David. As I reached the back lawn, I saw Sabena, her face dripping with tears, clutching her brother's hand. Seven year-old Danny towered over his sister, his expression nonchalant. They both stood at attention near the Adirondack chairs, Doc pointing at them like they'd arrived from outer space. David scooped them up.

Doc stopped jumping around and babbling to form a coherent sentence at last. "He *rappelled* down the side of the house with Sabena on his back. They could've been killed."

I noticed the rope dangling from a bedroom window, a gang of little boys sniggering there.

David deposited Danny in a chair and turned to Sabena, still crying in his arm. "Why don't you tell me what happened?"

She inhaled the tears. "I was missing my meeting. I overslept. Nanny Shirlene wouldn't let me go."

David shook his head, obviously trying to avoid smiling. "You know you're supposed to obey Nanny Shirlene."

"Yes." Sabena let loose another flood of tears. "But I was missing my meeting."

"You know you could've been hurt."

She looked at him like that never occurred to her. "That's why Danny brought me down. So I wouldn't get hurt."

Cisco let out a laugh and slapped me on the back. "When Cat asks you about this meeting—tell her it brought us all closer to God. Let's leave it at that."

~ *Annie* ~

We had such a wonderful gathering of women, it soothed my anxiety over leaving Buck alone to face Doc. I helped Debbie and Cat set out some food and beverages. Glori brought a pretty pitcher of water with lemon and mint. She poured herself a glass. "It'd be fun to be a fly on the beach. I'd like to see how they're gonna keep their eyes on God with a keg of beer."

We all giggled. Lisa surveyed the buffet table. "It'll loosen Billy's tongue a little. I hope he doesn't aggravate Mr. Rhodes. He's already in a bad mood from what I hear."

Glori loved gossip. "Oh, I know, hon. Word is, he's still in love with his ex-wife. That might be a good thing."

Cat interrupted with an invitation for everyone to take some dinner and an update to the notebook.

I wasn't especially hungry, so I settled on the couch with my notebook. Second Corinthians 1:22 caught my attention. A*nd he has identified us as his own by placing the Holy Spirit in our hearts as the first installment that guarantees everything he has promised us.*

So many thoughts swirled in my head. God had put a new heart and a new spirit in Buck. It was changing his life. God's promises were evident in Buck.

Debbie quietly took a seat beside me. I was pleased to see she had some food on her plate.

Glori sat on my other side, crossing her legs, demonstrating why she was a fashion icon even in blue jeans. "Okay, hon, I know this is all about keeping your eyes on God. I try every day. But sometimes it's hard to do when things go wrong."

Lisa took a chair and put her salad and ice water on the tray table in front of her. "Yeah, that's the truth. But Cat said God does the transforming, so I don't have to worry so much about messing up. I'm just a junior partner... that's the way I see this sacred partnership stuff. All I do is wake up every morning and say yes to God, so I set myself up for a better day. Things are a lot better than they used to be."

Ash pulled her chair near Lisa to share the table. "Uh... you sure sound like a dyed in the wool Diet Club partner." She turned to Glori.

"Before we start on all that, I have to say I *love* your jeans. Where can I get a pair?"

Karen spoke up from the buffet table. "And do they come in plus sizes?"

Cat looked a bit perturbed as she took her seat. Ellen gave her a glass of water and a comforting pat on the shoulder.

Lisa spoke even louder. "And can I afford a pair?"

Glori jumped out of her seat and strutted around the room. "This is our brand new line in honor of Cat. You know how we can never get her out of jeans. And she goes barefoot half the year. When she does wear shoes—it's riding boots or flats or sneakers. So I told Debbie we need to do a line for women like Cat, so they can be fashionable and comfortable. Welcome to our new line... Cat's Meow."

Cat slumped in her seat. "No!"

Glori bent down a bit to face Cat. I could only think her behind looked amazing. From the open mouths around me, I'd say everyone thought the same. "Hon, time waits for no woman—"

"Ugh! Where have I heard that before?" Cat covered her eyes with her forearm.

Glori turned to the rest of her audience. "We're all aging. Cat's Meow jeans give you help in all the right places... gentle... effective... shaping."

Cat was pink. "No!"

Glori was unfazed. "Hon, your charities stand to make a fortune on these jeans—not to mention your new footwear line. *Including* riding boots and flat, comfy shoes."

"Riding boots?"

So that was Cat's fashion weakness. Riding boots.

Glori giggled like she knew she was in the catbird seat. "I knew that'd get you on board. They're gorgeous. Even I want a pair—well, a pair in every shade." She demonstrated just how supple that denim material was as she bent down and dragged boxes from under and behind the couch. "Everyone gets shoes, boots, and jeans!"

The look on Lisa's face was priceless. I'd swear she won the lottery. Pandemonium ensued.

I noticed my sister turning every shade of purple, and gently rubbed her arm to soothe her.

"Glori promised me she'd wait until after the meeting." Debbie was near tears.

Ellen was beet red from laughing.

Cat jumped up. "Wait!"

The room went still. "Let's at least get one verse in—please." Everyone remained quiet. Cat read. "The first two verses of Psalm 62… I wait quietly before God, for my victory comes from him. He alone is my rock and my salvation, my fortress where I will never be shaken."

Glori broke the silence. "Cool."

Tuesday morning I met Buck at my office. As I was about to take his breakfast order, Amanda James called. Since he was busy on email, I decided to take her call. "Hi Amanda."

"Annie! Is everything okay with you?"

"Fine, thanks, how are you?"

She sighed. "Well, frankly, I'm a little peeved. Buck blew off our interview today. I was supposed to fly in to New York. Now my schedule is off. Can I come visit you in Marberry? I've got the full day free. I can get my blueberry pancake fix. How about it?"

I was confused. "He blew off your interview? About The Golden Bowl?"

Buck looked up from the computer, a faintly mischievous look in his eye.

"Well, partly about The Golden Bowl. This business model article he wrote is getting a lot of attention. His firm is on fire. Pardon the pun. I hear all the publicity is making him a hot commodity. I gotta say, Almighty Buck is a great tag. But I also wanted his take on this thing with Nathan Rhodes. The guy saved your life, and I can see how you'd have a crush on him. What's the scoop, Annie?"

I took a breath. "There is no scoop, Amanda. I don't have a crush on Nathan Rhodes, and he doesn't have a crush on me. I don't want to waste your time coming all the way to Marberry to watch Buck and me working here at The Golden Bowl. I'll be happy to feed you pancakes, and they'll be delicious, but it's probably not worth the trip all the way up here."

I saw Buck grin, but he gave me no advice.

Her voice deflated. "All right. I'll arrange another interview time in New York. Maybe I'll come up to Maine around foliage time."

"Sounds great. That's just around the corner. I'll look forward to seeing you then."

Amanda was gone, and I was at the desk in Buck's lap. I couldn't keep a straight face. "You blew off an interview with Amanda James?"

"I forgot all about it. I was preoccupied with a beautiful woman."

I must have been brilliant red by that point. Slow-the-bus-down-Annie took over. I picked up the phone and ordered a stack of blueberry pancakes in honor of Amanda James.

Over breakfast Buck happily explained there wasn't any more work for us to do. All systems were running smoothly. "I hope you understand you can take more time off."

"Okay Buck, if we don't have any work left, we should head to the beach."

He smiled that devilish smile. "We mustn't waste a perfectly good beach day."

At home, I ran up the stairs and into Glori. When she heard I'd be spending a free day with Buck, she insisted I wear my new "Cat's Meow" jeans. She followed me to my closet. Ever since Glori and Debbie arrived here this summer, incredible designer clothes would often appear there.

"Hon, I've got the jeans shorts right here for you." She pulled them out, threw them on the bed, and then went back for a top. "They're just the right length for you. Not too revealing, but shapely."

I stood in front of the mirror and held them up to me. "Does Cat wear these?"

She brought out an exquisite top. "Don't you worry, hon, I'll get her into 'em. The world'll be wearing Cat's Meow. Just like they wear our Watercolors line."

"I love your Watercolors line."

She waved the top. "This is Watercolors, hon."

The touch of the fabric was heavenly. "Oh, thank you, Glori. It's so pretty."

"It's yours, hon. Go have some fun today, and you know you'll look fantastic, too."

I put on the outfit with more encouragement from our fashion icon. It fit perfectly. But I'm not sure I'd have worn it if Glori hadn't pushed me out the door and down to the beach.

I was feeling a little self-conscious by the time I found Buck in a lounge chair, staring out to sea. I thought his eyes would pop out.

"I know, the jeans are a little tight, but Glori insists they fit correctly."

That devilish smile was back. "Not at all. You look beautiful, Annie."

I pulled my chair closer and sat. "Well, at least they have some stretch to them. They're from the new line they're doing for Cat. She didn't sound too thrilled about it when they told her last night. But Glori knows how to get her way. She said they'll make millions for charity."

"I'm sure that brought Cat around."

I giggled. "It helped. But Glori was quick to show her the riding boots and shoes. Very practical. I think that helped keep Cat's blood pressure down."

He took my hand and kissed it. I calmed down. "It's a perfect day, Buck."

"Any day with you is a perfect day, my dear. I hope to have a lifetime of them."

*Holding hands, looking out to sea, soaking up warm sunshine …"*I could get used to this." I'd met him almost a year ago. It wasn't such a long time, but the changes had been considerable. "Um… Buck… why did you avoid Amanda James? She said she wanted to ask you about the business article you did. I'm sure she'd get into the personal stuff, too. But I know you can handle an interview way better than I ever could."

He squeezed my hand. "I need some time away from the world. I want to be with you, Annie. It's as simple as that. And that requires time to work on myself so I'll be the person I want to be. The person you deserve. As you said, forgiveness is a process. At the least, I need to forgive myself, to be honest with myself. And I need time to think, to make better choices. A lot has happened in a relatively brief time."

I thought I'd burst with joy. "I understand. I'm so grateful you see what you need, and you can take the time to figure everything out … make the right choices."

He looked to the horizon. "This counselor Cat recommended … he's been very helpful. I keep returning to that night out on the rocks by The Golden Bowl. Cat invoked Holy Spirit to come into me and the dark spirits to leave. Frankly, that scared me. Why would I want any spirit to control me? Almighty Buck was always in charge, always in control. I wouldn't have it any other way."

He took a long drink of water. "But this counselor made me realize I was indeed giving up control to another power. That power was the addiction. In reality, everything else was in control. Not me. Not God. There finally came a time when Almighty Buck lost control of all those tenuous threads that orchestrated my life. I was one big lie. I'm grateful to you and Cat … and God … that I survived it all. I learned from it. I've made a change to save my life."

I inhaled tears of happiness. "I'm so glad. The way you were going, you could've killed yourself."

"I understand now that I was comfortable in addiction—it was an escape—a way to feel strong, successful, powerful. That's all I wanted. But look at the mess it created, the pain it caused. I'm sorry, Annie."

He pulled me onto the lounge, and I kissed him. "I forgive you. You need to forgive yourself."

"I'm working on it. I'm taking responsibility for my actions. Trying my best to set things right."

FIFTEEN

~ *Buck* ~

As Annie and I strolled through the cool water of the advancing tide, I felt content. I pushed away all thoughts of my firm, the deal I would make, and how I would execute it. Annie was the most important thing in the world, and she was by my side. I couldn't believe my good fortune.

The need to impress had evaporated. The world could melt away, as long as she was with me. It was only a short time ago when an interview with Amanda James would have had me on top of the world. Now it was well down on my to-do list. My priorities had changed. It was really rather shocking.

I briefly considered twenty years wasted with Deirdre, the wrong woman for me. She wasn't to blame, but she didn't help. I came out of that relationship well aware of my selfishness. Almighty Buck was the center of everything. It never bothered me. As a matter of fact, I'd celebrated it. Now I only wanted to give Annie everything.

"A penny for your thoughts." Annie smiled up at me, and I realized we'd been silent for some time.

"I'm thinking that I'm totally at ease, totally content with you. That couldn't have happened unless I was truthful. You've seen my ugly truth, and you still want me in your life. That's a miracle."

Annie stopped and reached up for me, then softly kissed my lips. "I love you, Buck."

The sweetest words—I'd waited forever to hear them. Exhilaration consumed me. Swept up in the emotion, I proclaimed my love. Ardor eventually became laughter, and we landed together in the sand. I held her close, listening for her voice above the tide.

"Every day, I think about your Valentine card … how you said for the first time in your life you wanted to come home … how you signed it 'Love, Buck' … how you said you'd plead your case for me." I tasted her tears. "Every day, I think about those things. Every day, I love you."

"Marry me, Annie."

I felt her draw in her breath. "I will. I'll marry you, Buck."

~ *Annie* ~

I don't think Buck expected to hear those words from me. I was a little surprised I could say them. He answered with an ardent kiss and professed his love. I almost let myself go in the emotion of it all, but I happened to catch a glimpse of Cat, walking on a rocky ledge above us, the evening light on her creating an ethereal image.

"Um, Buck." I pointed upward, but he was a little distracted. "Buck!" I pulled away, and the look of devastation on his face triggered a giggle. I pointed. "Cat's here."

"Huh?" He spun around, still gripping me.

I waved and caught her attention. "Come down here. Now!"

She made her way toward us with an impish little smile that made me laugh all the more.

Buck pulled me up and smoothed my hair back, as though he'd be charged with messing me up. I couldn't control the giggles.

Cat approached us, her backpack slung over her shoulder. She handed Buck a small piece of notepaper. "I've been praying for you, Buck."

He read the note, and his jaw dropped. When he found his voice, it was raspy. "Thank you, Cat. You've saved my life."

"God is good."

"Indeed." It looked as though there was a cauldron of emotion inside Buck. Curiosity as to what the note said consumed me.

Cat turned to me. "We're having dinner shortly. Care to join us?"

"I think we'll pass. Buck and I have a lot to discuss."

Cat's eyes were joyful. "I understand. God bless." She headed up the beach.

I tugged him in the opposite direction. "Why don't we walk a little?"

He exhaled a breath. "Sounds like a plan, my dear."

"So are you going to share that note with me? What is it?"

He stopped in his tracks. "It's the first—and only—prayer I've ever written and deposited in the gold bowl. What are the odds that Cat would have retrieved it?"

We both laughed.

"A hundred percent," I said.

He gave me the paper and took out a little penlight, shining it on the prayer.

God, you know my heart and its reasons—better than I. Grant me my heart's desire. "Buck, I'm gonna cry."

~ *Buck* ~

I convinced David that I should be allowed to take Annie for a drive. I'd been a sports car enthusiast for as long as I could remember. I was certainly capable of driving.

But then David took me under his wing and gave me a little secret agent training in evasive driving. The SUV he loaned me was suddenly fun. I took off for Ripple Lake, Annie riding shotgun. Our bodyguards followed in a duplicate black SUV.

Admittedly, I was nervous about my plan to ask Annie's parents for her hand in marriage. It was an important gesture, in my mind, but what if they rejected me as Doc had? Since Mike Auclair was a pastor, that would not bode well for me. Annie might reconsider.

It was a crisp September day when we drove into the blue-collar town of Ripple Lake where Annie had grown up. It was unimpressive. Aside from the natural beauty, there was evidence of poverty everywhere, and it dampened my spirits. Childhood couldn't have been too rosy for Annie.

I pulled into the driveway of a modest ranch-style home with a small garage attached, neatly maintained, though weathered. A friendly dog came out to greet us. He was obviously thrilled to see Annie. Mike and Millie Auclair appeared in the front doorway.

As we greeted them and entered the home, a blast of delicious odors told me Millie was preparing her special roast turkey feast. I was comforted. Annie was in her parents' arms, and then they reached for me. We settled in a parlor that wasn't any bigger than my bathroom.

Millie put out some appetizers. "I'm so happy you could take some time to come back home for dinner. Buck, I think you must finally have everything all set at The Golden Bowl. Now Annie can have some sort of a life—time to visit friends and family."

I smiled. "Exactly right, Millie."

She took a seat on the sofa beside her husband and turned to Annie. "Debbie sent me some huge boxes of clothing—beautiful things. We had an auction at the church and raised ten thousand dollars for our food pantry and soup kitchens. I almost fell over! People came from everywhere to bid. They said those clothes sell for a fortune in the stores. What a wonderful business Debbie and Glori have."

"They sure do. And they're incredibly generous. They've been so blessed, and they're a blessing to so many others. That whole family is. Between the music and the fashions—and I know Cisco donates millions of his own money every year."

Mike nodded. "He wrote a check the day they came to our church. He saw some crumbling masonry, the kitchen needed some help, and he spoke up to me about it and handed me a check. Ever since, the elders get a check from him on the tenth of the month. Like clockwork. They're good people."

Millie made a sudden exit to deal with something in the kitchen. Annie followed her. I was left, at a loss for words, with Mike. I began to feed the dog bits of cheese.

"Uh ... Buck?"

Spinning in my mind halted. I looked up at Mike. "Yes?"

"That ... cheese isn't the best for his digestive system."

"Ah! So sorry." I had no idea what to say. Nerves were getting the best of me. But now would be the time to bring up my hope for a future with Annie. Obviously she was keeping Millie in the kitchen so I could take care of that. The dog was becoming insistent, as he could see the plate still had plenty of cheese on it.

Mike rose, took the dog by its collar, and put it out the front door. He faced me. "I had an interesting dream last night."

"Really?"

He took the chair beside me. "I was standing at the altar—with Annie and you."

"Really?" Sweat began to bead on my forehead. "Funny you should say ... I ... we ... I came today to ask your blessing for Annie and me. We're planning to be married."

Mike smiled and shook my hand. "You have my blessing, Buck. Millie and I know you make our daughter happy. It's been ... a long time." He welled up. I handed him a fresh handkerchief, and he rubbed his face with it.

He took a breath. "Last night, in my dream, I was performing a marriage ceremony for Annie and you. There was water around us. There were tongues of fire above us. I'll never forget it."

"Fire?" My stomach lurched.

"Holy Spirit is with Annie and you. I know it."

A strange tingling came over me. *I will give you a new heart and put a new spirit in you.* "I ... I remember Annie told me so." Not that it was under happy circumstances, but perhaps it was best things happened the way they did. It may have been more comfortable for me to start our marriage hiding my lies, my past. But now that Annie knew the truth about me—and still loved me—it was an incredible feeling. There would be nothing we couldn't share.

"Dinner's ready!" Annie's call popped us both out of our seats.

I followed Mike around a small archway, and Annie pulled me into the kitchen. I wrapped my arm around her and inhaled the scent of dinner.

"This kitchen is dedicated to you, Buck."

"To me?"

Annie beamed at me. "I got the money to renovate this kitchen from the money I made at The Golden Bowl. The money you said was my salary, and we put it in different accounts. This kitchen couldn't have happened without you. I never saved a nickel until you showed me how. And Mom couldn't afford to update the kitchen ... well just a few new-to-her appliances when something died. So now Mom has her dream kitchen, and it's all because of you." The delight in her eyes transfixed me.

Annie's selflessness touched me once again. I wasn't at all surprised she'd do such a thing. But each of her actions and words filled my heart. I realized the emotion was joy—a feeling unknown to me until Annie.

We sat down in a well-worn dining room to the most scrumptious turkey dinner I've ever had. From the conversation and laughter, it was apparent no one but me was concerned that this room would need a renovation as well.

I understood as we drove home that day, Mike and Millie would never leave that house, that church, that town. "Annie, I want to give you a wedding present—an early one."

She looked surprised. "Early?"

"Yes, I'll order it this evening."

"What is it?"

"We'll renovate your parents' home—to go with the new kitchen."

A deluge of tears poured onto her face, and I nearly veered off the road. "Are you all right?" I went for the handkerchief I'd given Mike. "Wait! I'll find another." But there was only a tissue box, which she'd already found.

"Oh, Buck, you're so sweet." Her voice came in sobs. "Thank God you came into my life."

I was the one who needed to thank God.

~ *Annie* ~

Buck wasted no time in getting the contractor out to Ripple Lake. My parents were thrilled beyond words. They'd made no real renovations or improvements to the home since they'd bought it over fifty years ago. Everything had been repaired and patched and used until it was past used up. Now they'd have an updated, functional, *warm* home. Buck spared no expense. He understood this was the house they wanted to keep until their time on earth was up.

Although we didn't say a word about it to Doc, it was only a matter of hours before he found out. I think Dad told him.

It was not especially good timing. Paulo and family and their entourage were off to California for another concert series. I hugged my sister good-bye with more tears than usual. I'd confided to her and Cat that Buck and I were going to be married, but hadn't told Doc or the rest of the family. I thought it only fair that we inform Doc after Mom and Dad. Neither Buck nor I were keen on confronting Doc.

But it had to be done.

I found Buck on the beach with his trusty binder. I giggled as I took the empty chair beside him. "Are you hiding?"

He closed the binder and grabbed me out of my seat and into his arms. "Yes, I am."

Laughter welled up from my toes. "I love how honest you are."

He let out a guffaw. "I've learned my lesson."

I kissed him, then pushed myself off his chest to stand in front of him. "Everyone's gone, and Doc is reading his medical journal at the kitchen table." I took his hand.

He pushed his sunglasses up and squinted into the light. "You're sure there's no way we can delay this?"

I couldn't stop laughing—until we arrived at the kitchen door. I turned to Buck. "Okay, you're gonna do the talking, right?"

He made a face.

"Right?"

"Right," he said.

I didn't notice Doc was by the screen door, the journal tucked under his arm, coffee in his hand. "Oh, I was gonna have a seat in the Adirondack chair. But if you want to talk ..." He opened the door, and Buck hoisted me through.

I could feel my face on fire as I sat at the table. "Buck ... we have something we need to say, Doc."

He tossed the journal on the table, took a seat, and swigged his coffee. He glared at Buck, standing at the back of my chair. "Well, sit down and say what you have to say."

Buck obliged. "Annie has agreed to marry me."

"Congratulations, Buck, you win. I hope you're happy, Annie."

Waterworks started again, and Buck was prepared with a clean handkerchief. "I am happy, Doc. I hope we can all get along. I'd be even happier if you and Buck make peace."

Doc stared me in the eye. "Annie, you and Debbie are finally in my life. I can't say either one of you picked a winner, but I wasn't exactly a winner either. I made some big mistakes, and the biggest one was letting your mother go. So ... at least I admire Buck and David for going after the ones they wanted. Debbie is happy. You're happy. I can't argue with that anymore."

More tears poured. "Oh, Doc, thank you." I got up and hugged him. "I hope you know how thrilled Debbie and I are to have you in our life."

He patted the hand I'd draped over his shoulder. "Well, I'm going to try and make you more thrilled. Buck and I will be friends … at some point."

During the week the family was away, Buck conducted most of his business by phone, and oversaw the details of our new packaged food line for Super Club. It would be ready in time for a January launch, and was already creating a stir. Our website and blog were filled with testimonials from guests who'd tried the products at The Golden Bowl and The Bakery & Sweet Shop. Questions and comments suggested the launch would be huge.

Despite Lisa's gun-shy reaction, Karen and Ash enlisted her to help with the online promotion. Joe Harris was impressed. Lisa was surprisingly talented with social media videos.

Mom and Dad were elated that their renovation was progressing at a fast pace. Mom commented that she'd be able to host a small party of Ripple Lake friends to celebrate our engagement.

Buck and I took over my kitchen every night and made Doc's favorite meals. It wasn't long before his mood brightened. When we finally did cheeseburger night, I nearly killed myself laughing. I could count on cheeseburgers to improve the mood all around.

~ *Buck* ~

It was probably worth the effort to devote a week of dinners to Doc. We were now able to have civil conversations, and the occasional laugh.

Annie and I had spent some time discussing what to do with Doc after we married, but didn't come up with a solution. He would likely be living with or near us. I resolved to make peace with him however I could. So far, these dinners seemed the best avenue. Cheeseburger night was a breakthrough.

Doc had entertained us with stories of his years as a cardiac surgeon in New York. (I surprise myself using "entertained" and "surgeon" in the same sentence.) Never before would I have gone through a potentially uncomfortable dinner without the assistance of alcohol. Tonight I was drunk on Annie's laughter.

When Doc suggested we visit his old stomping grounds in New York sometime, I had a brilliant idea. "Why don't we go to Paulo's concert on Friday and spend the weekend in the city? We can stop by your old office, and see the sights."

Annie lit up. "That'll be great! I loved going backstage at their Boston concert. We'll have a blast."

Doc was all smiles. "Let's do it."

My phone blared with Paulo's latest hit, and I was sorry I'd left it on. It was my partner, Carter Lewis. "I need to take this call." I adjourned to the library. "Yes?"

"What's this crap about you leaving the firm? You can't leave."

I took a calming breath. "I can, and I am leaving."

I lowered myself into a comfortable chair as I listened to a barrage of curses. There was no sense in trying to interrupt. As he blustered himself out, I wondered when our friendship had ended. It was probably many years ago, though I never realized it. *Heart-shattering.* Come to think of it, the beginning of the end probably started with our blood pact. I'm sure that's what Cat would say.

"Buck?" Apparently Carter noticed he'd been having a one-way conversation.

I sighed into the phone. "If you listen for five minutes, Carter, I can explain how it's going to go."

He responded with more curses. I ended the call and shut off the phone. I returned to the dining room, walking past the liquor cabinet without a thought of it.

Annie had served slices of blueberry pie. Doc's was piled high with ice cream. Annie stood with her scoop at the ready. "It's honey vanilla, Buck."

"Perfect."

Doc retired for the night after we confirmed our plans with the family and made hotel reservations. For security sake, we'd all be in the same location. But Doc, Annie, and I would have our own staff to allow us to go sightseeing without concern.

Annie and I took a walk on the beach. The tide was out, and the sea was relatively quiet. September evenings were noticeably cooler. I wrapped my arm around Annie. "It's too early for winter to set in."

She laughed. "Come January, you'll be begging for September temperatures. We don't even have color yet. But when we get to New York, you'll appreciate how warm it is there, I bet. It's still technically summer."

"Hmm."

"I get it, Buck. You're thinking of taking some warm weather vacations. I can't blame you. I get sick of long winters here, too."

"That sounds promising."

Annie's phone interrupted. She took the call. "It's for you. It's William Brooke."

I let out a breath and took the phone. "Hello, Will. How are you?"

"I'm clueless, Buck. Clueless. What happened?"

"I've made a decision. I'm not interested in working myself into an early grave. I'm going to take some time to enjoy life. I'm sure your attorneys will find all the paperwork in order."

"Buck, from what I can see, that's all you've ever done is enjoy life. I don't get it. I know you've fallen for Anne Brewster, but that's no reason to quit this firm. We've put up with your crazy antics over her. We know you've turned things upside down over her. But your place is here. We understand that. We're willing to tolerate it."

My blood began to boil. How many times had I tolerated their antics?

He raised his voice. "Furthermore, you know it could well sink us. What kind of a legacy is that? Take all the time you want with her. Just don't leave your own company. We've been in this together almost thirty years. Carter and I know you're the rainmaker here. We know that. Don't walk out and sink the ship, Buck."

I felt a twinge of remorse. "You and Carter are perfectly capable of carrying on without me. You don't need to lift a finger to bring in new business. Janice is getting calls every day. You're growing, with or without me."

He let out a string of curses. "We know it's because of you. You're the one who's best friends with the Clementes. Everyone wants to be their best friend. So they call us. Then they can tell all their friends they use Paulo Clemente's friend Buck Wynn. You're no fool, Buck. You know that's exactly why we're getting the clients we're getting.

You even bragged about that at our partner's meeting—the night your apartment burned down."

I spoke in spite of the lump in my throat. "Have some confidence in yourself, Will. You're capable." I ended the call and shut off the phone. I had no intention of getting into a harangue with William Brooke in front of Annie. I turned to her. "I'm sorry."

She hugged me. "It's okay. Sounds like they're up the creek without you. What are we gonna do at The Golden Bowl?"

I held my hands to her face. "You mustn't ever worry over The Golden Bowl. I'll personally oversee your operations. Nothing will change. As a matter of fact, I plan on continuing to use my firm as your support. Regardless, I'm on top of it."

"Okay."

I kissed her. "What do you think of spending a couple of extra days in New York?"

"Fine with me. They're heading to the next concert in Philadelphia, so I have no plans."

I left Annie with her sister and friends at Glori's spa in New York. With David overseeing security, my mind was at ease. I came through the doors of Brooke, Lewis & Wynn unannounced. Again, I nearly collided with Lena Goodwin. This time she was more professionally dressed in a business suit.

"Hi, Buck!" She took me by the sleeve. "Come have a cup of coffee with me. Your partners are in a meeting with some lawyers." She tugged me to her office. "I've got my own set-up here. You'll like my coffee." She poured me a cup, and I took a seat.

She pulled her desk chair to face me. "Thanks for giving me a chance here. It means a lot to me. I promise you won't regret it."

"I'm sure you'll do a fine job, Ms. Goodwin."

"Lena."

"Yes. Lena."

"I'm not usually a saboteur or anything. It's just, you know, desperate measures and all."

I straightened in my seat. "Desperate measures?"

"Um, yeah ... well, not since I have this job, really. I mean I have a good income now. And an actual door on my office. I can even see when Carter is coming my way. I get up and close the door, and he knows I'm not interested in the employee experience."

"I see." I wasn't sure I wanted to know more about Lena Goodwin and her employee experience. I had enough on my plate as it was.

"Anyway, I heard Cat prays for the audience at her concerts. I mean, my friend told me she went last time they played in New York, and Cat went and sat in the nosebleed seats with a bunch of fans and they prayed together. She said people were healed. She said people get healed all the time at their concerts. Can you imagine?"

I cleared my throat. "Yes, I've heard that. I saw people in Boston and Chicago who claimed to be healed. But one doesn't know the truth. They may have been looking for attention for all I know. Cat certainly never makes any claims."

Lena leaned forward. "She's an honest-to-God saint. She doesn't have to make claims. I heard it's real. I researched some of those people. It's true. Cat Clemente changes lives. One way or the other."

Tingling began in my chest and gut, and I thought this was a most inconvenient time for all this spiritual stuff. I needed to focus on business for once. Annie's and my future depended on it.

"So Buck, I couldn't get a ticket. I tried, but they sell out like three minutes after they go on sale, and that's months and months ahead of time."

I noticed her hands were shaking. She put her cup on her desk. "Anyway, I'm taking the train to Philly for their next concert. I think I might be able to get a ticket from a scalper. I think it's a better chance to get in than in New York."

"Forgive me, Ms.—Lena. Why are you so desperate to pray with Cat?" I could see sudden panic in her eyes.

Her laugh was a bit hysterical. "Well, wouldn't you wanna be healed?"

In that instant I looked up to see Carter Lewis in the doorway.

"Hey, Buck, how are ya?"

I stood and shook his hand. "Good to see you, Carter."

He winked at Lena, and addressed me. "Why don't we head out to the conference room?"

I thanked Lena for the coffee and followed him.

SIXTEEN

~ Buck ~

Will Brooke stood at the table shuffling papers. As I entered the conference room, he reached for my outstretched hand, then grabbed me in a rather awkward hug. "I'm glad you're here. Maybe we can get this sorted out."

I laid my briefcase on the adjacent chair and took a seat. "There's really not much to sort, Will. We had our agreement thoroughly and legally written years ago. We planned for every contingency so the firm can continue on and prosper."

Carter landed in a chair at the head of the table and propped his foot on another. "That's just it, Buck, we're worried about the prospering part. You gotta stay."

Will cast an irritated glance his way. "Let's have a calm discussion, here. We're all friends—since we were kids. Buck, how about some coffee?"

Carter jumped up. "I'll get it."

By the time he was out the door, Will had his head in his hands. "Buck, you're the only one of the three of us with a law degree."

I let out a breath. "I took that degree for my own edification. I have representation here, as do you and Carter."

"Yes. But you're the rudder here. You always have been. We can't function at the level we did without you. It's as simple as that."

"You've several talented candidates for promotion right here. Give them a new title and a raise and let them run with it. You'll never miss me."

"Look, you can stay and lighten your load. Just bring in the business, give us a little advice from time to time. That's it. We won't bug you. You don't even have to set foot in the office. We'll pay you well."

He rose and poured himself a scotch, despite the early hour. "I've still got two kids in college and a wife that spends like a drunken sailor. I swear she bought half of Paris this summer. Let me get the kids through, and we'll all retire. The firm'll be worth a bloody fortune by then. We've already had a lowball offer from Nelson Scott."

"Really?"

"They see the blood in the water."

"How would they have had heard?"

"You know Carter has a big mouth. He's in a panic."

I sat back in my chair. Perhaps I was too hasty. "You're serious about basically licensing my name?"

"Serious as a heart attack. You can be a figurehead. I don't care what you do as long as you keep the business coming. And it will come as long as your name is on the door. You and Annie can cruise around the world for all I care. I'll promote the people you recommend. They can take on your clients—and more. You can help me get it so the three of us are expendable. You've always been great at that stuff, Buck. You can get this place running on autopilot, just like all the other businesses you advise."

I rubbed my chin. "You know Carter was expendable from day one."

He shrugged. "Yeah. But he was fun. And he is loyal, in his own way. How else could he make a living?"

I had to laugh. I put my head down on the table. Was I making the mistake of my life? I heard Carter fumbling with the coffees. What would Annie think?

I sat up. "All right, we'll work it out. It's going to be all my way. We're cleaning up this place. *Decorum* is the new watchword. And the first day I have a craving for a drink, I'm done with you. Understood?"

Carter's mouth was hanging open. "Sure, Buck."

Will chuckled. "Decorum has been the pretense here all along."

I looked him in the eye, then Carter. "No more pretending."

As I left my office building my focus went to the pub across the street—a client of Brooke, Lewis & Wynn and the location of far too many debaucheries on the part of my partners and me. I hadn't the faintest desire to enter there.

~ *Annie* ~

Glori was like a magnet. People came from everywhere to see this glamorous pop star fashion icon. Despite having the best security team in the world, I was seriously afraid we'd be trampled coming and going from the spa. By the time we made it back to the hotel, any relaxation I felt from all our treatments had disappeared. We settled in a parlor with the kids and some healthy snacks.

I asked the question that was on my mind all day long. "Glori, how come you're not at the hall with the rest of the band?" My sister giggled.

Glori wasn't fazed. "Hon, we've been doing this long enough to know I don't need to be there. What do I do? I sing 'ooo' and 'ahhh,' and I have my solos down pat. I make sure I look amazing, I walk in, they tell me where to stand, and I go to work. That's it. I'm way better off building my fashion and cosmetics businesses at the spa. We had photographers from every magazine and TV show you can name. You can't buy that kind of publicity."

"Wow. I guess you're right."

She poured a glass of mineral water. "Of course I'm right. I'm no singer, but I'm a great actress—and I have a head for business. At least the marketing part."

I had to chuckle. "Well, know thyself."

Glori smiled. "Exactly. It's one of my competitive advantages. And if I didn't have Cisco, I'd still be tryin' to figure that one out."

Glori's husband stood smirking in the doorway.

"Excuse me, ladies, I've got a date with the hottest guy in the world." She picked up her daughter and handed her to him. She turned back from the doorway with a wink and a whisper. "As soon as we put Christina down for her nap."

Sabena climbed up on the sofa with me. "Christina takes lots of naps."

Debbie burst out laughing, and that launched Sabena and me into a big case of the giggles.

It wasn't long until my nephews had reached the rowdy stage where Debbie was ready to call in the nannies. I sat gripping Sabena, wondering how I could dare to try and help without incurring an injury, when David and Buck walked in. There was instant silence, the boys frozen in place. Tears of relief filled my sister's eyes.

She was in David's arms in a second. "They were practicing their martial arts exercises."

I bit my lip. Though I never saw David lift a finger against the boys, Debbie always felt a need to defend them. He took it all in stride, mostly focusing on her with a comforting hug and gentle kiss.

His voice calm, he repeated to the boys, for at least the umpteenth time I'd heard this summer, "We don't practice martial arts in the parlor."

They all agreed, again, that they'd never do that.

Buck and I smirked at each other. I let go of Sabena, and she followed the rest of her family from the room.

Buck took a seat beside me and handed me a mineral water. We clinked glasses. "Cheers."

"I need to talk to you." He encircled me with his arm and encouraged me back on the couch.

"Tough time in the boardroom?"

"Not tough, but not what I expected, Annie, and I want to discuss this with you before I give my final answer."

"Okay. But you know I want whatever is best for you."

He squeezed me the way he always did when what I had to say pleased him. "I think this is best for both of us, as long as I don't take to drink. I made it clear I'm making my health a priority."

"You're staying with the firm?"

"I'm going to restructure the business, get it running in top form, and then I'll enjoy free time as the profits roll in. My name will remain on the door, but I'll rarely be there. I'll be with you. Wherever you want to be."

"Well, you look happy about it, Buck. Congratulations."

"My question is, are you happy about it?"

"I'm fine with it, as long as you are. But now you have your old job back, plus restructuring it, plus developing a class and teaching it in England, plus me and The Golden Bowl … and a wedding. I'm tired just listing all that stuff."

He took a thoughtful sip of water. "I see your point. But I have key people in New York and London who are underutilized. If they agree to the promotions I plan to offer them, I believe we'll make a giant step forward quickly. In the meantime, Will and Carter have agreed to an attitude adjustment, and they seem desperate enough to cooperate. If they don't, I'll be out in a heartbeat. They assure me they're on board with my plans. If we stick with it, I believe we'll be bought out for top dollar. Perhaps that day will come sooner than I think."

"Wow." My head was full of questions. "Does that mean you need to travel a lot?"

"No. You and I can spend some time in New York and London. But I'll conduct most of my business by phone. I won't be personally attending clients. My job will consist of strategizing, bringing in new business, hiring talented employees when necessary, and keeping my finger on the pulse. All with an eye to selling the business for a fortune. Enough to flood your charities with money and keep us financially secure."

"Sounds like a plan, Buck." I exhaled the million butterflies raging in my stomach.

The concert that Friday night was as spectacular as the one in Boston. But just like in Boston, I was distracted by Buck's situation. Back in June it was obvious that something was going on with Buck, to the point that he was called to a meeting with Cisco, David, and Nathan. It was much later when I realized it had to have had something to do with his gallery of girlfriends.

Now he was introducing his partners to our family backstage. It was apparent that Carter Lewis was drunk, and his date was probably someone from Buck's former gallery. William Brooke was married to a woman who was less than half his age. Even Glori made a face when she saw them together. I could see Doc was turning every shade of purple.

The only one who was cool, calm, and collected was Cat. Surprise, surprise. *Another redemption in store.* I guess her work was endless. It never ruffled her that I could see.

A hand wrapped around my shoulder. "Are you okay, Annie?"

My sister's voice soothed me. I turned and kissed her cheek, noticing David's grin, as he stood by her side. There was more than enough material to keep him entertained.

I tried to keep my voice in check. "I'm okay, Sweetie. Just a little concerned Buck is jumping back into the fray without realizing all the possibilities."

She was turning pinker. "You mustn't worry. Buck loves you. He wouldn't do anything to hurt you or worry you."

David's smirk remained in place. I was probably more in line with his thinking.

Cat emerged from a mob hand in hand with Cisco. She was in front of me, those eyes locking me in. "We're leaving for the hotel now, Annie. Will and Carter are joining us for dinner there."

Buck came up all smiles behind them. "Shall we go?" He took my arm. "This way, my dear."

As we left the venue, I barely managed, "Um … Buck?"

He brushed the side of my head with a kiss. Despite all the background noise I heard, "No worries, my dear. No worries."

"Um … yeah."

I quickly brushed my hair and powdered my nose, hoping to remotely fit in with rock stars and business titans and kept women. *Why?*

As I left my room I ran into Glori. "You look awesome, hon. Watercolors is your line."

"Thanks. I need all the help I can get."

She took my arm to stop me. "Hon, don't you worry about the way you look. You shine! And that's from the inside out."

I could feel my eyes beginning to water and my knees buckling. That was the nicest thing Glori ever said to me. "Oh! Glori." The waterworks began and my voice gave out. She pushed me back into my room, and we sat on the bed.

"Hon, William Brooke's wife was his daughter's college

roommate. And the coquette Carter Lewis is with gets paid by the hour. Don't you ever put yourself down. You're a billion times the woman they'll ever be. So you just remember that." She dabbed at my face with a tissue. "But your mascara is running. Hon, are you using my waterproof brand?"

I almost choked. "I don't think so."

By the time I made my entrance with waterproof lashes, I was remembering I was a still-young woman with a Master's degree. *Cold comfort.*

Buck had concern all over his face. He rose from his seat and escorted me to the table. "You look beautiful tonight, Annie."

I was shaking. "Thank you." I almost fell into the chair. Except for Cat and Cisco, there was no one else from my family in the dining room. Cat sat across from me, those empathetic eyes calming me.

She addressed Will and Carter. "I understand you attended the same preparatory school in New York, but never met Buck while you were there."

Will had a charming smile, not unexpected for an executive in the consulting business. "That's true, Cat. Carter and I were a year ahead of Buck at Charlton, and we never knew him there. Then we decided it'd be fun to study abroad. College is the time to do that stuff. So when we heard there was another Charlton grad at our university, we made a point of meeting Buck. It wasn't long before we decided to go into business together. We had plans for our firm well before we graduated."

"Did you begin in London?"

Will patted his distinguished gray hair. "We did. But we soon realized we needed a presence in New York. As it turns out, it was a great decision. Our business is global now."

I noticed Mrs. Brooke checking her look in a well-polished knife. It took all I had to stifle a sudden case of the giggles.

Cisco began a conversation about international currencies and how that must be affecting business at Brooke, Lewis & Wynn. Will made a comment or two, but the only one who truly kept the topic going was Buck. They lost me at Euro.

When the food was served, Cisco invited Cat to offer the blessing. Out of the corner of my eye I saw Carter slapping his date's fork to the table. Cat pretended not to notice, but I thought Cisco's smile was going to turn into a belly laugh. That almost set me off.

Buck turned to me, his eyes full of mischief. "Amen," he responded to Cat's prayer. His voice was low. "I didn't realize we've invited hillbillies to dinner."

I laughed until I coughed.

Once I was under control, Buck raised his water glass. "I'd like to offer a toast to Cat. We at Brooke, Lewis & Wynn are thrilled and grateful you'll be arriving Monday morning to bless our offices and any of our staff who wish to pray with you. Such a bold and wonderful new beginning for our company. Thank you, Cat. God bless you."

Carter's glass dropped to the table. Red wine soaked into the white linen tablecloth. I have to admit, I almost lost my grip on my water glass. Monday would be an interesting day for sure.

After dinner Buck escorted me to my room. "Um … Buck?"

"Yes, my dear?"

"You had this idea before you ever invited them backstage, didn't you?"

"Of course."

"Wow. You're amazing."

"Cat's amazing. There's no reason she can't do for them what she did for me. We'll drive the devil out of Brooke, Lewis & Wynn. We'll be sober as judges. No fooling around. Just impeccable client experience and profits to the sky. Coincidentally, our charities include The Golden Bowl and all your other charities, as well as Paulo Clemente's foundation."

There were some fireworks with our goodnight kiss.

"Wow. Just wow. Buck, you're amazing."

We were still nose-to-nose. "You're my inspiration, Annie. All of it."

Saturday we joined the family for a quick tour of New York, ending at the top of the Empire State Building. We returned to our hotel for lunch together, then went our separate ways. Paulo and the band would be performing that night at a stadium in New Jersey. There was so much demand for them, they had added Sunday afternoon at the same venue. Cat would do her visit to Brooke, Lewis & Wynn on Monday. Then they'd be off to Philadelphia for the next show.

Doc wanted to show us the office where he'd spent so many years, so Debbie, David, and kids joined Buck and me for that tour. The kids were on their best behavior and full of questions. As we drove by the various hospitals and universities where Doc had been affiliated, Sabena insisted we stop to view the lobbies. Once inside, she led us in prayer to bless the facilities, workers, and patients. Her brothers grew a bit impatient, but for the first time I noticed Danny admonishing them to settle down and respect their sister.

Cat would have been proud. Debbie definitely was. She was beaming. David, I'm sure, expected nothing less.

Buck surprised me with an invitation to dinner and dancing on Saturday evening. Of course we dined at one of Brooke, Lewis & Wynn's most exclusive clients. I could only imagine what the bill would amount to. But Buck rightly told me this was a well-deserved treat, and I must say it was an unforgettable experience. Buck was a great dancer. And of course, conversation was entertaining as always. We did it all without alcohol.

~ *Buck* ~

Monday morning bright and early Annie and I arrived at Brooke, Lewis & Wynn with Cat and Cisco. A contingent of armed-to-the-teeth security guards posted themselves by the doors. From the twisted look on Carter's face as he peered around the wall at us, I thought they might well come in handy.

Will rushed from the conference room and vigorously shook hands with Cisco, Cat, and Annie. Obviously, nerves were overwhelming him. Surprised and excited employees formed a mob around Cat and Cisco.

"Will, why don't you introduce our guests, and show them around? Let everyone know they're here to pray if they want prayer. I'll go talk with Carter."

"Good idea. He told me he hasn't slept all weekend. I don't know what's the matter with him. Maybe he's coming down with something." Will spun on his heel to intervene in a fan girl moment between Janice and Cat's handsome and wealthy husband.

With a nod to Annie, I headed to the conference room and shut the door behind me. When I saw Carter's face, I wasn't positive that was a good plan. There was something very strange about him. Very wrong. He sat straight up in his seat at the head of the table, a bottle of scotch in front of him. He'd rubbed his graying blond hair into a clumpy mess around his head. His tie hung loosely around his unbuttoned shirt. I believe he was still wearing the same suit jacket he had on Friday evening.

"Get out." His voice was different—threatening.

I took a seat at the opposite end of the table.

"I said, get out!"

Shivers reverberated through me. That was not Carter's voice.

I struggled to regulate my tone. "What's going on, Carter?"

A booming string of curses spewed out of him. His face distorted. As wild as Carter could be, I'd never seen or heard anything like this. It took all I had to remain seated there. Cat's voice repeated in my head, "Almighty Buck, the truth will set you free."

I raised my voice. "Carter, you're not yourself. Cat will pray with you. You'll feel better."

"No!" The mention of her name sent him into a rage writhing in his chair, waving the bottle about, spewing filth about her. He smashed the bottle on the edge of the table, spraying liquor about the room. I ran out and closed the door before he could reach me with the broken bottle. I kept my hand on the knob, listening to his curses, determined to keep him inside should he try and come after me. But he consoled himself with smashing things against the walls.

The rest of my staff were huddled at the end of the corridor, presumably engrossed with Cat and company. Their excitement was palpable. I hoped they were praying for their management team. Maybe that would tame Carter's ferocity. Now I sincerely wished I hadn't arranged this.

Annie broke away from the crowd and stopped halfway up the hallway. "Um … Buck? People are falling on the floor. Some of them are crying or laughing. I've never seen the likes of this. Do we have any pillows?"

"Pillows?" Bellowing from the conference room sent shivers

through me.

Annie clutched her chest. "Carter?"

Cat marched toward me followed by Cisco and Will. Will sounded desperate. "Is he gonna be all right?"

Cisco shook his head. "I'm not a medical doctor."

Cat stopped expectantly in front of me. "Shall we pray for Will and Carter?"

Did she not hear the growling coming from the conference room?

Will certainly did. "You know Cat—I went to church yesterday and spoke with the pastor. I'm all caught up. I'm not sure about Carter, but I said the prayer with the pastor word for word so I'd be all set."

Cat beamed up at him. "That's wonderful, Will. You can lead us in prayer."

Despite terror in my bones I thought I'd burst out laughing at Will's face and the sardonic twinkle in Cisco's eyes.

Cat wasted no time. "Shall we?" She pointed to the door. I cracked it slightly. The smell of scotch and sweat poured out. I grabbed Will by the arm and pushed him inside. Cat and Cisco followed.

Probably startled by the stench, Annie had her hand over her nose and mouth.

"I suggest you wait here my dear—at the ready to call the guards."

She coughed. "I can't miss this, Buck. I told Cat I'd be a prayer partner. I'll stand by the door in case we need the guards. I can run out fast."

"Annie—" She rushed in past me, and I grabbed her and seated her with Will at the head of the table by the door. Carter sat crumpled up at the opposite end, draped on the table.

"Is he dead?" Will asked.

Cisco helped Cat to a seat beside Carter. "You can see he's breathing," he said.

I moved up along the other side of the table, hoping to be of some use. In truth, I worried Cisco might kill Carter if he made a move against his wife. Though he hired the best of the best security, I'd seen firsthand that Cisco was a black belt himself. No matter how deranged Carter might be, he was no match for a six and a half foot black belt. He stood behind his wife.

Cat was unruffled. She put her hand on Carter's arm and it began to shake. He sat up at attention, the same demeanor as before. She kept her inscrutable gaze on his face.

"Carter, scripture tells us 'our struggle is not against flesh and blood, but against the rulers, against the authorities, against the powers of this dark world and against the spiritual forces of evil in the heavenly realms.' You are in such a struggle now, I'm sorry to say. You've opened wide the door to your enemy, the one who only wants your destruction. But you can be set free this very day, by the one who has all power—God."

"No!" Carter became evil itself. I sprung back against the wall watching the contortions of his face. His body gyrated, but surprisingly he didn't leave his chair.

Cat grasped his hand. "You've been believing lies since childhood, Carter. Satan is the father of lies and keeps you in bondage to those lies. Lies are killing you. You are God's creation, Carter. God loves you. Choose life, Carter. Choose God."

A hideous sound and a string of obscenities poured out of Carter, unnerving everyone but Cat and Cisco.

She gripped his convulsing hand. "In the name of Jesus Christ I bind up the power of these evil spirits and command them not to interfere with our communications or prayers. I further bind all interaction and communications of evil spirits as they affect Carter and all of us in this room. I break the assignment of any spirits sent against us and send them straight to Jesus to deal with according to his will. Thank you, merciful God, for your care, protection and guidance, that we may glorify your holy name."

Carter put his head down on his arm, weeping. Cat bowed her head in silent prayer. I turned to see Annie's head was bowed, too. Will sat staring, open-mouthed. Cisco took a seat, so I dropped into a chair and rubbed the sweat off my brow.

When Carter sat up his eyes were wet but clear. "They're gone." He looked at Cat. "The voices are gone."

Cat's eyes locked on his. "You have a choice, Carter. You can go on believing Satan's lies, listening to those voices, or you can make a choice to be free of them. God is the only way to freedom. Declare your faith in God and you become his child. You have his protection against these dark forces."

"I don't want those voices back. But they said they'd kill me if I listen to you. They said I should kill you. I ... they make me feel like I could do that." Carter sounded more himself for the first time in a long time, but killing certainly wasn't something he'd be capable of. This was all too strange and frightening.

Cat was unmoved by the threat of such violence. "They lie to keep you in bondage, Carter. Unless you welcome God into your heart, you leave yourself open to attack. You're free to walk out the door, but I hope you don't. I hope and pray you choose God."

He wiped his face with his sleeve. "I choose God. But I don't know how."

Cat radiated delight. "Let us help you. Scripture tells us to submit to God. Resist the devil and he will flee from you. Come near to God and he will come near to you."

For the first time, Cat turned to the rest of us. "I have prayer partners with me today, and we'll be praying with you Carter. It's as simple as that."

After lengthy prayers not unlike what she'd prayed with me, Carter looked to be his normal smiling self. He thanked Cat for helping him.

She took a small book from her backpack and gave it to him. "This is for you. I've highlighted some passages you may find helpful. And here is a card for a counselor I recommend." She cast a glance at me. "Different person, Buck, but I think you and Carter can help each other."

I nodded, but frankly I had enough to do to try and keep myself straight.

Carter stood, but he was shaky on his feet. Cisco took hold of him and led him out to his office.

Cat addressed Will and me. "Take him home and wash that smell off of him. Don't let him take a drink of alcohol. Clear all that out of his apartment. I'll call the counselor to get there as soon as possible. He'll be able to help Carter with his next steps. They'll likely move him out of that apartment. Security will be along to help you."

This wasn't happening as I'd planned. It never occurred to me that Carter would need more attention. I felt completely drained and weak at this point, and I had still more to deal with here. "What about Lena Goodwin? Did you see her?"

"Lena took the day off to go to Philadelphia for tickets. I'll find her at the concert." Cat jotted a note in a small book.

"Very well." I supposed we averted another scene with whatever evil spirits who had invaded Lena. "And what about the people falling on the floor?"

Cat looked up. "I'm sure they're fine. I gave Janice the information on some resources, should they be interested in following up."

"Very good." I propped myself on the table as I stood weak-kneed, then escorted Cat and Annie into the hallway. "Then it looks like your work is done here."

"Almost." She proceeded to bless the conference room and the three partners' offices.

I thanked her. "Now your work is done here."

Cat's smile reminded me of David's. "I believe it is. We're heading to Philadelphia this afternoon. See you soon in Marberry."

Exorcising demons from Carter—and probably Will, too, as Cat was at it—was wild enough. But I was not prepared for the maelstrom that was Carter's apartment. The entire place was trashed, and it smelled worse than he did. He landed on a couch in the middle of it, clutching his Bible for dear life.

"We can't stay here," Will said. "We'll be asphyxiated. And I'm sure not gonna clean this place up. We need a hazmat crew."

I couldn't disagree. I called the counselor and made arrangements to take Carter to a very comfortable rehab facility.

SEVENTEEN

~ Annie ~

New York was fun and more than exciting topped off with our experience at Brooke, Lewis & Wynn, but I was ecstatic to get home to my own bed. In the morning sunrise and surf beckoned me. I was a little surprised to find Buck sitting in the Adirondack chair, his tablet in his lap, phone in hand, and coffee perched on the arm of the chair.

"You're an early riser today." I greeted him with a kiss.

"Lots to do, Annie. I've already promoted three people in our London office today. From our conversations, I'd say it's a brilliant choice."

"Great news." I replaced his cup with mine. "Have a nice hot refill. I'll go get one for me." I headed back to the kitchen, smiling at his attitude.

There were some aspects of "Almighty" Buck that would never change. I was good with that. Buck was a born businessman. He thrived on it. Somehow it would all fit in our new life together. I poured my coffee and thanked God he was in charge of all that. The thought of Buck's "no worries, my dear" line made me chuckle. God was speaking through Buck. I'd take the advice.

I put on a heavier hoodie and took Sabena's notebook back outside with my coffee and a blanket for Buck. It'd be a relaxing time together by the ocean. As he worked on his tablet, I flipped to a verse for meditation.

But seek first his kingdom and his righteousness, and all these things will be given to you as well. Matt. 6:33

Countless blessings I'd been given flooded my mind. Now Buck and I were to be married—miracle of miracles. Here was a man who I never could have imagined "seeking first his kingdom." Yet God turned him around. Not only had Buck's life changed, but he'd gone on to inspire change in other lives. I let out a gasp of praise, up through a peachy September sunrise.

Buck closed his tablet and turned to me. "Care for a walk on the beach?"

I was out of my seat in an instant, and we headed down the stairs, hand in hand. "You're done with work already?"

"Taking a break. I spoke with a couple of people before we left New York, and they both have accepted their new positions. From the report I just received, I believe we're heading in the right direction. Everyone in the office was thrilled to have Cat visit, and it helped me in launching a new attitude for the firm. I've had a number of emails thanking me. Good feedback on that speech I gave before I left."

"That's awesome, Buck."

"Yes, things are falling into place." He took me by the waist and twirled me in front of him, sand spraying in the breeze. "Now, my dear, what about us?"

I let out a giggle. "What about us?"

"We have a wedding to plan and no date set."

"It's been a little tough, everyone's been so preoccupied. What's good for you?"

"Ten minutes ago is good for me."

I put my index finger to his devilish grin. "Then let's find your tablet and make a plan."

~ *Buck* ~

The Supernatural Diet Club was to reconvene on the beach on a brisk evening. Now that October had arrived, days were noticeably shorter and cooler. Annie and I arrived at the designated spot early and appropriately bundled. We huddled together under our blanket, sheltered from the wind by the rocks and cliff. The colors of the sky grabbed me. "There it is. Annie Blue!"

She giggled. "Annie Blue?"

"Yes, I've named a new color on the artist's palette. In it's true shade, it usually appears at the beginning and end of the day. I think the way the light works is what makes the difference. However, I've had to use my imagination on occasion when you weren't there."

She kissed me. "You're so sweet, Buck."

I drew her tight to me.

"Hi Buck. Hi Auntie."

Startled, Annie almost jumped out of my arms.

"You're early, Sabena." I wasn't pleased.

She dropped into the sand.

Annie struggled to throw off the blanket. "Honey, you're half-dressed. Did Nanny Shirlene let you out like that?" She tossed the blanket over the child.

Sabena was unfazed. "It's just as cold at home, Auntie. I don't need fleece in this weather. Papa and my brothers wear tee-shirts all year. We have to keep the house extra warm for Mama. She's from Beverly Hills, California."

Annie chuckled. I had to smile.

"Buck, I wish you could have come to more Supernatural Diet Club meetings. Did it help you so far?"

"It has helped me. Thank you, Sabena."

"I think it's been good. Sometimes it was painful, but God uses painful things sometimes. It brings us closer to God and to each other, too."

"Indeed." I had no intention of discussing the pain with a six-year-old, no matter how advanced and close to God she might be.

Just the mention of it threw me back to the tussle with Doc and my subsequent dream at The Birch Tree Inn. There was Sabena beside me tugging at my hand, her hair and nightgown aglow in the fire of the waves. *"Aren't we lucky to have grace and mercy, Buck?"*

Annie's voice brought me back to the present moment as she leaned over me to address her niece. "What was painful for you, honey?"

"Um ... when Auntie Cat made me understand about how God meets us where we are. We need to do that with people, too." She wiped a runny nose with her hand. "My brothers really love me.

Really a lot. No matter how much I bother them and get in their way."

"Here honey, use this." Annie produced a tissue from her beach bag. "You've always known that deep down. But it's good to be reminded."

Sabena blew her nose. "Yes. It's important to put myself in other people's shoes. Kindness matters, even if they're not kind to you. God is there in it all. That's the truth. That's what I want to talk about at our meeting."

I interjected like an enthusiastic student with the right answer. "Grace and mercy—God's kindness."

Sabena giggled. "That's right, Buck. We need to be more like God."

"Easier said than done," I said.

I'd guess that most everyone was relieved to have Sabena back at the helm on her lobster trap. It promised some semblance of decorum. Our last meeting had been a complete fiasco.

Rhodes handed me a hot coffee. "I hear that Lena took that job with Brook, Lewis & Wynn."

"Yes, I think she called me before she reached the New York state line."

He smirked. "Sounds like you made her a reasonable offer."

"I believe so. She's obviously quite capable, despite a long list of boutiques and hairdressing jobs on her resume. I imagine she has another list of employers she keeps secret."

Rhodes lost the smirk. "That's not for me to say."

It was my turn to grin. "You just did. Undoubtedly, she's worked for some nefarious organizations." Undoubtedly, that's why she needed Cat to exorcise some of those dark spirits that must frequent those places. "Did she ever meet up with Cat in Philadelphia?"

"I don't know—didn't know she'd planned on it."

My musings on Lena, Rhodes, and evil spirits were rudely interrupted.

Billy and Lisa created a stir by the lobster trap. "Lisa said yes! We're gonna get married." As Billy repeated the happy news, Lisa jumped to and fro waving a large diamond.

I slapped Rhodes on the back. "Congratulations to the best man."
He made a face.

I chose the assassin as my best man—after all, we were Diet Club
partners. If David could have changed enough to be blissfully married
to Debbie, I could be a good husband to Annie. He'd be my role
model.

"God help us both," I said to the sea breeze as I watched him and
his cohorts winding up a twenty kilometer run up and down the coast
of Maine. It was 6:00 a.m. and my coffee was only beginning to wash
away the cobwebs. I stood at the hedge looking down on the beach
below, grateful I'd somehow overcome the urge to become a forty-
nine-year-old SAS agent. It was a miracle Titan hadn't killed me.

Annie was inside, making breakfast for the troops. Now would be
a good time to catch him. I didn't want to turn this into a scene. I'd
ask him, he'd quickly nod his agreement, and we could adjourn to
breakfast. I headed down the stairs before I was awake enough to be
nervous.

The men were busy dumping each other into the cold sea, joking,
and generally horsing around. I took a seat in a beach chair, rather
clumsily sipping coffee, waiting. The bluest patch of sky caught my
attention, and the thought of Annie calmed me. I don't know why I
was so nervous. *Securing a best man should be the easiest of my tasks.*
Once Doc had agreed to the marriage, the rest would be simple.

My mind returned to the day David had me by the shirt, perched
on a rocky cliff not far from here. *"You're here today precisely
because I understand. I'm willing to give you the benefit of the doubt.
Don't try my patience. Treat Annie with respect. If and when she's
ready to be with you, I'll be making quite sure you're ready to be with
her. Understood?"* Sweat beaded on my forehead. I hoped David was
quite sure by now I'd be a good husband to Annie.

I watched him swipe the water off his face as he approached. I
motioned him to the chair near me. "Good morning."

He took the seat as the rest of the contingent ran up the stairs.

"You're not in a rush for blueberry pancakes?"

I slurped the coffee. "I suppose we should be. They look hungry."

His trademark smirk was the response.

I swallowed hard. "David, I'd like you to be my best man. Annie and I would both be pleased to have you and Debbie as our witnesses."

He looked a bit surprised. "You have a brother."

I cleared my throat. "Yes, but I haven't seen him in years. The last time I was in Portland, we never managed to get together. I doubt he'll even come to the wedding."

His expression was unreadable.

I could feel the coffee percolating upward. "I'd very much appreciate the favor."

There was a hardness in his eyes that made me wonder if he wanted to shoot me. I tripped over the words. "Perhaps ... you'd consider it a ... a favor for Annie."

"Have you made amends with your brother?"

My coffee landed in the sand and my hands covered my face. "Suddenly everyone's a therapist." I couldn't believe I'd said it aloud.

David's voice was softer. "You're lucky you have a brother."

Regret choked me. "I'm terribly sorry, David. I ... I didn't mean it." I took a breath. "That was rude of me."

He shook his head. "I dealt with that a long time ago. But what I mean is—you need to deal with it. You need to make peace with him, whether or not he's your best man."

My stomach churned. "I will. I promise. I'll speak with him soon."

He stood. "I hope so." Then he headed up the stairs.

I put my head in my hands. *Brilliant*! Why hadn't it occurred to me that David had lost his only brother in a plane crash as a child—*before* I came out with that remark? *I need a drink.* I took some deep breaths.

I knew David was right. But I only wanted to marry Annie. *Put her first.* Everything else would work out in due time.

Deep breathing was not helping.

At this moment, it seemed nothing was easy without vodka. I regretted the liquor cabinet was now impenetrable with a Special Forces team at breakfast in the same room. I considered a trip to Marberry's liquor store, though it'd be hours before they would open.

Was there a sympathetic neighbor in the area?

Focusing on the logistics of finding a drink, my gaffe with David and my brother disappeared from my thoughts. It was a little while later when I felt her hand on my back. I sat up. "Annie."

She landed a kiss on my cheek and took a seat. "Not in the mood for pancakes?"

I let out a heavy breath. "I was trying to recruit a best man." I reached for her. "He recommended I contact my brother. That could delay the ceremony considerably."

Annie smiled sympathetically. "It's not that David won't do it, Buck. He's trying to be helpful. We don't have to delay the wedding."

I let my frustration show. "The Supernatural Diet Club runs amuck. Everyone is concerned that there's no possibility of me taking a drink ever again. I'm to make amends with the world, I suppose, before our wedding. How many steps did David do before he married your sister?"

Annie made a face. "Buck, it's not some competition. They're concerned for you. And so am I. You'll straighten out your relationship with your brother when you're ready and able. Let's not worry about it."

She tugged me up from the chair, and we strolled the beach arm in arm for quite some time before I could let the words out. "I left home for boarding school in New York when I was young. I leapt at the chance to leave. I left my brother there to fend for himself. I never forgave myself, and he never forgave me. I hate that I did that. I hate the person I was. I don't want to discuss it now. I don't want to be reminded. I don't think he does either."

Annie stopped and wrapped around me. "It's okay, Buck. It's all in the past. It's over. You were just a kid. You couldn't fight off your dad. You and your brother were both victimized. It's not your fault."

"I could have done more."

Annie sighed. "Just like Doc. He could have done more to keep my birth mother from marrying someone else. You could have done more to keep your brother from beatings. I could have done more—more to make a million things turn out better. But we're human, and we make mistakes. We admit our part in the mess. All we can do is give it over to God and move on the best we can. I know I'm sounding like a broken record, but the most important thing right now is to put down the alcohol, forget the gallery of girlfriends, and live a healthy long life. With me."

Her understanding made the difference that morning. Relief improved my outlook. I took out my phone. "I'll call Cliff now."

Annie smiled. "It's 4:30 in the morning in Oregon."

"I'm sure he's awake. He gets an early start. And I don't want to lose my nerve."

She planted a gentle kiss on my cheek then headed down the beach to give me privacy. I watched her gaze at the horizon and drop to her knees in the sand.

There was a voice on the phone. "Hello?"

Nerves fired. "Cliff."

"Buck?"

"I … I'm sorry it's been so long. How are you?"

"Fine. You?"

"Fine. And the family?" I couldn't remember their names for the life of me.

"Fine."

"Good. I … uh … I'm calling … well I've finally taken some time to take a good look at myself. I need to tell you how sorry I am. I treated you badly. I … apologize."

His voice was even. "Mother called. She told me about your visit. She sounded much happier."

"Glad to hear it."

"You don't need to apologize to me, Buck. I ran, too. I couldn't stand up to him either."

"You were a child."

"We both were. Forget the past. From newspapers and TV—sounds like you have a good future."

I kept my eyes on Annie, who most certainly was praying for me. "Annie … agreed to be my wife." Each time I said those words I could barely believe my luck, and joy welled up through my chest.

"Congratulations."

"I wonder if you'd agree to be my best man? Come out here—bring the family—they'll love Maine."

~ *Annie* ~

Buck was trying his best to be accommodating to me and to my extended family. He would have much preferred a quick trip to a Justice of the Peace to marry me. But he knew I'd want to have a wedding conducted by my dad with everyone present to celebrate with us. He patiently waited until I confirmed a date that suited the world. Even his brother was on board as best man.

So I happily consented to accompany Buck to New York City on the spur of the moment one day when Paulo and entourage were touring the South. Unbeknownst to me, our very first stop was an exclusive jewelry store where we were ushered to a private room. We sat in posh chairs at a cherry table. As an elegantly dressed saleswoman brought out a box, I began to shake.

"Um … Buck?"

He reached his arm around me. "Annie, I chose a few engagement rings I thought you might like, but I wasn't positive. So I thought it best to have you select the stone and setting that you want."

My jaw dropped when I saw the diamonds. I nodded politely at the woman and turned to Buck, whispering, "Um … just a plain gold band is good."

The woman graciously disappeared. Buck turned to me with a grin. "Annie, I'm sure you could use the money I'll spend for some great humanitarian purpose. You might even end world hunger with it. But I insist on giving my bride a proper engagement ring."

"Bride" sounded so weird. "I'm forty-eight years old, Buck."

"And?"

I knew he was right. This was me being silly. Why not have a proper engagement ring? Age shouldn't be the issue. I took another look at the eye-popping selection. "They're all gorgeous. Which one do you like?"

He smiled. "You first."

I pointed to a dainty—if you can use that term with precious gemstones—diamond surrounded by sapphires. He put it on my finger and a thrill went through me. Tears welled up. "It's perfect, Buck."

He took my hand. "It is. A perfect ring for a perfect woman." He kissed me. "Your sister designed it. Apparently she knows your taste."

I almost fell off the chair.

I sat nestled at Buck's side staring at my left hand as we drove through New York. How had Debbie known this would be the perfect ring for me? I looked up when we arrived at Brooke, Lewis & Wynn. He helped me from the car and security escorted us upstairs to the office.

"I have some paperwork to sign, and I'll need a few moments for updates, but then we'll be free to enjoy the day, my dear. Think what you might like to do."

I had to smile. "Is this your way of showing me you're not going back to a crazy work schedule?"

He brushed my cheek with a kiss. "Indeed." Then we entered the hallowed doors of Brooke, Lewis & Wynn.

Will Brooke instantly drew us to the conference room and shut the door. "Spiritual warfare! That's what my pastor said it was. So did Carter's counselor. That's what they said."

Buck helped me to a seat. "All right." He sat and turned a quizzical face to me. "If that's what they said. They know more than I. Seems like a reasonable term."

Will landed in the chair with the files piled neatly in front of him. He rolled in our direction. "Carter looks better than he has in years. You can tell it's him in there again. This is in a matter of *days*. And the staff—they're doing all kinds of nutty stuff. I mean … they're doing prayer meetings together … they're being nice to each other … they're enthusiastic at work … making good suggestions on how to improve things … giving clients the VIP treatment you talked about. They're supporting each other. They're smiling! It's like Cat waved a magic wand. They all fell on the floor, but man, they were changed when they got up."

Buck nodded. "Glad to hear it, Will."

Will kept rolling. "I had to get this figured out. I had to know more, and I wanted to make sure all those demons were out of me and my family, too." He poured three glasses of fruit-infused water from a crystal carafe and slid them to us. There was no scotch in sight. "So anyway, I called Cat. She invited me and my wife to tea with her and Cisco. We met at their hotel in Atlanta. The only reason my wife went was to have tea with a rock star and a billionaire. But at least it got her there. By the time we were done, Cat prayed with her, and she had her in with a women's book study group right here in Manhattan."

"Excellent," Buck said.

Will looked Buck straight in the eye. "I'm grateful to you, Buck. It was some tough going there for a good long while—at home and at the office. But I can see the light at the end of the tunnel. This time I know it's not a freight train. It's *good*. And it's all because of you—and Annie."

He nodded at me. "You both set an example—that salt and light stuff Cat was talking about at the concert. She explained it better to me, and it all makes sense. My wife and I, well, I think we have a chance now. I really do. And she told me she's willing to work at it. I noticed she was watching Cat and Cisco—paying close attention. Those two were meant for each other if anyone ever was."

"Indeed." Buck seemed deep in thought.

Will rifled through papers. "I left the stuff in my office. Be right back." He left the room.

Buck squeezed my hand. "We have a real shot at it, Annie."

I guess I looked confused.

"We have a real shot at a life together—as good as Cat and Cisco. It's all because of you. You brought God into my life. It seems to make all the difference."

I had goose bumps. "It does, Buck."

The next day we met Amanda James at Brooke, Lewis & Wynn. Buck settled with her and the cameras in the conference room for the interview. Amanda stuck with business questions for the most part, but when she had to ask about the wedding, Buck summoned me in front of the cameras. I reacted with schoolgirl enthusiasm. Exactly what Amanda wanted.

In all, Buck was very pleased. The interview would show his firm in a good light and bring in clients. And our conversation about The Golden Bowl would keep it front and center in people's minds— always a great thing for business and our charitable causes.

A day after we returned to Marberry, the family returned from their tour. After a big celebratory dinner, I took a brief walk on the beach with Buck then headed to bed for a good night's sleep. I found a room full of women gabbing and laughing. There was a wedding dress and a long white silk and wool cape hanging by my fireplace.

My eyes filled and my hands flew to cover my open mouth.

"Surprise!" Everyone yelled. Debbie and Glori ran to embrace me.

"Debbie had to design your gown, hon. You had to know that." Glori pulled me toward the dresses. "We've got her bridesmaid's dress here, too. Your favorite shade of purple."

Then she showed me my flower girls' dresses. I couldn't stop smiling. They were nothing short of dazzling. Sabena and Christina would definitely steal the show.

It couldn't have been more perfect. We spent the rest of the evening chatting about wedding and honeymoon plans, and admiring the dresses.

~ *Lisa* ~

Being invited to Annie's engagement party was so cool. Glori actually gave me an outfit to wear. It was a pretty blue silk suit, and she said it'd work for interviews and things like that, too. All I needed to do was accessorize it the right way. I got a little nervous about that, but then she gave me all the accessories and explained what to do with what. I wrote everything down so I'd remember what to wear for what occasion. It's not like I had many occasions.

When I walked in to the party on Billy's arm, she caught my eye and came over. "You look awesome, hon."

I thought I was going to cry, I was so happy. "Thanks, Glori, thanks for everything."

She straightened the neckline of my blouse to line up with the jewelry. "No worries, hon, we're Diet Club partners."

I giggled and Billy gave me a smile.

"Did you hear the news?" Glori always had the scoop on everything. That's one thing I loved about her. She loved gossip.

"Probably not."

"Let's go get it from the horse's mouth. I'm not sure I've got all the details." She tugged me by the hand, and I pulled Billy with me over to Annie and Buck.

Before Glori could say anything, Annie had me in a big hug. "Thanks for joining us today, Lisa. It means so much to me."

"Sure Annie, I wouldn't miss your party." Even thinking I could possibly have anything better to do, well, only Annie could do that. She was so sweet.

Glori had Buck by the arm. "Hon, tell us again about the Super Club."

Buck shook my hand. "Congratulations Lisa, you and Ashleigh have started yet another successful venture at The Golden Bowl. I'm sorry to say I was rather distracted when Ashleigh first presented the idea. I didn't realize the power in it until I was chatting with a guest at The Birch Tree Inn. She was there to attend the wedding of the Secretary of State's daughter, and she also happens to be best friends with the First Lady."

I had no idea what Buck was getting at, but I had to sound like I did. After all, the Clemente's foundation was paying for my nursing school, and I was supposed to represent them. "Cool." I figured if that worked for Glori it'd work for me.

"Indeed. Long story short, this woman had visited The Golden Bowl this summer and brought the Super Club to the attention of the First Lady. She loved it. So she wants to do some national publicity on healthy eating with the Super Club. We'll be coordinating menus with some other restaurants and soon packaging a line specific to the Super Club. We'll call upon you and Ashleigh to spearhead our campaign with some public service announcements."

"Wow. Spearhead?" I got the shakes.

Annie giggled. "You two can start off doing my show. Then you'll be all set for Hollywood." She winked at me.

I gulped. "I don't think so, Annie. I know I can be a good nurse, but not a TV spearheader." For some reason, everyone thought that was funny.

"No worries, hon," Glori said. "You can do a dance video. I can help if you want. It'll be fun."

That idea made me smile. "We can wear your new Cat's Meow

jeans. It'll be awesome!" For once I'd found jeans that made my butt look good. "I bet we sell the jeans, too."

"That's right, hon, everyone's gonna want Super Club meals if they can look that good. And don't you know … I'll be telling the world we're wearing those jeans. Public Service Campaign Glori-style." She strutted off to her next conquest, some poor woman dripping with diamonds who obviously needed fashion advice.

The very next day Glori had Paulo's new dance music for Super Club. She said he dashed it off in like five minutes. It was incredible. Glori had her choreographer in the employee lounge with me, Ashleigh, and Karen, all wearing Cat's Meow jeans. We had a blast dancing away and making up words for the music, but I dreaded seeing the video they took.

Glori played director and guest celebrity dancer. Of course she was the center of attention. Next thing you know she recruited some kids and a bunch of Golden Bowl employees and took us all out to the beach. We danced practically the whole way down the lawn to Miller's Way and then to the water. Paparazzi and happy customer spectators were everywhere, and even they were dancing. It turned into a cool flash mob thing. I didn't know if it would sell anything, but we sure had fun.

Annie invited us all to dinner one night before Thanksgiving because Sabena wanted to wrap up our first season of The Supernatural Diet Club. As the adults nibbled on appetizers, Sabena stood on an ottoman in the living room in her nightgown. Her dad warned her she had only a few minutes to do her thing. Then it'd be off to bed for her, and our Diet Club wouldn't meet again till next summer.

She held her arm to her forehead in a woe-is-me gesture that cracked me up. "We've been together from summer to autumn to winter, and I'm grateful to God for bringing us all together to share and learn and grow. Just remember, the journey of the *Supernatural* Diet is not natural in our day. But our minds are being renewed, and we are stronger now. Trust God. Be courageous. Now is the time for action. God is calling us. Remember Isaiah 60:1."

She spun around pointing to each of us. "Arise, shine, for your light has come, and the glory of the Lord rises upon you."

Sabena jumped off the ottoman and ran upstairs to cheers and loud applause led by Glori.

Ash grabbed my arm. "That kid should run for office."

~ Annie ~

I wanted a simple wedding, although it would involve a huge number of people. It was important to me to have my extended family, friends, and employees share in the occasion. Buck was happy to extend that invitation to his—with the exception of his father. I didn't push that, knowing it would be challenging enough to include his mother and his brother and family.

In the end it was anything but simple, but the people made it a joy. I'd scheduled December 3ʳᵈ, the first Saturday of the month, and prayed for decent weather. Paulo's U.S. Golden Bowl Tour was complete, and Thanksgiving was over.

On top of our usual charity events for the Thanksgiving holiday, everyone in my extended family joined us to serve the needy and then share an evening dinner. Buck's brother and his family flew in the next day. They had quality time together and mended some fences before their mother arrived the following Monday. His family couldn't have been more gracious and accepting. Even Doc took to them right away. That was a huge relief to me.

It felt like endless parties between engagement celebrations in Ripple Lake and Marberry, and a rehearsal dinner at The Golden Bowl. Saturday morning Dad conducted our wedding at his church in Ripple Lake. Then we returned home to a reception that spilled into every room on the first floor, out to the well-tended still-green lawn, and down to the beach. The weather cooperated beautifully, and the party went long into the night.

I have to say I was good and ready for a honeymoon in Hawaii. Buck would get his warm weather holiday, and we'd celebrate his fiftieth birthday in the sunshine.

~ Buck ~

Our wedding day was the best day of my life. Annie was an

inspiration in a simple silk gown and a delicate floral crown that caught up her hair in a beautiful twist. Our guests included the most diverse group of people I'd ever seen in one space—all ages, nationalities, and occupations, from every socioeconomic background. Most importantly, they were having fun celebrating without tearing the place apart. Even Carter Lewis comported himself with decorum—and not a drink other than mineral water.

I found my wife in the foyer admiring Debbie's painting of us engrossed in our White House dance. Annie's image was perfectly and naturally proportioned, looking almost as lovely as she did today. Relief washed through me. I hadn't dared to look for that painting after our break-up, though I'd often wondered about it.

I took Annie's hand, and she stood on tiptoe to kiss me. Her shoes had long since disappeared.

Her hand brushed the neckline of the violet gown she wore in the painting. "Um, Buck ... you know you can't fool with prophecy."

It was a strange statement, but I knew exactly what Annie meant. She burst into laughter, and I literally became hot under the collar. It was the last secret I thought I'd kept.

Her smile, the look in her eyes, could not have been more loving. "The truth will set you free, Buck."

"Indeed." I'm sure I blushed. "When did you know?"

"When Debbie kept complaining about the neckline on my gown. Debbie never gets it wrong. I didn't want to upset her, so I asked Cat about it. She told me Debbie must have picked up on your fantasy. We had a good laugh. Men!"

There was a tremble in her smile. "Sure enough, after your accident on the way to The Birch Tree Inn, Debbie fixed it, no problem. That's when I knew you'd truly changed—down deep inside. That's when I knew this is real. Us. You and me, Buck."

I was speechless.

She smoothed my hair with a gentle touch. Her voice wavered with emotion. "And that ... night ... we broke up ... it broke my heart when I found out our painting was one of your many. But when you asked me if Cat's prayer for Holy Spirit to help you was real, I knew in my heart your heart was changed. I knew we'd be together somehow ... sometime. Even though it sure didn't feel that way." Her eyes filled. "This painting—it reminds me of the day I fell for you.

And now it reminds me of the truth—love that's true. You and me, Buck."

Love rejoices with the truth. I saw my heart in her blue eyes. "You and me, Annie. Let's dance."

The truth has set me free. I can honestly say there isn't—has never been—a more perfect, more beautiful woman.

The Cast of Characters in The Golden Bowl:
THE SUPERNATURAL DIET CLUB

The Golden Bowl:
Anne Auclair Brewster (Annie), owner

Staff
Ashleigh (Ash), Manager, First shift
Brianna (Bree), Manager, Second shift
Karen, Confections Manager, The Bakery & Sweet Shop
Gerald, Manager, Food Prep Facility
Tracey, Customer Service Manager
Lisa Quinn, Dishwasher

Annie's Family and Extended Family:
Dr. Craig Westcott (Doc), birth father
Pastor Mike Auclair, adoptive father
Millie Auclair, adoptive mother
Debbie Lambrecht, sister, fashion designer, artist
David Lambrecht, brother-in-law
Cat Clemente, David's cousin, rock star lyricist, philanthropist, prophet
Cisco Clemente, Cat's husband, billionaire businessman and philanthropist
Paulo Clemente, Cisco's youngest brother, rock star, composer
Ellen Clemente, Paulo's wife
Sabena Lambrecht, Annie's niece
Glori Coulson Dusseault, fashion icon, pop star

The Consultants
Buckminster Wynn (Almighty Buck), Brooke, Lewis & Wynn
William (Will) Brooke, Brooke, Lewis & Wynn
Carter Lewis, Brooke, Lewis & Wynn
Janice, Administrator, Brooke, Lewis & Wynn
Joe Harris, Agent, entertainment industry
Amanda James, Journalist

The Security Team
David Lambrecht
Nathan Rhodes, Director
Billy Foster
Keith
Roger

The Townspeople
Peg, Lisa's babysitter/friend

Other Books by
Maeve Christopher

The Golden Bowl Series:
A Ring and a Prayer (Book One)
The Supernatural Diet Club (Book Two)

The Redemption Series: read in order 1--5
Killer Cupid
Fame, Fortune & Secrets
In the Name of Glori
Last Tangle in Paris
Mercy's Pen

Find links to retailers at
MaeveChristopher.com

About Maeve Christopher

Ordinary people in extraordinary situations fuel Maeve Christopher's imagination. Keep asking "what if" and "why," and the plot thickens. What could be more fun?

Her bestselling Redemption Series is part family saga, part suspense, and part love story—with the touch of the Supernatural. Tongue firmly in cheek, it deals with the age-old question: What happens when an assassin falls for a woman who is trying to kill herself?

Maeve's new series, The Golden Bowl, is set on the scenic coast of Maine. This unusual restaurant caters to the body, soul, and spirit. A large gold bowl on the front porch gives the establishment its name and invites patrons to leave a prayer and take a prayer. When they do: lives change.

Maeve lives in Massachusetts with too many characters and a number of messy subplots. She loves to hear from readers. Subscribe to Maeve's Email Updates for exclusive content, contests, special offers, and more on her website.

You can also find her on Facebook @maevechristopher

Maeve enjoys hearing from her readers. She can be contacted through her website MaeveChristopher.com

A Note from Maeve

If you enjoyed The Supernatural Diet Club, I'd be honored if you would tell others by leaving a review on the site where you purchased this book.

Thank you!
Maeve

www.ingramcontent.com/pod-product-compliance
Lightning Source LLC
Chambersburg PA
CBHW061217170626
46809CB00007B/2515